MEGAN GAMBLE, SING OUT

DEBBIE ROMANI

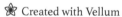

For my kids and my husband, who have (thankfully) never asked me to sing backup for an arena show.

1

Megan Gamble edged onto the stage at the empty LA arena, the seats fading into the distance and her famous son almost directly in front of her. Just this morning she had decided that this time she was really going to do it: she was going to take charge of her life and change things up.

Apparently, life had taken that resolution pretty literally.

Kyle heard her, but instead of saying hello, he turned to his buddy and bandmate Li-Fang. "Jesus, fuck. You asked my *Mom* to sing backup?"

Not what she wanted to hear, but far from a surprise.

Her relationship with Kyle had been so bad for so long that she could barely remember what it was like to have a normal conversation with him. So this morning, when she'd made a two-item list of things to fix in her life, the sour relationship with Kyle had been one of them. The other? She was going to find a job that didn't involve working in the same office as Jaimie Somerset.

Li-Fang turned. "Mrs. M! You made it!" Unlike Kyle, Li-Fang stepped forward, his arms open wide. She remembered the first time they'd met, when Li-Fang had been an earnest kindergartener. He'd told her, "Li-Fang, rhymes with song. Not *fang*. I don't have super big teeth, see?" And the five-year-old had smiled wide, pulling back his lips.

Her heart both lifted and broke. She'd met the rest of the band, but Li-Fang was the only other person on the stage she knew at all well, and while she was happy that he was glad to see her, she hated the contrast with Kyle's behavior.

"Great to see you Li, everyone," Megan said. She waved at the rest of the band and ducked under the neck of Li-Fang's electric violin for her hug.

Then she pulled away and asked, "Kyle, did you say I'm *singing*?"

Kyle looked at her, eyes wide, then spoke again to Li-Fang, shaking his head at his buddy. "You didn't tell her? Li-Fang, you said you had a vocalist who would be perfect for this, and then you just expected Mom to, what? Figure it out? Go with it? What is with you these days?" He spoke into his mic, the sound carrying over the empty arena. It was as if staring at thousands of empty seats was as normal for Kyle these days as staring at the posters on the wall of his old bedroom had been, back when he'd still lived at home.

Great. Now Kyle was pissed off at Li-Fang, too.

Li-Fang held his bow down at his side, facing Kyle. Standing tall. "No, I didn't tell your mom. I asked if she was flying down for the concert, and when she said yes, I figured we were set. I didn't want to freak her out." Li-Fang turned and looked at Megan with classic puppy-dog eyes. Those eyes made younger women do very foolish things, at least according to social media. But Megan had known Li-Fang for too many years to react that way to this man.

"You'll sing, right?" Li-Fang asked.

That zing she felt? That was adrenaline shooting through her body. It had been more than twenty years since her last sound check, which had been in a church multi-use room when she'd done backup for a bunch of Christian rockers. But apparently Li-Fang had promised Kyle that Megan would sing today.

Li-Fang had always been a sweet kid. She didn't want to let him down, and maybe singing would help ease the tension with Kyle. So she nodded yes, figuring it was just a sound check. The normal backup singer must have had a conflict this afternoon, and Kyle was a perfectionist when it came to his music. He'd want to make sure the balance on the mics was right, run a few things before tonight's show.

"You want me over here?" she asked, stepping to the stand mic near the rear of the stage, careful not to trip over the loose cords. After they finished sound check and finalized the setup, the roadies would make sure everything was taped down, but now they were still adjusting equipment.

She leaned into the mic. "Testing. One. Two."

Speaking those words felt like coming home and like jumping off a ten story building all at the same time, perfectly normal and utterly insane.

Kyle didn't even look over his shoulder. "Mom, you gotta get closer."

She crowded the mic, close enough to smell the metal grid protecting the pickup. "This better? Check, check?" If this wasn't close enough, she'd have to put the thing inside her mouth.

Kyle nodded, back still turned.

Come on, Kyle. Turn around. Look at me.

The jeans he was wearing looked exactly like a pair she'd bought for him when he was thirteen. Maybe they actually were. His hair was longer than she remembered, the stage lighting making pale highlights stand out against the deep brown of his natural color. And clearly Kyle had been working out between gigs; the shoulders that hadn't filled out until late in high school were broader now, and his arms seemed thicker.

There were a lot of tweets about those shoulders. And that voice. And the cut of his cheekbones.

Tweets about her kid.

"Mic's picking you up just fine, Mrs. M." Li-Fang put a bow to the strings of his violin and wailed out a line.

On Kyle's first day of kindergarten, she'd waited with the other mothers to pick up their kids. Kyle, dressed in a YMCA Super-Camper T-shirt, standing next to a cute Asian boy with a shy smile and an awful haircut, their shoulders practically touching as they avoided the girls to either side of them.

"Is that your boy next to mine?" the woman beside her had asked, gesturing with a tiny movement of her hand.

That was how Megan had met Jiao. By the end of that first week, Megan had invited Jiao to join the weekly coffee date she had with her best friend Keiko, and the three had been friends ever since.

Keiko and Megan met in college. After passing the bar, Keiko had joined the law firm where Megan was already a paralegal, and the two of them had worked there for almost twenty years. But not for much longer. Because this time she was really going to quit, find a new job, and get away from Jaimie, even if it did mean leaving Keiko. Thinking back on what she'd learned about Jaimie this morning, she was flat out pissed with herself. She'd deluded herself about him for far too long.

"You ready, Mrs. M?" Li-Fang asked.

Five-year-old Li-Fang had called her Mrs. M, because Kyle had his dad's last name, Marshall. Her own driver's license read "Megan Gamble," but she'd always be Mrs. M to Li-Fang.

Megan looked up from the set list taped to the floor in front of her mic and nodded toward Li-Fang, then just missed catching Kyle's eye. Darn. *Look at me, please.*

Kyle glanced past her to the drummer upstage and to her right, actually smiling for a change, probably looking forward to the music. "Zane, count us in."

Zane, a beefy man with a shaved head, smashed his sticks together four times.

They conjured music out of the air, and the sound twitched the sinews that held her bones together. She'd defy anyone who thought they could resist this visceral pull to move. She couldn't stand still, that was certain.

As her body loosened up and she waited for her entrance, she took in the empty seats of the arena, the water bottle on the floor next to Charlotte's array of keyboards, the dim lights at the sound boards in the middle distance, where three men with headphones manipulated hidden levers and dials.

Damn, this was the experience of a lifetime, to hear a band as incredible as this one do its thing when she was standing literally in the middle of the action.

The beat pulsed through her, spreading from her core to her legs and shoulders. She let her head move in time.

The Sutter Boys had always been good, playing the kind of high energy music that made her forget she was in her forties now—the kind of music that made her dance, sweat, and sing at the top of her lungs. She'd been to countless concerts, starting back when the band was playing tiny venues in the Bay Area, and she knew all their music, acoustic versions to studio recordings, even the extended bridges Kyle liked to throw in during a live show.

But she'd never been on the stage with them while they were working their magic, and singing even just for sound check dialed the thrill up to eleven. She wasn't sure exactly why their normal singer had flaked, or why they had needed Megan to stand in, but this was incredible!

At the chorus to "Days of Broken Glass," she crowded the mic again and grabbed it with both hands, the metal cool on her palms. This was the mic where what's-her-face would be swaying later tonight, but for now, it was Megan's voice adding to the mix.

5

Of course Megan knew the harmonies. Every fan did, and some of them could hold pitch, make their voices ring with Kyle's. Megan's own voice, as rusty as it was, was perfectly suited to Kyle's. The timbre of the voice was encoded by the genes, and she shared half of Kyle's DNA. She was his mother, and could lock a harmony with her boy better than anyone on the planet. That was a powerful high for a music addict like her.

Too bad no one would ever hear this except the band, the crew, and the arena staff. Okay, focus. Kyle wasn't messing around.

He ran the sound check like it was an actual rehearsal.

"Someone get Mom an in-ear monitor," Kyle said at the end of that first piece, but there was already a tech heading her direction with a pair of the devices in his hand, pulling a genuine smile of appreciation to her son's face. He said, "On top of things as always, I see. Thanks, Erik."

Once Megan seated the devices, they were off again.

Kyle asked for a faster tempo on "No More You," and then praised the bass player, Theo, for a silky new addition to his line on that piece. He winced when their keyboard player Charlotte threw in a minor seventh to the bridge on "Finding Livvie," and tossed the word, "Nope," over his shoulder. He made them redo the number, of course. He also corrected Megan at least three or four times, which was kind of mortifying. She'd forgotten what it was like to sing for someone who demanded perfection. It had been that way back when she'd been with 2 Samuel 6, and apparently it was that way with Kyle.

It was kind of odd that Kyle was nitpicking her performance, because it didn't matter, unless maybe he thought her mistakes would throw off the rest of the band. But the comments kept coming.

Kyle had a great ear, and he was mostly right when he called her out, so she sucked it up for the sake of self-improvement. Her entrance *had* been sloppy on "No More You." Her vowel matching hadn't been great at the start of "Running"; not nearly as good as it had been in the other numbers. She swallowed her pride, listened harder, mimicked him more closely, and admitted to herself that the music sounded better after she made the changes. Kyle even nodded her direction once, and while it wasn't a Grammy award, she knew that there was professional respect there.

She glowed.

But then Kyle told her to lose the scoop before the chorus of "Days of Broken Glass."

"I like the scoop," she said into her mic. All the band did it, using the mics instead of raising their voices to make themselves heard.

"You may like the scoop, but I don't," was all Kyle said. "Drop it."

She said, "Yes, sir," and threw a mock salute at Kyle's back. Theo, the dark-haired, lanky bass player, caught the motion, and raised an eyebrow. She felt like she was in on the joke with one of the cool kids, but then Theo held her gaze for a tad too long. She wanted to roll her eyes; he was far too young to be paying this much attention to the old lady on the stage.

She wasn't really old; she knew that. But being around twenty-year-olds didn't make her feel any younger.

Zane counted them in again, and this time she didn't slide up to her entrance.

Kyle didn't cut any of them any slack. Even Li-Fang, who had been playing the violin since he was four, got called out a couple of times, though Kyle also tossed Li-Fang an awed, "Smokin'!" after one particularly nimble-fingered run.

Kyle was spot-on with his comments (except for that scoop, of course, which would have sounded great), but did he have to be so cold with her?

Sound check lasted almost forty-five minutes, but finally

Kyle was satisfied. He handed his guitar to a hovering tech, and Megan sagged. Her feet were tired, and her ribs were almost sore; clearly the breath support she'd once had was shot. Megan turned to Charlotte, the keyboardist, and said, "God, I'm wiped. I don't know how you all do this five times a week."

Charlotte flipped a switch on one of her boards and gave Megan a warm, gap-toothed smile. "You'll get the hang of it."

That comment struck Megan as odd, but she was too focused on finding some water to think much of it. Her throat wasn't exactly sore, but if she didn't get some liquid down, her vocal chords were going to start talking to her.

It had been a long day. She'd been in her closet of an office at six this morning plowing through files for her firm's attorneys, trying to get ahead so she could grab her midday flight from San Jose to LA. And then Jaimie had blindsided her with his news, making it almost impossible to concentrate and spoiling her productivity.

She was so exhausted now that her body felt almost hollow. The adrenaline that had been keeping her standing was shutting down hard.

Well, the concert tonight should perk her up again. After that she could head to her hotel and collapse. The alarm was going to go off awfully early if she was going to catch her flight and get home in time to make her regular Saturday morning gab-fest with Jiao and Keiko. Wait until she told them that she'd sung at sound check!

"Good work, Mrs. M," Li-Fang said. "Grab you a water?" He dug around in a big plastic bowl filled with ice and canned drinks. The bowl was identical to the one her office kept in the big cabinet over the fridge, which she hauled out for afternoon meetings and filled with exactly the same selection of beverages.

It struck her as pretty funny. Weren't these rock-star types supposed to have gold-plated trays and crystal glasses and caviar? Maybe not.

Kyle grabbed an ultra-caffeinated energy drink, pried off the top, and glared at Li-Fang. "I'm guessing you owe Mom more than a bottle of water that's already been paid for."

Kyle had bags under his eyes. Later someone would give him guyliner, and they'd probably use concealer as well, but up close, her hot-shot kid looked pretty beat-up.

The rest of the band drifted off, leaving the three of them at the edge of the stage. And a couple of roadies. And that guy with the headset. And the group of three very young women sitting on amp cases just off the stage, feet dangling like they were still sitting on playground swing sets. Instead of sneakers, their feet were in obnoxiously high heels, criss-crossed straps showing off painted toenails. The women eyed Kyle and Li-Fang, but turned away pretty quickly when they caught Megan staring in their direction.

Li-Fang tapped Megan's arm with a sweating water bottle, then held it out for her. "Here you go, Mrs. M." His eyes followed Megan's to the girls offstage, and Li-Fang dipped his chin slightly, smiling in their direction.

Megan took the water and frowned. Li-Fang and Kyle were young, but surely those girls were too young, right? Were they even eighteen?

Li-Fang gave each of the women a long, head-to-toe look, even with Megan standing right there. She elbowed him. "Weren't you dating your backup singer? And where is she, anyway?"

Kyle snorted and ignored the second part of her question. "I guess that's one way to describe what he was doing."

There was no doubt what he was implying. But Megan's feet hurt, and she'd been putting up with him barking orders at her for almost an hour. "Kyle. Stop that. You've been a grouch to me all afternoon, and you haven't even had the decency to really say hello. You're not a toddler. Come on. Do better."

His sulk was familiar, like the classic expression of a fourteen-year-old, but now it was laid over a fleshed-out face that needed a shave. He stared at her with dead eyes and spoke with a completely flat voice. "Hello."

She blinked rapidly, her eyes suddenly watery.

What had gone so wrong with their relationship? They'd been a team, once upon a time, and now it was like he was permanently mad at her. And she never been able to figure out exactly what she'd done.

Resolutions, baby, she told herself. Two resolutions: new job, and fix whatever was wrong with this relationship.

The silence stretched out for a beat. Kyle put his energy drink to his lips and tipped his head back, which the young women seemed to find fascinating.

Li-Fang gave Kyle's other arm a light punch. "Jesus, man. Show maybe a little respect for your mom, okay? Stop staring at the girls. You know they'll be there later."

Kyle lowered the bottle and glared at Li-Fang. "You're really going to go there, and hassle me about the groupies when your inability to keep your dick in your pants is why we're in this situation at all?"

Megan's chin jerked forward and her eyebrows leapt upward. Wow. He really wasn't holding back. But maybe he was even cruder when she wasn't around, because this was really not the way she had raised her boy.

Li-Fang beat her to the punch. "Language, man. And don't be calling me out. At least Katya was almost a girlfriend. Unlike the way you and Theo go through women."

"Well, if Katya was your girlfriend, why were your pants around your ankles when that groupie was on her knees last night in San Diego, huh?"

Megan coughed into her hand. Okay, that was definitely worse than Kyle just using the word "dick."

Li-Fang said, "Pot, have you met kettle? Weren't there two girls in your dressing room last night?"

"What if there were?"

"Right here," Megan said, but the guys barely flicked their eyes in her direction, still glaring at each other. "Maybe you two could dial this down a bit."

After a beat where he visibly forced his shoulders to relax, Li-Fang said, "No problem, Mrs. M."

"No, the language isn't the real problem, now is it, Li?" Kyle took a step forward, crowding his buddy. Li-Fang had almost two inches on Kyle, but Kyle was behaving like he was calling out an employee who'd been way out of line. "The real problem was you and Katya. Resulting it the lack of Katya. And your lack of control, which put us in this position in the first place. Now, if you'll excuse me, I'm going to go talk to the ladies for a minute while *you* fix our problem."

Li-Fang looked from Kyle to Megan, then back at Kyle. "She's your mom!"

"Your problem," Kyle said.

"What problem?" Megan asked, looking between the two men.

Kyle just raised the corners of his mouth, then actually leaned over and kissed Megan on the cheek. "Just a lovely little surprise from Li-Fang. See you." He strolled toward the girls, who slipped off the cases to stand and giggle. One of them flicked her hair back over her shoulders and leaned in to run a hand over Kyle's arm.

It was downright nauseating to realize that the kid she'd raised all by herself was now an object of lust. These girls were really young, which was certainly concerning, but it could have been worse. Women her own age (and older) fan-girled for her boy. And men, too. People her own age? She shuddered. That was where her stomach wouldn't let her mind go.

Li-Fang said, "Yeah. That must be hard to watch, but I swear he'll tone it down."

She could shake it off, right? "I'm just here for tonight, and of course I'm going to catch the San Jose show tomorrow. So I won't have to put up with him for long." Which was good, because she didn't think she would be able to stand watching Kyle behave this way night after night.

"We-e-ell." Li-Fang stretched the word out and grimaced. He fiddled with the label on his bottle of water, pulling a loose corner free from the sweating plastic. He hadn't drained much of it. "You remember Katya?"

Megan nodded. "I just covered for her. Of course I remember her. Where is she this afternoon, anyway?"

Li-Fang looked back out at the arena, and Megan wondered if maybe Katya was sitting in one of the distant seats. Then Li-Fang turned back to Megan and ran a hand over his face. "I don't really know. She kind of quit last night."

Ah. Pants around his ankles. A groupie giving him a blow job. Right.

"She quit, huh? But who's going to sing tonight?"

His eyes got very wide. Pleading. "You? We don't have anyone else, and I knew you would be here." Li-Fang looked down, scuffing the edge of his shoe against the dusty floor. At some point he'd stopped wearing Vans and started wearing dress shoes.

"Thanks for the tickets, by the way." Kyle certainly hadn't thought to comp her any.

"You're welcome. But you don't really need them now, not if you're going to sing."

Why did he keep saying that? "You can't be serious."

The foot scuffing was back. "I'm dead serious. Who else are we going to get in time for the show? Lots of people would jump on a chance to sing with us, but Katya quit *last night*, less than twenty-four hours ago. We all thought she would cool off and show up this morning, but she didn't. So now we've got a show in a few hours and no backup singer. No one knows our set list better than you do, and you were gonna be here and I knew you'd want to help us out. You caught every one of our shows when we were still local in the Bay Area. And of course you can sing—you did sound amazing at sound check, by the way. We don't have time to teach someone else all this music. And you saw what Kyle was like with you. Can you imagine how stressed he would be if it was someone who barely knew our stuff? Please, Mrs. M. Eventually we'll figure something out, but we can't figure it out today. I guess Katya never wants to see my sorry ass again. I mean, she was pretty upset."

Megan thought of the lovely image Kyle had painted. "I can't imagine why."

"Yeah, well, kinda probably shouldn't have done that, or at least I should have been more careful."

"Li-Fang!"

"Right. Shouldn't have done that."

Megan nodded. "That's right. You shouldn't have." She really didn't want to talk to a man she'd known since he was five about the fact he'd let some random woman blow him, and pissed off his girlfriend in the process.

"So, will you sing?" He had the label all the way off his water bottle now, and was working at the little patches of glue still stuck to the side.

"Do I have much of a choice?" She shook her head to clear it, thinking about the empty seats beyond the stage and feeling her stomach drop. "How many people does this place seat?"

"Oh, I don't know exactly. Maybe ten thousand? More?"

"Jesus!" Now she was the one swearing. Great. "I can't possibly do that. Ten *thousand* people? They'll probably sue you guys for their money back if you throw an old lady onto the stage."

"Well, they'll certainly be more pissed if we cancel the show."

"The band would cancel the show if I said I wasn't going to sing?" Megan couldn't even imagine that. When the car had dropped her off there had already been people lined up waiting for the doors to open. There had to be more of them by now.

"No, I guess we wouldn't cancel. But we sound way better when we have a backup singer, and you totally rocked the rehearsal."

"So that's why Kyle ran so much of the set. I was wondering about that."

Li-Fang nodded. "C'mon, Mrs. M. You're an old pro, right? I mean, not *old* old, but you've performed before."

She put her hand to her temple. God, her head hurt.

Maybe caffeine would help. "Yeah, I've performed, but for something like a hundred people in a church multipurpose room. Not with a band like yours." She waved her hand around, trying to indicate the size of the venue, the sheer number of people on the payroll here in LA and touring with the band. The social media. Everything. "You guys are way, way out of my league. I was a good-enough-for-a-tiny-bar singer, nothing more. So it's not quite the same thing. Besides, the last time I performed was more than twenty years ago."

And boy, had her days with that band ended on a sour note. It wasn't just that life and a new baby had gotten in the way of singing. She didn't want to think about that band ever again. Not if she could help it.

Li-Fang backed up a step, and she realized just how loud her voice had gotten. Then the idiot actually got on his knees. "Please, Mrs. M? Kyle was about ready to kill me when we realized that Katya really had bailed. Why do you think he was so pissy at sound check? He's stressed. There's a lot riding on this for the whole band. We could really use the help. Please."

How had she let things with Kyle get so bad that he wouldn't even ask her for a favor in a situation like this one? Her boy's band needed her, and now Kyle was nowhere to be seen. Instead, he'd sent Li-Fang. "Well, why didn't you clear this with Kyle before? It seems like he had no idea I was showing up for sound check."

Li-Fang looked even more uncomfortable. "I probably should have, but..." He stopped.

With a sigh Megan said, "But you knew how much he hates being around me. I used to think it was the normal way adult kids drift away from their parents, but ever since he visited home the tour before last, it's been really bad. I'm guessing you just didn't want to risk telling him."

"No, can't say that I did."

"Well, I get that." She took a deep breath and looked back toward all the empty seats in the arena beyond the stage. She wanted a better relationship with Kyle, not to piss him off even more. And as much as she hated to admit it, she could probably survive for a show, if that's what it took to get this tour back on track. She took a slug from her water bottle. Her vocal chords were going to need a lot more love if she was going to sing tonight.

Her breathing sped up. That whole arena, full. "Ten thousand people?"

"Maybe more?" Li-Fang looked very guilty.

"What are you going to tell your mom?"

She was thinking how appalled Jiao would be if she ever heard exactly how Li-Fang had managed to piss off his girl-friend, but that wasn't the question Li-Fang answered. "I'll tell her that Mrs. M bailed me out again? I can't tell her the whole story, that's for sure."

"Yeah, I don't think she'd love that." Jiao Wang, hearing

about her son getting interrupted in the middle of a blow job. Nope. That would not go over well at all.

"Please."

She closed her eyes, not wanting to look at the empty arena when she said the word. "I can't believe I'm going to say this, but...okay."

2

After finishing makeup and wardrobe, Megan stepped into one of the backstage hallways and almost collided with a roadie carrying an open cardboard box of concert tees. The box went flying, but Kyle had just emerged from a different door and somehow grabbed the box before it hit the ground.

And then he went on to behave so differently from the way he'd been treating her. Instead of yelling or getting upset, Kyle held the box while the other man picked up the handful of T-shirts that had fallen out and tossed them back. Kyle returned the box with a smile.

His quick save reminded her of a time when she'd almost flipped one of Kyle's pancakes onto the floor, and he'd caught the flying food with the plate he was holding out. He'd been about seven.

The roadie said something, and Kyle gave the man's shoulder a brief squeeze, saying, "No problem, man."

That was the boy she'd raised.

She was just a few feet away when Kyle noticed her. Mother and son now had matching eyeliner and skinny jeans, but her heels were three inches higher; and while he was in a T-shirt, she was in something a bit like a tank top, but with snaps, and leather, and hooks, and enough support that even Dolly Parton could have gone jogging in it.

"Jeez, Mom! I should've hired you a while ago. You're going to be fighting them off with a stick."

That was his first comment? Yikes. Not exactly the conversational opening she was looking for. "Thanks, I think. Good to see you, by the way. How've you been? Things going okay? It's been a long time since we had a chance to catch up."

"And you think now is a good time, what, twenty minutes before we go on? I don't think so. Not when you can't even make time for me when I'm back at your place for an actual visit." What did he mean by that, exactly? He turned as if he was about to walk away, then faced her again. "Maybe you should be taking this gig a bit more seriously, you think? Instead, here you are, acting like singing your first arena show is no biggie, like we should just hang out and chat."

It wasn't kindly said.

She told herself to suck it up. Kyle was stressed, and rightfully so. His backup singer had quit, and he must be worried about how Megan was going to do. She could be a total disaster, humiliate herself, and maybe even mess up the show for the band. So if Kyle was way too brusque with her, she could understand why.

It hit her again, after the whirlwind of wardrobe and makeup and getting her inner ear monitors better calibrated: she was going onstage soon. It got very hard to swallow, and suddenly her mouth was full of saliva.

She tried again. "Yeah, this isn't really the time, is it. Any chance you can come by the house before the San Jose show tomorrow? We could catch up then."

"Sorry, Mom. Radio spots all day."

Okay then. She'd have to try some other time. Maybe they'd have a chance backstage before tomorrow's show. The band would have another singer by then, so at least Megan wouldn't be dealing with stage fright.

A guy with a clipboard brushed past, and Kyle said, "Oh, hey, Deke, sorry to interrupt, but could you let the arena know the lock's busted on the bathroom door in my dressing room?"

Deke pulled out a pen and scribbled a note. "Sure thing, Mr. Marshall."

The grin crept all the way to Kyle's eyes. "Enough with the 'Mr. Marshall' stuff. Come on. My name's Kyle. I don't bite, you know."

"Right," said the roadie, looking pleased. "I'll make sure they check it out for you. Broken lock."

"Thanks, man." Kyle gave him a mock punch in the shoulder, and Deke continued toward the stage.

One of the girls from earlier came out of the same door as Kyle had and swung a skinny arm over his shoulder. Her hand snaked down toward his pecs and gave his upper chest a leisurely stroke. "Who's that, babe?"

Kyle shrugged away from her touch and the woman slid her hand back to his shoulder. "That's my mom."

The woman's eyes were on Megan. "Your mom's kinda hot for an old lady."

Megan took a step forward. "Excuse me?" It sounded far too much like the line Jaimie had used before she hooked up with him the first time, both of them drunk at a Christmas party days after his wife had kicked him out of the house. Well, after the first time his wife had kicked him out. She didn't like being reminded of Jaimie at all.

Kyle reached for the girl's hand and moved it off his shoulder. "Leave it, babe. We're on in twenty. Still plenty of time." He smiled down at her, touching a finger to her cheek, and the girl grinned up at him before shooting Megan a rather triumphant smile.

Yeah, it was pretty clear that Kyle wasn't going to be interested in a mother-son heart-to-heart any time soon. How was she going to reach him? She had to do something if she wanted a real relationship with Kyle. And that woman seemed awfully young.

"Kyle," Megan said, "Can I speak with you for a minute?"

Kyle turned the girl's face toward him with one hand and used his other to tap her three times on the tip of her perky little nose. "Wait. Right. Here." When he turned back to Megan, he dipped his chin and looked out from under his eyebrows, appearing determined to stare her down.

Megan pulled him away from the little minx, realizing she was holding a leather cuff at his wrist. Yep, her son now wore leather jewelry. "Is she even legal? I do hope you know something about consent. And protection."

Kyle's eyes got wide, and then he just shook his head. "Really? You want to give me a little sex ed lecture a month into tour? Because you think I've been doing...what, exactly, during the last five years of my career?"

Okay, so talking to him about protection had been pretty stupid, but the age thing wasn't obvious, at least not to her. "How old is she?" Megan asked.

"Jesus," Kyle swore, then looked over his shoulder at the girl. "Babe?"

"Yeah?"

"Mom wants to know if you're into me or not. Seems she's worried about consent. And you being old enough."

The girl oozed back to Kyle's side and tried to glue her body to his. When she turned to look at Megan, light flashed off the tiny rhinestones dotted under the girl's eyebrows. "Totally legal. And you may be his mom, but you're not mine. So don't be in my face about what I do with my body."

"Well," Megan said under her breath. "I guess she's consenting."

She felt queasy, but who was she to judge any else's sex life?

Her own was too screwed up for words. For years she had heard how rocky her boss's marriage was, and how it wasn't going to last. She'd listen and sympathize, and time and again Jaimie would sweet-talk her into sleeping with him, telling her she was the only one who really understood him.

Sometimes Megan thought she and Jaimie were headed for a relationship. But that never happened.

They'd sleep together for a few weeks, even months, and she'd get comfortable. Then one morning Jaimie would lie in her bed, sated, and casually mention that his wife had let him move back home a few days earlier. Funny how he never mentioned it before they had sex.

Then Jaimie would pretend they'd never spent time together, and that she was just some paralegal who happened to work for him.

The weeks right after one of their interludes were always the worst. Megan would be pissed off and ashamed that Jaimie had manipulated her again, but she'd also be depressed. Would no one ever love her for being herself? Did she just deserve to be treated like that?

A few months later, Jaimie would be back at her office door. He only pulled that sort of thing when the two of them were the last people in the office, and then he'd appear, shaken and emotional, saying his marriage was over for good this time.

And the cycle would start over again. Comfort. Seduction. Betrayal. At this point, she didn't even like Jaimie.

Especially not after the bomb he had dropped this morning. Next spring, Jaimie was taking a month out of the office—a month!—to take his "beloved" wife on a luxury cruise to celebrate their twenty-fifth wedding anniversary. Just ten days earlier, Jaimie had told Megan that his divorce papers were all but signed.

So no, she wasn't in a position to judge anyone's sex life. She should cut Kyle a break, surrounded by women like this one, living his life in the tabloids. That had to add a level of stress that Megan could only begin to imagine. Why shouldn't he sleep with these women if they were into it and it made him happier?

"Sorry," Megan said. "None of my business."

The girl nodded and tucked herself further under Kyle's arm.

Kyle continued to stare Megan down. "Nope. Not really your business."

She hated that her relationship with Kyle had come to this, vaguely hurtful comments made in passing, and then months without any contact. He barely texted.

She'd supported him and his career every way she knew how, and they'd been so close when he was small, the two of them against the world. Now there was just this animosity, ever since the tour before last. And she was never with him for long enough stretches to fix anything. She needed more time with him.

Kyle told Megan, "Have Li-Fang or someone show you where your entrance is. He's always stashing girls offstage. He'll know the best spot. Right now, I've got someplace I'd rather be." Kyle ran his hand along the the woman's arm, opened the door she'd just come through, and the two of them disappeared.

Okay. That had just happened. Her son had basically taken out a billboard to say that he was going to use the spare few minutes before the show to screw this young woman.

Megan tried to get her breathing back under control. Maybe she and Kyle could connect after the show. Hopefully they'd both be calmer then.

Calmer.

After the show.

She didn't even know where she was supposed to wait for her entrance. She was pretty sure she was supposed to stay offstage until the band started the set, then come out just in time for the chorus during their first song, but she should ask.

She looked at that closed door. Yeah, not asking Kyle.

Right. Find Li-Fang.

Megan took off down the corridor, making a mental note to stay out of earshot of the room where Kyle and arm-candy had just disappeared.

Li-Fang lounged on a greenroom couch, his arms thrown over the shoulders of the girls sitting to each side. *Women,* Megan reminded herself. At least, she hoped they were old enough to qualify. Each of them sported a backstage pass, just like the one Megan had around her neck. As a performer, she didn't technically need one, but since none of the crew really knew her, she figured it was better to keep her pass on. Stay on the safe side.

Just like Kyle had, Li-Fang did a double take when he saw Megan. He disengaged from the girls and stood, taking Megan's hands and turning her side to side. "Hot damn, Mrs. M! Looking fine!"

An eye roll seemed to be the only appropriate response. At least his sweet talk took her mind off how badly things had gone with Kyle. "Hush, you. Stop humoring me. Kyle said you would know where I was supposed to stand?"

"Yeah. I can help you with that. Shannon? Marcy? Give me a minute. I'll be right back."

From the couch, the two girls appeared to be ogling Li-Fang's butt, but they paused long enough to nod and simper. "Hurry, 'kay?"

"You're both eighteen, right?" Megan demanded, giving off a pretty strong "Mom" vibe.

"Yeah." Sulks registered in their voices.

"Duh. What are you, the band grandma or something?"

Li-Fang whipped his head around to stare at them. "Hey! Respect a little, okay? You sure as shit better hope you're this hot when you're the same age as Mrs. M. I'm pretty sure neither of you have a mom that looks this good. And you haven't even heard this lady sing yet. She's saving our butts tonight, so no lip from either of you now...if you want any lip from me later."

The girls—women!—smiled at that one, and Megan tried hard—really hard—not to picture the image that comment called up. "I sure wish you'd learn to keep it zipped. Or at least not talk about it around me. You know tomorrow's my weekly coffee date with your mom, right?"

"Sorry, Mrs. M. You're not going to tell her about this, right?" He changed the pitch of his voice to the one he'd used to use when he and Kyle had gotten in trouble, and the two of them were trying to talk their way out of Megan ratting Li-Fang out to his mom. She'd been so young when she had Kyle, just nineteen, that she'd been the cool Mom: the one the other kids related to.

And Li-Fang had been a nice kid, and had grown up into a pretty decent man, all things considered. She wasn't going to rat him out to Jiao.

She shook her head no, and his relief showed in the breath he let out. Then he gave a mischievous little smile, one that some fan somewhere would probably describe as incredibly hot. "Honest to God, these girls make it pretty hard to resist."

He gave the women an altogether different smile, and then led Megan back into the hallway.

But wait a minute. The reason she was here, dressed in someone else's clothes and ready to go onstage was because Li-Fang had been two-timing the last backup singer with a groupie. It wasn't even twenty-four hours later, and he had two more girls waiting for him on the greenroom couch? Jeez. No wonder he didn't want her talking to his mother.

At the end of a long corridor, Li-Fang lifted a thin metal chain that served as the only barrier between where they stood and the space immediately off of the stage. Just to make things abundantly clear, a sign dangled from the low arc of the metal: "Performers and Staff only past this point. NO BACKSTAGE PASSES." Megan ducked underneath, and then Li-Fang stepped over it with his longer legs.

"Li-Fang, at the risk of sounding like your mother, who doubtless is still hoping you're going to marry a nice Chinese girl and finish your engineering degree, just be careful with yourself, and with these women. I'm glad you at least know their names, but remember these are people. They've got dreams of their own, so treat them with some respect."

"Mrs. M, yes. I swear that every woman I'm with makes it very, very clear that she's totally into it. I mean, you've seen them, right? I know this sounds horrible, but none of us have to work hard to convince women to spend time with us. We're not taking advantage of anyone. I'm not! And neither is Kyle, if you're worried about him."

"Li-Fang, I was a mom before I turned twenty, and totally on my own when I was barely old enough to buy a beer. Can I point out that there's *wanting* it, and then there's living to regret it? Maybe these girls are all excited to hook up with you now. You're a celebrity, and you're a good-looking guy. Just, please, for me, do your best to remember that they're someone's sisters or cousins or best friends. Be a good guy, not a jerk."

"Don't have to do much jerking." She glared, and he threw his hands up like he was protesting his innocence. "Sorry," he said. "Don't worry. I always wrap it up tight, and I know Kyle does, too. At least, not like I've... Shit, that went down the wrong track pretty quick, didn't it?"

Megan grimaced. "I really wish I wasn't having this conversation."

He led her past a long row of empty equipment cases to the edge of the stage, not ten feet from Zane's drum kit. Techs were still moving around, doing whatever tech crews did before a show. The lights were low on the stage, which somehow highlighted the noise coming from the arena floor. The opening act had wrapped up, and the audience was swelling as late comers arrived and early birds got back from buying drinks and hitting the bathrooms.

She swallowed hard, wishing she'd grabbed a water bottle, and tried to adjust her top so things were a bit less on display. It sounded more like an approaching thunderstorm than a roomful of sympathetic fellow human beings—all of them would be staring at her, and, heaven help her, listening to her sing.

Too bad she didn't believe in God. This would be a handy time to have a divine power at her beck and call.

Megan honestly didn't have many qualms about her voice. Her voice was decent, judging by the compliments she'd received over the course of her lifetime. But for every person who'd listened to her sing at a show back in college, there were a hundred people in the audience tonight.

Intimidating.

She pulled at the shoulder strap of her top again, then looked up at Li-Fang. "How do you guys do this every night? Aren't you nervous as the dickens right now?" He was going to be shredding on the guitar and wailing on the violin. And singing.

Li-Fang gave her the grin she recognized from the band's posters. "Wrong question. The real question is how do we stop? Just you wait, Mrs. M. The biggest high you've ever felt is about ten minutes away from hitting you in the face. You're never going to want to go back to real life." He paused, eyes unfocused. He must really love being on stage.

Eventually he looked at her and said, "Wait here. The band'll enter from the other side, but your mic is on this side of the drum kit, so it's better to wait here than where we'll be. Closer for you. Just hide back here until we get to the chorus of 'Finding Livvie,' but be on that mic in time. You don't want to set yourself up for one of Kyle's post-show rants, trust me… especially not at a big show like LA. Lots of people here tonight. Lots of fans."

He stared off past Zane's drums like he couldn't wait to step out there and hear them screaming his name.

She hopped up onto a black case just out of sight from the stage and Li-Fang disappeared. Letting her feet dangle and recover from the trauma of these damn high-heeled boots, her mind drifted, watching the rather ratty-looking crew still hustle through the final moments of set up. The guys in the band, and Charlotte, of course—they were young and gorgeous, but the roadies were a different story. They were the sagging middle of the music world; the part that didn't age well, and didn't look pretty. They were also the crew that made things run. Just a collection of beer bellies, droopy jeans with back pockets bulging with cigarette packs, and T-shirts from bands from a generation gone by.

Why had she let Jaimie dupe her for so long? Why did she always give in? He never took her out to dinner, never treated her like a real girlfriend.

She was really going to do it this time: she was going to find a new job. She was one final exam away from finishing her undergrad degree, and after that, she'd be able to find something better, especially with twenty years of experience as a paralegal. If she stayed at the firm, she just knew she'd end up with Jaimie again. He knew exactly what buttons to push, and she'd be back in his bed.

A man who took his wife on a months-long cruise was not a man who was going to leave that wife for his paralegal. She had to make a change. She was going to make a change.

"Oh, no you don't," said a voice behind her.

A hand grabbed her elbow and she turned, almost falling as someone yanked her hard off of her perch.

"Watch it," she said, attempting to get her ridiculous heels back under her. "You trying to make me break a leg or something?"

"I swear to God, I don't need to deal with this right now. Did Li-Fang stash you here? I'm gonna have to ream that kid out one of these days."

She was too startled to notice much about the man holding her arm, but a touch of silver gleamed in the close-cropped hair about his ears. He must be close to her age. The hair above his forehead was all loose dark curls, longer than she'd expect from a guy in a suit.

And this guy was not only the kind of guy she thought of as "a suit," but he sure could wear one. Why was a man backstage at a rock concert wearing a coat and tie? But here he was, his tie a perfectly-knotted powder blue. She caught a brief glimpse of his eyes in a shaft of light falling in from off the stage, and realized they were a mossy green, heavily shadowed by dark lashes.

And then her attention was back on the hand gripping hard around her bare elbow. He began hauling her away, just as Zane started giving the count.

She shook him off, but he had moved her a fair distance already. Now he was blocking her way and scolding her like she was a naughty teen. "Backstage passes aren't full access to anything and everything. You're nuts if you think I'm going to let you run around back here!"

Kyle started singing. "*I'd been searching for days, never knowing if I'd find her/Thought I'd lost her for good when she first drove away.*"

She still had time, but not much.

Suit Guy looked her full in the face, eyes hard and almost dangerous; not someone she'd want to meet on a dark street. A scar ran white across his upper lip. "Don't think about running out there. I don't care if you are one of Li-Fang's little friends. The VIP area's that way."

He pointed the opposite direction from the stage, which helped her tear her eyes away from that scarred lip.

"Li-Fang told me to wait here." She wasn't keeping her voice down, but neither of them were likely to be heard over the sound pumping from the stage.

"I swear I'm going to have to renegotiate part of that idiot's contract. Girls try to make a break for the stage, and he knows that. I'm not having Li-Fang's arm candy spoil this show."

She slapped him, because, excuse her? Arm candy?

She rubbed her stinging right hand on her leg and was glad to see Suit Guy put his own hand to the reddening patch of skin on his jaw. Nice to see she could pack a wallop. She stood as straight as she could, glad for the extra inches of the uncomfortable gladiator boots, and tried to glare down at a man still six inches taller than she was. "I don't know who you are, or what you think you're doing, but no one talks to me like that. Now get out of my way, or I'm going to have you kicked out of here so fast it'll make your head spin."

He just raised his eyebrows. "Really? You've got a cheap backstage pass, and you suddenly think you're in charge? If anyone's getting kicked out, it's going to be you. Hey, Charlie?" He called to an enormous guy lounging on another of the cases that littered this part of the backstage area. "Come escort this *woman*," at this point Suit Guy's voice almost caught in his throat, as if he couldn't believe he had to use a polite term in reference to her, "to the nearest exit. And make sure to confiscate her pass. Actually...." he said, reaching for the dangling tag.

She whipped her arms across her chest, because it sure as hell seemed like he was trying to cop a feel. Her breasts were far too exposed in this ridiculous bustier wanna-be she was wearing.

When he kept reaching she slapped him again, this time on

the hand, and the man yelped. "Jeez, lady, what's with the slapping thing you've got going?"

Before she could answer, Kyle's voice launched into the song's chorus. "*It was Livvie I saw./It was Livvie that day.*"

Megan and Mr. Suit both whipped their heads toward the stage. She made a break for it, and an arm like an iron bar against her stomach stopped her mid-step.

This chorus was always supported by harmonies, but Kyle's was the only voice singing.

She almost felt it when Suit Guy realized what was happening, that no one was singing backup.

This was no man just dropping in for the show. This was someone who knew everything about the Sutter Boys and their music.

She started shaking her head. "Damn it, you idiot. I've missed my entrance."

"Your entrance?" Those green eyes of his widened. "You're the singer Li-Fang found for tonight."

"Yes, fancy pants. That's me."

He really looked at her, and took in the bustier. The shoes. The tight jeans. The make up.

What did he think, that the audience would pay to hear a band where the women were in frumpy sweats or ratty T-shirts? This industry sold women like sex objects, and now he was judging her for it. "Eyes up here, bud."

He raised his eyes, and might have blushed. "I'm sorry. Go! You'd better get out there, hadn't you?"

Before she could move, though, he grabbed her hand. "Wait! Your pass," he said. "Don't wear your pass onstage."

She ripped off the stupid thing and held it out.

"Break a leg out there," he said.

She barely registered his words, still incredibly pissed he'd made her late. She was not looking forward to Kyle's reaction.

She had left him hanging for that first chorus, and he was going to be furious.

At least one good thing came from those last aggravating moments. By the time Megan marched onto the stage, she'd completely forgotten to be nervous.

3

She strutted into the lights, trying to look like she hadn't just missed her entrance.

She was appalled that she was late, but she would be darned if she let the audience in on that secret. So she faked it, threw back her shoulders, and moved like she was doing exactly what she was supposed to be doing. This part of performing couldn't be forgotten; this body-memory still singing through her muscles, even though she hadn't been onstage she was pregnant with Kyle. And looking like she *owned* it was even more important in a moment like this one, when things weren't going as planned.

Kyle hadn't blinked; just kept playing, which was exactly what he needed to do to cover her missed entrance. And right now, she had a job to do, too. They were all here to give this audience a great show. She'd never forgive herself if her late entrance ruined that.

She had missed the entire first chorus by the time she got to the mic, so she stood motionless, trying not to look out past the lights. It was incredibly hot on stage, the lights painting her body with solid waves of heat. Toward the end of the second verse, just before she needed to come in, Kyle glanced over his shoulder, presumably checking to see if she was there.

He glared—she deserved that, she'd been late—then turned back to his mic and gave a very exaggerated pelvic thrust to punctuate the last line of the verse.

Right. Message received.

She should be dancing, not standing stiff as a board.

Trying to free her body up, she shifted her balance between her feet to sway a bit, and ended up feeling like a complete idiot. At least the motion loosened her up enough that her breath came more easily. She got a good, solid lungful before her first chorus and then came in, supporting Kyle's melody:

> It was Livvie I saw,
> She was fading away.
> Like the light of her smile
> Had nothing to say
> To the world any longer.
> She moved farther from me
> And the ash from the sky rained down.

She leaned into her mic with one hand on the stand, the other just skimming the top of her left thigh, and set her voice free.

And then everything was better. Singing got her out of her head and made everything better; even a song that had as much pain as this one.

Suit Guy had moved forward along the side of the stage, closer to the audience but still hidden from their view. He was level with Kyle, so it was easy for him to catch Megan's eye and smile at her encouragingly. Even against the glare of the lights, Megan could see that the expression took over his whole face: mouth, cheeks, and eyes all shone. He even lifted his fingers to his forehead in a silly little salute as she sang.

Huh.

She got looser, both in her voice and in her body, the way Kyle clearly wanted. Made sense. She needed to be part of the show, get the crowd excited and moving. Good lord, the number of people watching her, listening to her!

Time sped up. Every moment on the stage felt like the first moment she'd ever been alive, vivid and demanding and just pulling her forward, one beat of music to the next. She gave that crowd everything, and after her first thirty minutes, Megan was as sweaty as if she'd been training for a 5k. She also felt higher than she'd ever been in her life.

Deeper into the set she was able to take in her surroundings a bit, not quite as petrified that she was going to miss a cue.

Kyle and Li-Fang both had a certain look which they laser-focused on women in the front row, a look that was way more obvious to her now that she was onstage. They would tuck their chins slightly, so they could look out from under their eyebrows, and it made the women scream and fan themselves. It looked like the way the model on the cover of a romance novel would glower at the camera, and she'd never seen either of them do anything remotely like that growing up, so it had to be completely fake. She found it darn funny.

She glanced at the keyboard player, Charlotte, during one of those "smoldering" looks from Kyle, and caught her shaking her head and hiding her own grin. The fans might have thought Kyle and Li-Fang were sex gods trying to melt female panties, but apparently Charlotte also knew how phony those tilted heads and lowered eyebrows really were. From then on, whenever either of the male leads made their "sexy eyes" at the audience, she and Charlotte would exchange glances and try not to laugh. Charlotte had been with the band for almost five years, and though Megan didn't know her well, it felt in this moment like they might have similar senses of humor.

What had that old boyfriend of Charlotte's been named?

Stu? Stan? Something like that. He had been a truly terrible bass player. The only good thing he had done for the band was encouraging Kyle to add Charlotte. When Charlotte and what's-his-face broke up, Kyle kept Charlotte and kicked out Steve. Then Theo, their current bassist, had answered an open audition call posted in the music building at San Jose State, and the lineup had really gelled. Zane had been part of the group from the beginning.

When Megan wasn't mugging at Charlotte, she danced to the solid beat coming off of Zane's drums. Every now and then she whipped her head around, and could almost feel drops of sweat shaking free from her hair. Heat pulsed off the bodies dancing in the pit just below the stage, adding to the intensity of the lights. She was suddenly grateful for the sleeveless bustier, tight jeans, and heels. At least she was relatively cool.

Kyle kept glancing over his shoulder during the show, looking annoyed if he caught her standing still. But she was getting a tiny bit more comfortable with this ridiculous night, holding her own on vocals, and trying to rile up the crowd with her movements. She danced like no one was watching, like she was in the crowd. She jumped, tossed her hair, and strutted in her best impression of Madonna in the Vogue video.

That dated her, didn't it? But, face it: that was a woman who could entertain a crowd.

It was so freeing to dance onstage. Back when she'd been in the band with the Marshall brothers, dancing hadn't exactly been encouraged, but she loved to dance. Moving took the joy she always felt when she was singing and amped it up even further.

She gripped the mic stand, the metal blessedly cool against her fingers. Tonight, no matter how much fun it was to move, her main job was to sing, and that required a balancing act. She had to convince the audience that this was no-holds-barred movement, while still keeping her heart rate under control. And the longer the set went on, the more out of shape she felt.

She stopped jumping and just moved her hips, and her heart rate slowed by a welcome beat or two.

"Free Again," started with a descant, just an open "ooh" that floated above the bassline. During sound check, Kyle had told her not to be shy. So she let loose, feeling her sound reverberate while Theo's bass danced under her voice.

Li-Fang had the violin again. He pulled out an intricate line with his bow, ornamenting her descant; his violin was sweetly soprano, her voice just lower—mezzo warmth, but high in her range—and the two of them floated octaves above Theo's steady, silky bass.

Kyle watched them over his shoulder, clearly pleased. He let the rhythm build while Li-Fang's fans screamed their appreciation. While Li-Fang preened and played, Charlotte snuck in on the keyboard so subtly that even Megan didn't notice exactly when she'd started.

They spun it out into something almost earth-shaking, until the music needed to break open just to sustain itself. Only then did Kyle wail in on the rhythm guitar, enormous swings of his arm across the strings, those cheekbones of his catching the light.

He leaned in to the mic and sang.

This was a song the band had written the night they called the 2020 election, back when it felt like the hospitals were going to overflow with Covid patients, and that no one was ever going to dance in a crowd like this again.

Megan went wild, along with every other person in the venue.

We're free again.
Free to live our lives.
We're free again.

Free to love, free to dance,
Free to raise our heads with pride
And carry
Hope
Into the world.

She poured her soul into the chorus. She could growl a bit on this one, let the rasp color her voice, really dig into the sense of renewed promise they'd all felt that night.

During the bridge she closed her eyes, holding the mic, letting the crowd's emotion carry her into the song's darker turn. It gutted her, the way Kyle spun music out of nothing. Zane pulled things back, bare thumping bass drum on the downbeat, until Theo's bass grew insistent and Zane began to tease the high hats, bringing music back to the final chorus. The energy built until she couldn't keep her eyes closed, and she sure as hell couldn't keep her body still. Just outside the harshest glare of the lights, Suit Guy leaned against the wall that separated backstage from the vastness of the arena, staring straight at her, the tiniest of smiles softening his lips.

What did that mean?

Damn him. She could dance if she wanted to. Kyle had basically ordered her to cut loose. Suit Guy over there wasn't going to destroy her mood.

So she danced harder, threw a body roll into the beat, let her bum curve its way through the melody. Offstage, the man's eyes widened.

See if you can find someone better at this than I am, she thought, throwing one more glance off of the stage.

She rolled her hips and let her voice wail behind Kyle's until Kyle actually turned and stretched out his arm, palm up, acknowledging her in front of the crowd. She waved back at them, looking away from the wings, sending her soul into the audience.

Zane moved to the toms, leading into the next number, and Theo wove a new bass line.

God, the way the bass thrummed through her body when she was in the middle of the band, stage monitors blasting the sound at her, her in-ears carrying Kyle's voice more clearly, at the front of the mix. She could hear how often Theo had listened to the Red Hot Chili Peppers. He'd picked up Flea's love of a moving line, and man, that boy had just gotten better since they'd added him to the band.

Theo caught her watching him. He strolled across the stage toward her, leaning in to play his bass inches away from her. While Megan danced, Theo kept his eyes glued to her body. He had been staring at her for most of the set, but now that he was right in her personal space, Megan got damned uncomfortable. It felt like he was essentially propositioning her in front of a packed arena, and she had to play along. The way these songs played up everyone's sexuality, wasn't blatant flirting what the crowd wanted to see?

Off stage, the guy in the wings folded his arms across his chest, the set of his shoulders growing tighter. The cuff links at his wrists caught the light, but her eyes instantly flew to his, given the stare he was fixing her with. Was he upset? By Theo, or by her? And then she looked back at Theo, who mouthed the words, *"I'd do you. You up for it?"*

Good lord, Theo was literally the same age as her son, and he was—what?—asking her for a hookup live on stage? Her jaw dropped, and her mind went blank.

So maybe it shouldn't have surprised her that she missed her next cue, leaving Kyle hanging on the vocals. Again. She'd been late to start the set, thanks to Suit Guy over there in the wings, and now Theo had messed her up again. Okay, well, it was the only time she'd performed in front of a crowd this large, so maybe mistakes were to be expected. The first one certainly hadn't been her fault. But this one was. Kyle covered the glitch, but she knew she'd missed her cue. So did Kyle; and so, apparently, did the guy in the wings. Now both of them were glaring at her. Theo just gave her a cocky little smirk, like he enjoyed rattling her.

Men and their egos.

She jerked her chin at Theo, hoping he would take the hint and go back to his own spot on the stage. After another moment, he finally did.

That hadn't been fun. Had the crowd noticed her second gaffe? Did they all think she was an idiot for being up here, prancing around and pretending she actually belonged onstage with their favorite band, with all the hard young bodies and camera-ready faces and flamboyant clothes?

The show continued, and she was pretty sure she eventually redeemed herself. Kyle wasn't throwing her dirty looks anymore, Theo was playing nice in his own corner of the sandbox, and even Suit Guy offstage had loosened up a bit.

Who was he, anyway? Someone from the label?

At the end of the show, she was covered in a layer of sweat. The many straps of the bustier felt like they had been individually super-glued to her torso. A few strands of her hair had escaped her ponytail and floated near her ears, but the rest of it was plastered to her scalp. She now felt a profound appreciation for the makeup artist who had insisted on waterproof makeup.

Her whole body buzzed.

Before the show, Li-Fang had told her she'd be high on performing, and he had not oversold. Good God, that was like nothing she'd ever experienced before, and she'd only been singing back up! What did Kyle feel every night, hearing them scream his name? How did it feel to know that his lyrics and his vocals could pack a stadium—even now, after a pandemic had made crowded indoor spaces feel threatening and dangerous?

She didn't want to leave the stage, but they'd finished their last number. The crowd was still cheering for the band, and she didn't want to hang around like an interloper, so she retreated offstage, feeling a flush of pride in Kyle and the band. Their musicianship and plain old stamina was incredible; after that show, she appreciated it more than ever.

She dropped her hands to her knees, trying to catch her breath; then pushed herself upright again and clapped. God, this band was amazing.

From in front of the crowd, Kyle searched until he spotted her in the wings. He beckoned, but she shook her head, no. He shrugged and turned to the crowd. "Hey, LA, any of you notice the awesome backing vocals tonight? I'd like to invite the talented Megan Gamble back onto the stage, and thank her for subbing at the last minute. And give her a very warm welcome, would you? Because she also happens to be my mom."

The crowd made so much noise that he broke off, smiling and holding an outstretched arm toward her until she had to walk back into view.

Kyle said something in Li-Fang's ear, then shouted something to Zane on drums. While she was waving, the band launched into what was apparently going to be tonight's encore: Panic at the Disco's, "Hey, Look Ma, I've Made it."

She laughed and grabbed her mic stand. The original didn't have backing vocals, but there was an awesome trumpet line that she could cover.

One last chance to sing and feel this incredible high, and she enjoyed the hell out of it.

At the end of the encore, Kyle shouted, "Thank you very much, LA! You've been a great audience! We can't wait to get back here again!" He led the band offstage with the crowd roaring, stamping, and clapping their approval.

Maybe now that she'd done Kyle a real favor, he'd finally make time to actually talk to her.

In the greenroom, she collapsed onto one of the couches,

wishing she could open a bottle of water and pour it over her head to cool off. But guyliner and men's hair reacted better to that sort of thing, and it was clear the women in the room didn't mind the wet T-shirts or bare torsos of the young guys, while they sure as heck wouldn't appreciate it if Megan did the same. Then again, at the moment the guys were too pumped from the performance to pay the women much mind.

Suit Guy—the one who'd tried to kick her out, and then had smiled at her while she was onstage— stood near the catering tables talking into his phone. He hadn't done her any favors with Kyle, making her late like that, but he was awfully easy on the eyes.

When there were men that looked like Suit Guy in the world, why had she wasted years on an affair with her married boss? Her mind jumped to that damned, gut-kicking announcement this morning about the cruise. She'd been played.

But right now? Right now she felt strong. Jamie might not know it yet, but Megan was going to tell him to take a hike. She was going to cut him off for good. After that show, she felt like she finally had the strength to walk away from him. Because she deserved better.

Tonight had been incredible.

She took a slug of her water, then pulled at one of the bustier straps where her drying sweat was plastering it to her skin. She needed a shower something bad.

Suit Guy lowered his phone and focused his green eyes on her. There was no expression on his face, which pissed her off; he owed her an apology for making her late.

But then he nodded at her, and she had no idea what that meant. Suddenly, Megan was hyper-aware of herself in these skinny jeans and high heels, and a bustier that must look ridiculous now that she was off the stage. Was Suit Guy checking her out?

As she fidgeted with one of the straps of her top, Kyle

walked in. Where had he been? Suit Guy caught Kyle's eye, then took in the rest of the band. "Five minutes, guys, Charlotte; then you've got the meet-and-greet. So if you're going to grab a clean shirt, do it now. Showers later, okay? The bus leaves at midnight." He glanced at his wrist. A watch glinted—the kind that cost more than her mortgage payment. "That's just under two hours from now, people, and it's a long drive to the Bay Area. Be ready."

Tour manager? Band manager?

Man, this guy was seriously gorgeous. And it wasn't like she was missing a point of reference on the handsome scale. She'd raised Kyle.

Kyle's looks had been drawing attention since his toddler years. When he was two, a man hauling a long-lensed camera approached her in a park while she was pushing Kyle on a swing. The photographer told her he'd be happy to do some test shots of her toddler if she wanted to get him into modeling. She'd found the experience rather creepy, and had thrown away the card as soon as she got Kyle back to their apartment, but it had happened again and again over the years. Even during middle school, at the age when normal humans look awkward and frightened of their growing bodies, Kyle had smirked confidently at the camera, and the camera had loved him for it. That eighth grade photo? The one with his hair almost hanging in his eyes, and that dimple of his highlighting his smile? She had that one framed and sitting on the little table in her entryway.

That's what she needed to do! She should dig up their old photo albums and bring them to the show tomorrow night. Kyle would make time to go through old pics with her, right? Though clearly, he was only interested in ignoring her at the moment. Why should she expect it would be easier to bond by looking at photos than singing together to thousands?

Well, she had to try something.

Megan looked between Kyle and Suit Guy. The contrast was remarkable: Kyle was lean and, like a lot of musicians, looked like a bit of a bad boy in the dark, sweaty, and close-fitting clothes of a musician fresh from a concert. Suit Guy, on the other hand, looked perfectly groomed, like he could step directly into a board meeting. He was larger than Kyle; his breadth showed in the tailoring of his suit's shoulders and chest, and he also had an inch or two of height on Kyle. While Kyle had the charisma of a performer, Suit Guy had the confidence of a man who'd worked hard and by virtue of sheer competence had found his place in the world.

Why was she even looking? Even if she really, truly managed to walk away from Jaimie for good, a man like that would never bother with a woman like her: a college drop-out, old enough for a couple of lines on her face. Nothing like the pretty young women that followed a band like this.

And if he was the manager, he could have his pick of most of them, right?

Okay, enough ogling. God, she was tired. Maybe she should just get out of here and catch up with Kyle tomorrow in San Jose. Or not, depending on his mood.

Photo albums. Bring photo albums.

Was she supposed to use a driver to get to her hotel, or maybe just Uber? Could an Uber even get to the stage entrance for a pickup? She needed her phone.

Kyle looked her way and shouted, "Mom!"

After the high of the show, it was its own sort of smaller high to have Kyle acknowledge her. "Yes, Kyle?"

"I think you can skip the meet-and-greet, but meet me in my dressing room, okay? We need to talk."

Tired as she was, she could hold off on getting to the hotel for a bit longer, especially if Kyle actually wanted to see her. She nodded her agreement, but wasn't certain Kyle even noticed. Suit Guy was already shepherding the rest of the band out the greenroom door. Maybe he was the tour manager?

Music still pumped in through the speakers, but without the band, the greenroom felt desolate, like the moment after a party when everyone's gone home and there's nothing left to do but pick up red plastic cups and throw away the disgusting mess of dip still left at the bottom of the bowl next to the empty chip basket. She almost started to gather the trash on the table when she realized she didn't have to; the arena or the band would have staff for that.

The day really hit her, like the lights in her body had all gone out. She wanted to curl up on the couch, pull a blanket over herself, and sleep. Sadly, there weren't any blankets, and the couch was probably covered with some pretty disgusting stuff. Worse, the sweat drying on her arms and under the bustier had started to turn into actual salt crystals, scratching away at the sides of her breasts like fine-grit sandpaper.

She wandered back into the hall and turned away from the noise of the fans. Maybe there was a shower in Kyle's dressing room.

Megan found the door where Kyle and Little Miss Blonde had disappeared before the show, and opened it. Bingo: Kyle's acoustic guitar on the floor near a couch, lying in its open case; a hot mirror on one wall, like the one where they'd given her boy his eyeliner. How odd was that? She had washed crap off his face so many times when he was a tot, and now people were actually getting paid to layer it on him. And, yes! The door at the back led to a tiny private bathroom, with a shower stall stocked with tiny bottles of shampoo and conditioner and shower gel. There was even a fresh towel.

Megan stripped off her drying clothes and stepped under the hot water, letting it stream over her head and shoulders. She ran her hands through her product-ridden hair and then paused, water hot and glorious. And the day hit her again.

Holy shit.

She had just been onstage.

At a rock concert.

Singing.

In front of what, ten thousand people?

Holy shit.

She tipped her head back and closed her eyes, her arms limp at her sides. Unbelievable. When she could move again, she worked the shampoo through her hair and started singing loudly, the way she did at home. She had just rinsed her hair when the door to the bathroom banged open.

Suit Guy stood in the doorway, and there was nothing but a partially fogged up shower door between her body and those green, green eyes.

"Shit!"

She actually didn't know if she had sworn or if he had.

4

What had been the chorus of "Finding Livvie" turned into a scream.

She jerked one hand down to cover herself, while Suit Guy threw his hands over his face and swore. An endless instant later, her hand finally connected with the towel, and she dragged it across the front of her body.

He was already backing out of the door. "Sorry! Sorry! No one was supposed to be in here!" He shut the door with one hand while the other hid his eyes.

God, this was humiliating. She raised her voice. "What are you thinking, barging into a bathroom without even knocking?"

Megan had no desire to give the guy more of a show. Maybe there were women who'd relish the chance to show off their toned bodies, but she wasn't one of them. Plus, he'd hidden his eyes like he'd been recoiling in horror. She remembered the moment in *There's Something About Mary* when a peeping Tom thinks he's got his binoculars trained on the pretty twenty-year-old, but instead gets an eyeful of a seventy-year-old's naked breasts.

The only reason she'd been onstage tonight was because Li-

Fang couldn't figure out whether to keep his hands on the last backup singer or a random groupie. Then she'd been pretty brutally confronted by her son's sexuality, seeing him waltz off with the bimbo of the hour. And now that she was naked in front of Suit Guy, all she could think of was how her body compared to the bodies of the twenty-somethings crawling around the backstage area.

Megan wasn't twenty.

So what, this guy was cowering in fright? He'd never seen a naked woman old enough to toss her fake ID? Maybe she was repulsive.

Furious and mortified, she wrapped the towel around herself, letting her hair drip in stringy clumps onto her shoulders. She stormed out into the dressing room. "What did you think you were doing? Haven't you heard of knocking?" She stalked toward him, thinking that if he hated her body, at least it was a tool she could use to shock him or get him to back off.

And back off he did, retreating as she got nearer, despite the fact that she was only five-two to his six-foot-something. He ended up with his back to the couch and the storage shelves next to it.

"I'm sorry, alright? That girl Kyle's with left her phone in here, so he sent me to get it, okay? And then I heard the water. Why didn't you lock the door?"

She got to the middle of the room and stood as tall as she could. "The locks's broken. And it's not okay to walk into a bathroom like that. Get the hell out of here!"

She made a shooing motion with one hand, the other keeping her towel in place. As she waved her arm, she spotted the bag with her street clothes behind Brandon, on the shelves against the wall with the door. Why hadn't she brought them into the bathroom with her? Now what was she going to do? She wasn't going to change back into a sweaty wanna-be corset, that was for sure.

He edged sideways toward the door to the room, still between her and the bag with her clothes. Then he took a visible breath and tugged at his collar. He dialed back the volume on his voice and actually sounded contrite. "I'm sorry. Look, we've had a few problems this tour with the newer roadies. They like to dare each other to do stuff, silly things like grab a shower in one of the band's dressing rooms. That's why I busted in. So I'm really sorry."

She clutched the towel tighter, trying to figure out how to get past him to grab her clothes, when the door to the hall opened, and of course—yes, of course!—Kyle stood there, the girl from earlier tucked under his arm. Because what Megan needed was more of an audience, clearly.

"There's my phone!" said the girl, heading straight for a phone on the dressing room's couch. As if she didn't care that Megan was standing there in a towel, dripping wet.

Kyle looked back and forth between his mother and the man in the room. "Mom! What the hell? You? And Brandon?" Kyle's hand motioned between the two of them, asking the question.

"No!"

The guy (whose name was apparently Brandon) spoke over her. "No! I swear, Kyle, I had no idea she was in here. And I apologized. She couldn't lock the door."

Brandon shot a glance her way, still looking guilty. When she shivered, he looked away, searching for someplace else to focus his eyes.

Megan still couldn't figure out why the room was suddenly full. "Kyle, weren't you supposed to be at that fan thing? I hope you didn't shortchange them."

The girl hadn't taken her eyes off of Megan, which was starting to make Megan's skin crawl. She shivered. Her arms were wet, and water dripped from her hair onto the industrial-grade carpet under her feet. She could practically feel athlete's foot leaping off the carpet and into the spaces between her toes.

The girl stared straight at Megan and said, "He didn't short-change anyone."

Charming. Just the kind of girl everyone wants to bring home to mother.

At that point the young woman turned and looked up at Kyle possessively. Megan's stomach churned. Next thing, the girl would be posting on some social media site saying, "I just had sex with the lead singer of the Sutter Boys. Happy to share details." Way to ride the claim to fame.

Her son sure knew how to pick them.

Kyle stepped away from the girl and calmly said, "Cool it. That's my mom."

It wasn't an apology, but at least it was better than his atti-tude had been before the show, when he'd stomped off so he could get laid.

Megan looked longingly at her bag of clothes on the shelves between the couch and where Kyle was, at the door. Right next to Little Miss Obnoxious, who was now looking down at her phone. Brandon followed Megan's gaze and immediately moved toward Megan's bag. "Are these your things?"

She nodded, and Brandon plucked the bag off the shelf. He took two steps toward Megan and pressed her clothes into the arm that wasn't holding up her towel without her having to ask.

"Thanks," she said quietly, beginning to move back toward the bathroom.

"So, Mom," said Kyle before she'd made it more than a step or two, looking between Megan and Brandon. "I'm glad you're both here. I wanted to talk to you about tour."

Brandon shot him a glance. "Let your mom throw on some clothes, and then we'll talk."

"Nah," said Kyle. "This should only take a second, right?

She can think things over when she's getting changed. 'Kay, Mom?"

Standing there on the hairy edge of shivering from the cold, for some idiotic reason all Megan could think to say was, "Could you at least introduce us or something?"

"Sorry, Mom. Mom, this is Shell. Shell, this is my Mom."

The girl smiled and started to say something, but Megan jerked her chin toward Brandon. She sure as hell wasn't going to risk letting go of the towel to gesture, and she was holding the bag in her other hand. "Not her. Him!"

Kyle did a small double take. "Wait, you haven't met?" Kyle glanced again between Megan and Brandon, like he was trying to understand why his mom was wearing a towel in front of a guy she didn't know.

Brandon stepped forward, that pressed shirt and perfect tie looking so out of place in the grunge of the tiny room. Did he have to be so damned attractive? God, after years where the only man to touch her had been Jaimie, why did she have to meet a guy who looked like this—looking like this? And why did it have to happen in front of her pissed-off son and this girl he was hooking up with? She was pretty sure Kyle didn't even know Shell's last name.

Megan shivered again, and her nipples did that thing that cold nipples do. She held her arm firmly across her chest.

Yep. She was definitely beyond *mortified*.

"Mom, this is our new manager, Brandon Thatch. Brandon, this is my mom."

Of course this was a guy who was important to the band. Not just the tour manager, but someone who'd be around for the long haul. She recognized his name, but they'd never met.

And now, because of the introduction, the guy who had been horrified to see her in the shower was basically forced to look directly at her. She was holding the bag in front of her chest, but her legs were on full display, and the curve of her hips was only hidden by this thin towel.

He lifted his eyes to her face and put out his hand, trying to pretend he hadn't been looking where he'd definitely been looking.

She tried to free her right hand by shifting her left to hold up both the bag of clothes and her towel, and then wondered what the hell she was thinking.

Brandon saw her problem and lowered his own hand. "Megan Gamble," he said, using her real name, not Kyle's last name. "It's a pleasure to finally meet you. And Kyle, let your mother go put her clothes on while I try to explain about earlier."

Dang it. She couldn't leave now. "Kyle, about that, I'm really sorry I missed my entrance. I was trying, but Brandon held me up."

Brandon chimed in. "I saw her offstage, and thought we might have another crasher. You remember what happened back in Vegas when that girl ran onstage, right? I was taking away your mom's pass at just about the time she was supposed to be getting on mic."

"But I'm still really sorry, Kyle. It was my job to be there on time, and I messed up. No excuses. I apologize."

"Just don't do it again," said Kyle.

Megan did a double take. Her hair was at that awful stage between actively dripping and drying in unflattering hunks, and she was crashing hard after the long day. She really wanted to get dressed. But what the heck was he talking about? "What? How would I possibly miss another entrance? It's not like I'll ever be singing a show with you again. Look, can you just call me tomorrow?"

"No, because I wanted to talk to you about tomorrow night. And I think this is better in person."

The girl huffed and dropped onto the couch, tired of being

ignored. Kyle kept his eyes on Megan, which she took as confirmation that this woman was a one-night stand at most. After a moment, Kyle looked toward Brandon, who shrugged, then shook his head quickly.

The two men seemed to have some sort of mind-reading thing going on. Brandon said, "Nope. Nothing yet. I know you want to hear Greta, but she's under contract right now. I can't get her in for an audition for a few days, so the next few concerts we're just gonna have to fill in however we can. Then again, it isn't like Li-Fang gave us much time, did he?"

Kyle shook his head. "No, he didn't." Then Kyle shifted his attention to Megan and finally really looked at her. Sure, he'd noticed Megan when he'd come into the room, but now there was actual eye contact, the kind he hadn't had with her in years.

What had she done to blow up this one relationship in her life that really meant something to her?

"Mom, your late entrance aside, you really did us a solid tonight. And I trust you. We need a replacement singer until Brandon can find someone permanent. We've listened to some voices, but no one feels like a good fit. Brandon's got a great lead on a singer we think would work, but for right now, we're in a bind unless you can step in. You're here, and if you'll just stop flirting with Theo on stage, you can totally save our butts."

"Wait, you're blaming me for that thing with Theo? That was his fault. He started it!" Megan said.

And now she sounded like a toddler. Wonderful.

"Maybe it isn't fair, because Theo was pretty in your face, but he does that on stage. And if you can keep your libido in check and all, maybe you could—" Kyle looked at Brandon again, who nodded—"Could you hop on the tour with us? At least until we can hire someone else?"

Was he nuts? He had to be high.

Actually, she hadn't seen any sign that he was drugged out, so there was that. Still, this was a crazy big ask.

"I do have a job, you know. And—dammit, Kyle!—I have to take my last final on Monday."

"Well, get an extension or something. I never finished my degree, either."

"Yeah, but you have a career now. And I never wanted to sit around working as a paralegal for my whole life, and I need to finish my BA before I can get a better job. I'd be giving up a lot to go on tour, even for just a few days."

Kyle's face changed, got meaner somehow. "Well, your day job does have some perks you seem to enjoy."

Her eyes widened. Kyle couldn't possibly be implying what he seemed to be implying, could he? First of all, he had no idea she had ever slept with her boss. Well, she was pretty certain he didn't know that. No one else did. And sleeping with Jaimie wasn't exactly a perk. More like an unhealthy addiction. Jaimie played on her sympathies until he finally got what he wanted. They'd scratch their mutual itch, and she'd wind up so disgusted with herself that she couldn't face her two best friends for weeks.

Okay, so she needed to ignore his insinuation. "If you mean, for example, that they're going to pay for law school if I ever get this damned BA finished, yeah, it does have some perks."

Brandon tucked a hand into his pants pocket and raised his eyebrows. "That's quite the benefit. You're lucky to work at a place like that."

"Are you implying that I don't deserve my job because I never finished my BA?" He'd actually been pretty nice to her before, but she'd always been pretty insecure about dropping out.

Brandon raised his hands. "No! Not at all. It just sounds like a firm that takes care of its people, which is a good thing."

Kyle interjected. "We're getting off the topic. And Mom, I know the timing sounds like shit for you, with the exam, but could you at least try to ask for an extension, or take it online or something? We really need someone on tour, and we don't have a lot of options."

She turned to Brandon. "Isn't that your job, to find someone?"

His voice was almost defensive. "Yes, but while there are vocalists lined up to sing with a band as hot as the Sutter Boys, we can't use just anyone. Based on the demo tapes, the voice we've liked best actually belongs to my fiancé's little sister, Greta, who's a damned good singer, right Kyle?"

Kyle nodded, and Brandon continued, looking at Megan like he really wanted to convince her of this. "Greta's on another tour right now. Once that wraps up, she can start with the Sutter Boys, assuming the band likes what she does in her audition."

"And do I have to audition, too?"

Kyle stared at her. "What do you think this afternoon was? Tonight? Jeez, Mom, you're hired if you want the job."

That's right. She hadn't even thought about it, but they would probably pay her, so she should be able to afford the time off. It wasn't like a vacation or something.

Assuming she could talk Jaimie into letting her use vacation days. Which would mean she'd have to be nice to him. All she wanted to do was to spit in the man's coffee when he wasn't looking, and now she had to ask him for a favor.

This still seemed like a crazy idea. Megan looked back at Kyle. "I still think you're out of your mind. You're asking your *mother* to join your band on tour? Won't the macho police come and rescind your hot guy card if you do something like that?"

Brandon made a strangled sound. "Macho?" Brandon looked at Kyle, who shrugged.

And there is was. She was mortified. *Again.* Mortified on repeat.

Pretty much like she'd been feeling for what felt like an

hour or two. "Okay, so maybe 'macho' hasn't been a thing for a while. I probably sound like I'm pushing sixty."

Brandon said, "Well, you sure as hell don't look it. But I'm pretty sure no one has said the word 'macho' since sometime in the 1980s. And no, I don't think Kyle is going to sacrifice one ounce of his street cred. Not if we keep you dressed in stuff like you wore tonight."

Kyle broke in. "Okay, Brandon, maybe can we not talk about Mom like she's a sex object? Really don't want to go there."

Megan tightened the towel again, careful not to let too much leg or hip show as she readjusted the cloth. "Double standard, much?" She looked at the woman playing phone on the couch, and made sure Kyle followed her gaze.

"Okay, I get it, but I don't have to like it." Kyle sighed, sounding exactly like he had six or seven years ago when he was still a pouting teenager, not a musician with paparazzi stalking his every move.

Kyle dropped the whiny tone but tried to plead his case. "Mom, you were planning on hitting the San Jose show tomorrow night anyway, right? And after that is Sacramento, which is a reasonable drive from your place. Maybe you can just sing for those two shows, and Brandon can work on trying to find a singer who can cover until we make a permanent hire. I mean, it's gotta be tempting, right? Basically the choice is to go back to your firm and a paralegal job you've been complaining about all my life, or come on a national tour with us. And this isn't just a favor. You'll probably make more on tour than you do at the firm."

"Pretty much a given," Megan said.

She twitched the towel again, trying to cover a bit more of her body.

Brandon's face became slightly less stern. "In case you're interested, the contract's per show, with additional per diems for travel days." Then he dropped a number which was pretty impressive.

"That sounds fair," she said, and took a moment to think.

This wasn't the kind of decision she wanted to make in thirty seconds, but if she wasn't going to sing, then the band would have to scramble for another sub to cover the next night's show, and that seemed like a pretty big problem. If she did sing, it would certainly help out the band. And being on stage had honestly been one of the most incredible experiences she'd ever had.

Ever.

But could she really do this? She stalled. "I'll have to call in to the office, get my boss to give me leave or something."

Kyle said, "Isn't Keiko a partner now? I'm sure she would put in a good word with Jaimie. Not like you need it or anything."

Again with the comment. Did he suspect that things between her and Jaimie weren't entirely professional?

God, she hoped not. She wasn't proud of how she broke down every few months and slept with Jaimie, and her son was pretty much the last person on the planet she wanted to suspect that. But Jaimie was so good at pleading his case, and making those sad eyes at her, and telling her how miserable it was at home; how he was really, truly leaving his wife for good this time.

Well, going on tour would certainly help break her of that habit, now, wouldn't it?

"You really want me?"

Kyle and Brandon exchanged looks again.

Brandon answered. "We really do. Please. Obviously you have your own life and responsibilities, but this is really important to us, to the band. If you could at least cover us for the next couple of shows, it would give me a bit of breathing room to check out a few more leads, let Kyle listen to a few more demos.

Better still, it might give us a chance to convince you to join the tour for a bit longer, until Greta can get free."

Why the hell was she hesitating?

Maybe because it was patently ridiculous. A woman her age should NOT be onstage with the guys in this band. But why did she keep forgetting about Charlotte? These boys were the definition of pretty; even her own son, with his shaggy hair, too-high cheekbones, and body so ripped that she could understand all the fans who gushed over him, as creepy as it was to think that way. Kyle looked so much like his father! She sent up a silent thank you to Jason, because being objectively attractive certainly helped in a career like music. She followed her thanks with the automatic "may you rest in peace" that always tagged onto her thoughts of her long-ago boyfriend.

Well, maybe she'd contributed a bit to Kyle's looks. Their eyes were not only the same color of gray, but they were also the same shape.

It was just that—young men like these, these pretty boys that every woman (and plenty of men) lusted after—they shouldn't be performing with someone ordinary like she was. She wasn't hideous, standing here nearly naked in this damn towel, but she was nothing like the kind of woman these guys put in their music videos.

She didn't fit into this world, but Li-Fang had been right earlier. Being on stage was a drug like no other. No wonder so many musicians ended up with substance abuse problems, she thought.

Remembering the high of performing made something click inside her. She wanted this, more than she'd wanted anything in a long, long time.

Well, duh. She needed to start thinking about herself; this was exactly what she'd been thinking about this morning, after hearing that Jaimie was going to take his wife on that cruise.

And going on tour sounded pretty damned sweet. Literally the opportunity of a lifetime.

"Yeah, I'm in. At least until this other woman can start. I'll get in touch with my office, get some sort of leave." She looked back toward the bathroom, hoping she could finally sneak away and get herself dressed.

Both Kyle and Brandon seemed to relax, tension she hadn't been aware of dropping away. "Great," Kyle said. "Brandon will set you up with the contract."

"Contract?"

Brandon covered his smile with his hand and turned away for a moment. The smile lines at the corners of his eyes still showed when he turned back, and she heard fondness in his voice when he spoke. "Yes, princess. We do this strange thing where we sign agreements with the people we hire." How could a man look like a menswear model and tease her like this? He managed to wipe away his smile and make that face that catalog models wore, the sort of *I don't care about anyone or anything, but don't I carry this suit well* expression that was in so many ads.

"I know what a contract is." She hated being teased, so she just plowed ahead, even if Brandon probably didn't deserve it. "Just because you've got some fancy suit and probably some fancy degree, just because I never finished college, none of that gives you the right to look down on me. I raised a kid all on my own, with no help from anyone. So don't you go lording it over me, Mr. La-di-dah Manager."

"God, I just can't seem to say anything right, can I? I'm sorry I walked in on you, and I'm sorry if I implied you didn't understand what a contract was. And I'm really sorry I couldn't get this stupid son of yours to at least let you get dressed before we had this conversation. But anyone who can stand up for herself while wearing a towel has my respect, that's for damned sure."

Which actually made Megan feel better.

"Thank you," she said. "Kyle, maybe you could apologize for making me stand around like this. It's freezing in here!"

The girl on the couch looked up from her phone, finally amused enough by the real world to pay attention.

"Yeah," said Kyle. "Sorry, Mom. Go ahead, get dressed. You're flying home in the morning, right?"

She nodded.

"Okay, so you can meet up with us in San Jose, right? Maybe show up around four, so you and Brandon can go over stuff before sound check?"

That hadn't been much of an apology, but it was a step in the right direction. At least she'd have a chance to spend some more time with him.

Megan tried to stalk the few short steps to the bathroom, but it is hard to look powerful and in control when you're five foot two, wearing a damp towel, and have your hair hanging in clumps.

But she tried.

5

The next night in San Jose, the man at the backstage entrance folded his arms across the Celtics jersey covering his bulky chest and stood straighter, staring down Megan and Keiko. With the belly on him, he probably outweighed the two of them combined. "Passes?" he asked.

Megan held out the new pass Brandon had given her last night, and the man flipped it over once, then looked at her like she was nuts. "Okay, lemme explain something. This is a single pass. One." He waved a thick finger in the air between her and Keiko, then held up a second finger. "You are two people. One pass. Two people. Nuh uh." She could barely understand him through his Boston accent.

Keiko edged past Megan. "One pass, one person," Keiko said, gesturing to herself and speaking slowly. Next Keiko pointed Megan's way with her thumb. "She's on the list. With the band. Supposed to be here."

Mr. Beefy Celtics Fan looked down at his clipboard, and Megan reached into her pocket for her phone, thinking maybe she should text somebody.

The guy started shaking his head, but then focused on

Megan. To her surprise, he broke into a smile, and Megan saw a hint of a goofy middle schooler gone to seed. He shook his thick finger at Megan again. "Wait a minute. You're that lady from last night, the one Brandon wanted me to throw out. Remember me? I'm Charlie." He stuck out his hand, a cheerful smile revealing smoke-stained teeth.

Oh, my God. Not exactly a moment she wanted to remember, but she took his hand anyway. If she went on tour, she'd need a friend or two in the crew. "Well, Charlie, how could I forget? You gonna let us in, or what?" She tried to keep a smile on her face. She was sort of pissed at the guy for being part of team Make-Megan-Late-and-Piss-Off-Kyle, but of course the blame should just fall on Brandon. Even if he had apologized.

Brandon with the impeccable suit.

"Sure thing, little lady." He punched a code into the pad beside the door, opening it but still blocking their way. Then Charlie wiggled his eyebrows at Megan and smiled as if he was sharing a joke. "By the way, I heard about that little shower snafu. The whole crew was talking about it! I guess you gave Brandon quite the eyeful. Lucky man, getting that kind of a show. But if he comes Tom-Peeping around again, you just let me know. I'll make sure he knows that is a no-way, no-how, no-go situation."

The blood rushed to Megan's face. "Thanks. Let's just hope that won't be necessary."

"Of course. But I've got your back, you remember!" He stepped aside, finally letting them pass and then calling after them as the heavy door began to close. "Just save me a seat for the next show!"

Keiko hauled Megan through the door before Megan could think of a comeback.

"Oh my God," Keiko said, then added with air quotes: "'Save him a seat?' I should sue that guy for sexually harassing you."

"He was joking. Probably just the way these guys talk back-stage." Megan looked over her shoulder at the now-closed door, way too aware of the kind of speculations the crew might have made.

Keiko folded her arms. Even in a swingy tank top, torn skinny jeans, and heels, she looked like a lawyer used to winning these fights. "Maybe, but that doesn't make it right."

"Well, maybe I deserved it."

Keiko jerked her chin sharply. "Wait, you deserved to have someone barge in on you when you were in the shower? Not in the world I live in. Why would you even say that?"

Megan shook her head and started walking. "I should just shake it off. There are so many pretty young women hanging out around the band that I'm the last person anyone is gonna hassle."

Keiko stopped her with a hand to her elbow. "Okay, so, what? You're gonna ignore his comment so guys can, what?—just be left with younger women to hassle? Because you know it's even harder for them to stand up for themselves."

Yeah. Megan knew that pretty damn well, thank you very much.

Keiko wasn't done. "And why are you dissing yourself? Have you looked in a mirror lately? Guys our age—the ones who have outgrown Tinder and want more than a hookup—those men would be ecstatic to be seen with you. An ugly woman would never have given birth to a guy like Kyle, one who all the teen magazines want on their cover. So stop with the 'I'm so old and ugly' BS."

Megan supposed she could feel old and unattractive without belaboring the point, so she shut up and followed the signs for the greenroom, where Brandon planned to meet her. She hoped she could catch Kyle before the show, because she'd actually remembered to bring one of their old photo albums. She'd like to look through it with Kyle, to remind him of how close they used to be. Maybe break through whatever wall he'd thrown up between them.

At the greenroom door, Keiko stopped. She waved a hand at the grungy hallway with its dirty concrete floors. "So, this is where the magic happens, huh? It doesn't look like much, but it's pretty cool to think we're inches away from rock gods."

Megan gave her friend a joking backhanded slap across the arm. "Chill. You were with me for my ultrasound when I was pregnant with Kyle. And you were there that time when he pooped his diaper so hard that it squirted out the top *and* bottom of his PJs, and we had to stop the car by the side of the road to strip that baby naked and use diaper wipes to get it out of his hair, and it was about forty degrees out, and foggy and windy as all get out. You don't get to freak and pretend he's some hot shot, untouchable star."

"But he is!"

And that was the odd thing. He was.

It was like Kyle was two different people. On the one hand, he was the boy she'd known all his life. On the other, he was a complete stranger: this construct of a person who showed up in magazines and on the Internet—famous, untouchable, and really, really good at making music people couldn't get enough of.

"But it's still just Kyle, okay? If you act weird, he's gonna think you're nuts."

"Fine."

Then Keiko looked through the greenroom door and said, "Holy shit! Who is that guy?"

"Um, Keiko? Pretty sure all those boys are way too young for you."

Keiko shook her head. "That's not a boy. That's a man."

Megan looked.

Inside, Brandon sat on one of the couches, his phone to his ear, the other hand dangling a water bottle over the arm of the couch. His suit today was midnight blue, which meant his eyes would probably look darker, too: more forest than emerald. His beard was perfectly groomed, and the cast of light from above made the angle of his jaw even more pronounced, like it belonged on a movie star from the Classic age. Megan didn't even want to imagine the pull of muscles under that suit, but it was like trying not to think of an elephant sitting smack in the middle of the room. The only thing she could picture was the way his pecs would curve above that flat stomach, and she wondered if they were rough with hair or completely smooth.

"Ah," Megan said, pulling her head quickly back into the hallway. She swallowed. "Yeah, so that's Brandon."

Keiko stuck her own head around the corner, then pulled it back. "*That's* the guy who found you in the shower? Damn."

The man was good-looking, to be sure, but he worked for the band. It would be a huge conflict or something to crush on him, right? Off limits. And wasn't she a little old to drool over someone just because of his looks? There was so much more to life than standing next to someone who was easy on the eyes. "Focus, Keiko. Yes, that's the guy who made me more embarrassed than I've felt in decades. He's also the man who has my contract. Brandon's the manager, not a guy posing for a magazine ad. I need you to help me make sure he's not stiffing me."

"Nice choice of words."

Megan put both hands over her face. "You are the worst friend ever. I hate you. Why did I give you my pass again?"

"Because you can't live without me, and I can't live without you. So: stiff upper lip, think of the Queen, and let's go take a look at what's on the table. Or maybe just at the guy sitting behind it. Is he single, do you think?"

Megan shook her head, laughing. "Oh, my God. And no, he's not single. He's got a fiancée. And he works for the band, so that's kind of a conflict, right?"

"Shame, that. How long has it been since you even went out

on a date? That last guy was Phil, right? The dentist? Was that last spring?"

"You are horrible. No, that was the spring before Covid." In other words, a very long time ago.

The thing with Jaimie was more of a booty call. Which probably had something to do with why Megan couldn't find a real relationship.

"I hate dating," she continued. It was about as much fun as clipping her toenails.

Back when she'd been younger and at the age to turn heads, with the hope of maybe finding a decent guy, she'd been an exhausted single mom. Now that she'd edged into her forties, the only eligible guys seemed to be divorced men who ignored their own families, or men so far out on the geek spectrum that she didn't have the patience to deal with them, no matter how sweet or lovely they might be. Not to mention that she had her own emotional baggage.

Keiko said, "That's a poor excuse, and you know it."

Megan walked through the door. At the moment she'd rather deal with Brandon than Keiko.

He was still taking up space on the couch, talking on the phone. He held up a finger when he noticed them enter, and his expensive watch peeked out of the edge of his sleeve, all elegance against the grimy background of the greenroom. "Let me get back to you on that," he said into the phone, then ended the call.

He stood, buttoning his jacket as if he were about to give a speech. "Ladies."

"Hi," was Megan's brilliant response. "You wanted to talk about my contract? Oh, and I should introduce you. This is my friend, Keiko Matsue."

He extended a hand. "Brandon Thatch. A pleasure to meet you."

Keiko snuck in a glance at Megan before she shook Brandon's hand. "The pleasure's all mine."

Brandon opened the portfolio at his side and fished out a few stapled pages. Just as he was about to hand it to Megan, Brandon's phone rang again. He looked down and said, "I'm sorry, ladies. I need to take this. Give me a minute while you look this over?"

Megan took the document he was still holding out, and she and Keiko began to look through the pages. The contract seemed pretty benign, but Megan was glad Keiko was there. Megan's own experience was with trusts and estates, and with custody situations. Family law. Outsiders sometimes assumed all lawyer stuff was related, but in reality, there were tons of specialties. As a paralegal, Megan hadn't seen anything like a basic employment agreement, and this one would be more complex. It had to cover things like rights to songs and photos of the band. Privacy and intellectual property sort of stuff.

Keiko practiced in the same area as she did, but at least she'd gone to law school and studied other types of law, not to mention passing the California bar exam. So Megan definitely felt better knowing Keiko was reviewing her contract. She didn't want to sign and then wonder if she was being taken for a ride. Not that Kyle would do that to her, but still.

"What do you think? Is it okay?" Megan asked after they'd reached the last page, heads bent over the paper together like they were seventh graders sharing a teen magazine.

"Yep. All good."

It hit her, then: if she actually passed her last class at San Jose State, she could go to law school and learn what was supposed to be in agreements just like this one. Maybe that was a good goal for a new profession. Music law.

Brandon wrapped up his call, and asked, "We set?"

"Yep, all set," Megan said. "Do you have a pen?"

He pulled one from the inner pocket of his jacket.

Her fingers should not have sparked that way. Not from taking a pen from the hand of an engaged man. She was not messing around with a taken man. She'd learned that lesson, hadn't she?

Down, girl.

She had just finished signing when the band burst into the room, filling the space with the energy of twenty-year-old performers itching to get back onstage.

"Hey, hey, hey, Mrs. M! Brandon, my man! Let's get this party going!" Li-Fang was in high spirits; she wondered how he could be so alert after sitting on a tour bus on the overnight trip from LA, especially after he'd been hanging out with those two girls after the show. "Auntie Keiko!" Li-Fang gave Keiko a warm hug hello.

Kyle headed straight for the bucket of ice filled with cold beers and soft drinks, grabbing another energy drink and cracking it open. He gave Keiko his own hug, then flopped onto the middle of the couch across from the one Megan and Brandon sat on. "Auntie Keiko," he said, sounding far happier to see Keiko than he'd sounded last night about seeing his mother. "Good to see you. Glad you made it."

Kyle reached across the space with one hand held in a fist, and Keiko leaned forward to bump his fist with her own. "There's no way I would have missed it."

Li-Fang sat next to Kyle, and Kyle jerked his head at his friend and lead guitarist. "Not like this guy's mom, huh? I swear, Auntie Keiko, it's like you and Mom and Auntie Jiao are joined at the hip, except that Auntie Jiao never shows up to the stadiums."

"Well," Li-Fang said. "If I'd just stuck to classical music she would probably have sat through any concert anywhere. But we hurt her ears. You know that, man."

Jiao and Keiko's friendship had really taken off about ten years ago, when Keiko's first child was born—God, had it been that long? Keiko and Jiao compared Japanese and Chinese parenting styles, and both boys used the word "Auntie," even if the term still sounded a bit odd to Megan's ears.

"Kyle, do you have a second?" She reached into her bag and pulled out the heavy photo album. "Look what I found!"

Kyle shook his head. "I don't have time to look at old photos, not before the show." He looked completely indifferent, but Brandon glanced at the heavy book in her hand, as did Li-Fang.

Trying not to show her disappointment, she stowed the book back in her bag. "Well, maybe some other time, then." She was going to get through to him somehow, even if it killed her.

Kyle finally seemed interested. He leaned forward. "So, Mom, 'some other time?' Does that mean you're all signed up for the tour?"

"Yep." She and Brandon spoke at the same time. She was going to ignore how good Brandon looked in that suit. Especially when compared to these young kids in their T-shirts and jeans and leather bracelets and nose piercings. "Just until you find a better option. Like this sister of Brandon's fiancée, if that works out."

Brandon's expression changed. Why would talking about his fiancée and her sister make him deflate like that? "Yep, Greta will be in Seattle when we roll through, so the band can see what it's like to sing with her. She wouldn't be able to join the tour until we get to the East Coast, so I'm hoping Megan can stay with us until then."

"I'll have to check with my boss," Megan said. "And you all probably need to hear how I do tonight before you get all excited about me joining the tour for a while, right?"

Li-Fang shook his head. "Nah. You're good. Right, Kyle?"

Kyle didn't look particularly happy, but he agreed. "Brandon, can you give Greta an incentive to join us earlier?"

"I can try," Brandon said, "but she's touring with Lara, and I don't think she'll give up that gig even for us."

Charlotte took a seat next to Kyle, and he threw an arm around her shoulders. She shrugged it off and leaned toward Megan. "Well, I for one, would love to have you on the tour, Mrs. M. It'd be great to dilute the excess testosterone around here."

Li-Fang tossed a bag of chips toward Charlotte, but Kyle grabbed them out of the air.

Megan shook her head. The boys really hadn't changed much in some ways. She grabbed a bottle of water from the bucket on the floor next to her couch. When she straightened, Brandon touched her on the arm. "Welcome aboard."

Those weren't tingles, were they? It was probably just the warmth in his eyes as he spoke that made her believe he wasn't just happy to have solved the problem for now, but that he was happy that she, Megan Gamble, was the solution. "I'm glad I can help out," she said.

———

Then time flew, and she was onstage again; and just as suddenly, Kyle was waving goodnight to the crowd, and the band was heading off the stage.

She was sweaty and completely exhilarated, so high on performing that she wanted to celebrate, to jump up and down and squeal like a thirteen-year-old. Happily, just the right person was waiting for her backstage. She made a beeline for Keiko, who caught her mood and her body, lifting Megan off her feet. Beside them, Brandon seemed to stifle a smile.

"Megan! Oh, my God! That was incredible! *You* were incredible!" Keiko's face glowed. She had always been that kind of friend, generous in celebrating with Megan whenever something went well in her life.

"Yeah, really? I did okay?"

Keiko nodded fast and hard, her grin still splitting her face in two. "Way, way better. You were amazing."

At that moment, Kyle threw down his empty water bottle and walked past them toward the rope line. Keiko said, "Hey, Kyle! Great show!"

He threw the word "thanks" over his shoulder and headed straight for a group of women standing with the backstage pass holders. After a very short moment, he grabbed the hand of a curvy girl and pulled her down the hallway. The woman laughed and threw a look at her friends, all of them giggling, while Megan and Keiko tried not to let their jaws hit the floor.

Megan remembered the grip of a male hand on her own wrist back when she'd been about that woman's age. But this woman was smiling. "At least she seems into it. But, Keiko, is this normal? Would most men act like this around their own moms?"

Keiko shook her head. "I don't think so. It's also not really like Kyle."

Theo was close enough to catch the comment. "Uh, actually, this is pretty much Kyle's MO after a show." He gave Megan a rather pointed look. "Any chance I could drag you off to a closet, too?"

Brandon, who had been hovering near Keiko and Megan this whole time, crossed his arms over his chest, and stared down Theo.

Megan shuddered. "I think not. Go find someone your own age to play with."

Theo's face broke into a very broad smile, one eyebrow raised and a dimple showing. "Playtime. My favorite."

He strutted off to the remaining group of girls, drawling, "Ladies," and making a little half-bow as Megan, Keiko, and Brandon watched. What was it with these guys and their over-charged libidos?

Brandon turned back to Megan. "I'm sorry you had to see that," he said. "But since you asked, yes, it is pretty much how things go down after a show. It can't be easy to watch."

"I'm a big girl. I can handle it."

"But you shouldn't have to. I'll talk to him later."

That was kind of him, assuming he was thinking of her feelings. But maybe he was just making sure things didn't get too wild. Because this was going to be her life for the next few weeks.

Rather different from spending her days in a law firm office in a strip mall, that was for sure.

6

Megan drove home and packed her bags, making sure to include her two precious photo albums. Given how difficult those early years had been, she was pretty proud she'd saved enough photos for even that many. God, he'd been such an adorable kid. Smiles. So many smiles. That tiny belly, all soft warmth under her hands when he was a toddler. Blond hair darkening over time to the deep brown he had now.

She turned the pages, remembering; then collapsed into her bed, where she appreciated the hell out of one last night sleeping on her own pillows.

The next morning she emailed her professor to explain that she'd be traveling for business—which, oddly enough, was actually true—and to ask, could she take the final remotely? She studied for an hour, then found he'd already responded: she could download the final whenever she wanted, but after that, she'd only have four hours to get her results uploaded, and he needed the completed exam by 6pm on Friday.

She thought about the band's schedule. Okay, so today was Tuesday and the Sacramento show was tonight; tomorrow they played Portland, and then Seattle on Thursday, followed by a long bus ride to Salt Lake City. The connection would be spotty on the road, so she should really take the exam while she was sitting in one place, and in Seattle they had that new singer audition.

So, Portland it was. She'd sing the show tonight, study on the bus, grab a power nap in Portland and then do the exam in the afternoon before the show.

Yikes. That did not sound like a very rock-n-roll way to kick off a tour, did it? But she wouldn't skip the final after turning in everything else this semester. She was so damn close to finishing her degree, she just wanted to be done.

Megan Gamble, BA.

So much better than Megan Gamble, college dropout. Because she sure as hell was no Mark Zuckerberg who could quit school and found a company that made a gazillion dollars. She was just a woman who put her head down, did her job, raised her kid, and tried not to let her past destroy her present.

Megan locked her house, and thanked God for a good friend like Keiko who would drive her the 125 miles to Sacramento. Keiko's parents lived in the central valley, so she planned to drop Megan at the arena and then head down to her folks' place in time for dinner.

"It was my pleasure," said Keiko, when Megan thanked her profusely, unloading her roller bag at the entrance to the arena after two and a half hours on the road. Megan gave Keiko a hug through the window, and from the backstage door, Charlie the roadie waved at Keiko before she drove off.

It wasn't easy to watch Keiko's car pull out of the lot. Keiko and Jiao were such rocks in her life, and it was going to be weeks before she'd see them in person again. She was really going to be adrift on this tour, completely a fish out of water, even if it was the opportunity of a lifetime.

Hair, makeup, and wardrobe were easier tonight, now that she and the team were getting to know each other. *Hannah and hair start with the same letter*, she told herself, trying to remember who was who. Kryssa was wardrobe. It was easier to tell them apart than remember their names; Hannah had bright orange nails, and Kryssa dyed her hair. Today it was lime green, but had been purple for Megan's first show in LA.

"Nice color," said Megan to Kryssa, adjusting tonight's version of the corset-top.

"Thanks," she replied. "I thought it was time for a change."

Megan thought suddenly of Kyle's first professional haircut, back when he was about two. He had been delighted with the chair, a bright red toy car that raised and lowered on a regular stylist's pedestal, and Megan had loved the results. There was a photo of that day in the album.

The show that night—Megan's third—was another sweaty, wonderful experience. She was getting to the point where she actually enjoyed Theo's aggressive onstage flirting. When they were backstage, he flirted a lot, but he also backed off really quickly, which made his onstage behavior felt less like harassment and more like misguided but good-natured teasing. So she just roller her eyes at him and did her job.

Tonight was the night she'd actually get on the bus, and she had to admit she was looking forward to it. Maybe it would get old; but right now, the thought of being a real touring artist sounded even better to her than the letters BA after her name.

"You got a minute?" Brandon poked his head into the dressing room she and Charlotte were using. He'd given one quick knock, and she wasn't naked, but he really needed to stop doing that.

"Knock first. Wait for answer. Open door. Not too hard to remember, is it?"

"You're totally right. My apologies." Brandon even sounded contrite.

She turned back to the mirror and finished gathering her hair up into a ponytail. It was still wet, but at least it would be out of her way for the bus ride. She watched Brandon in the mirror.

He leaned against the counter behind her in the narrow room, not looking entirely comfortable. "Before you get on the bus, I wanted to tell you one more time how sorry I am that I made you late for your entrance that first night. You really impressed me, how well you handled yourself onstage that night, even though you probably should have been rattled. You absolutely owned that performance. And, obviously, I'm mortified that I walked in on you in the shower." He looked down and fidgeted with the cuff of his shirt where it peeked out from under his suit coat. "I know you don't know me well, and you have no reason to believe me, but I try to do the right thing and that night I really messed up. Twice. I don't like the way the music business used to be run. Women should be able to perform without feeling like they'd get ahead faster if they put up with leering looks and outright abuse; I believe that, and I always have. I really, truly should have done better that first day."

Her hair was up now, so she had nothing left to do with her hands. "Well, I was pretty mortified, myself." Her face showed pink in the mirror.

"Again, I'm so sorry. Can we start over? Make peace? I could show you the bus, get you settled?"

She stood. "That would be great. Thanks."

It took a brave man to apologize. She couldn't think of a time when Jaimie had done anything remotely like it.

She reached for her roller bag, but Brandon got to it first.

For a moment the edge of his pinky brushed hers, leaving that tiny patch of her skin feeling very alive. Megan settled her breath and hitched her purse higher on her shoulder. She was near enough that she caught a tiny whiff of his scent, something like sandalwood and citrus. Light. Barely there.

Attractive.

It felt superficial, but after spending hours with the band guys in their guyliner, she also appreciated that Brandon didn't have a stitch of makeup on his face. She was getting used to seeing it on Kyle and Li-Fang and Theo and Zane, but she didn't much like it.

Brandon had good skin, and—another bonus!—he wasn't sweaty. His suit and tie were still pressed and sharp, even after the show. He clearly had his act together. His fiancée was a lucky woman.

"Not to pry or anything, but what've you got in this bag? It's heavy."

The smile lines at the corners of his eyes showed when he looked over his shoulder at Megan as they walked through the maze backstage. The corridor widened, and she caught up to walk by his side.

"Oh," Megan said. "A textbook for the final I have to take, and some photo albums. I was hoping Kyle would look through them with me. I'm hoping to lure him in, get him to talk to me a bit more than he usually does."

"Well, even if Kyle won't make time, I bet the rest of the band would love to see them."

They probably would. But the band laughing at Kyle's childhood pictures wouldn't exactly help her get back in his good books.

They continued down the corridor.

"What're you studying for?"

"One last class to finish my BA, and then I'm going to apply to law school." Huh. When had she decided that? "The firm where I work said they'd pay for me to get a JD, but I have to finish up undergrad first. I think they want me to go into trusts and estates, but I might like to try something different."

"Yeah?" he asked. He stopped and turned to lean against a wall of the corridor, facing her.

She rested against the opposite wall, hitching her purse up to her shoulder again. "Singing these last couple of shows, I've realized how much I've missed music. If I get a law degree, maybe I can do something music-related. I think I'd love that."

He smiled, and it did lovely things to those green eyes.

He said, "I can see it now: Megan Gamble, power-attorney to the stars. Requires a bit of a different wardrobe than singing backup, doesn't it?"

At that comment, she thought of the first time Brandon had seen her, when she had been wearing that stupid bustier thing that had shoved her boobs higher than they'd been in a decade. Her cheeks flamed. "Well," she said, trying to cover her blush. "Since I work at a law firm, most of what I own would work."

"Not much of a partier, huh? I feel like I should apologize in advance for what your life is about to be like. These guys, on the road? They're not exactly a tame bunch."

Megan put a hand on her hip and gestured to herself with her other hand, pretending she was insanely attractive. "Are you even kidding me? I hit the clubs at least three nights a week. Because everyone knows Fridays don't really count as work days, right?"

She was completely spoofing. She hadn't been to a club since the last time the Sutter Boys played in one of the smaller venues, but teasing was fun.

Even through the slight scruff on his cheeks, she could see him blush. "Sorry. I'm totally making assumptions."

She stared at him, pretending for a moment longer, until he fidgeted his heel against the wall, rubbing it back and forth while the ball of his foot stayed planted. "I'm not making this better, am I?"

She laughed, then pushed away from the wall to walk to the exit, trusting him to follow. "Nope. Not making this better. But I'm totally pulling your leg. I never go out; not really, so it's going to be a huge lifestyle change, getting on that bus. Thanks for the warning."

Brandon shook his head. "You devil. You had me going. I'm sorry to say, you're really in for it. These guys can be animals, but hopefully they'll tone it down a little. At least while you're with the tour."

He was kinda adorable when he was flustered. Good to know.

She had missed this, mild flirting with an attractive guy. That tantalizing hope that maybe this one would actually like her, want to spend time with her. And maybe they'd have something to talk about.

As nice as Brandon was being, though, she was pretty sure he was way out of her league. She couldn't exactly date the band's manager. He must travel all the time, and she was going to go home and get a new job and apply to law school and dating Brandon obviously wouldn't work—because look at the women who followed this industry.

Once she got back to her real life, she needed to let Keiko and Jiao set her up on a few dates.

Brandon pushed open the door, and they stepped out into the cool of the Sacramento evening. What a contrast to the afternoon, when the central valley was blazingly hot. Thank God for the sea breeze which came in every afternoon like clockwork, dropping the temperature fast.

A few fans still lingered. When Megan and Brandon stepped through the door, the sparse crowd outside shifted and craned forward and generally acted like they were ready to scream for selfies. But once they realized that neither Brandon nor Megan was one of the headliners, they slumped back, no longer paying attention. Still, walking past the thin line of people was slightly creepy, like carrying dirty sheets to the laundry room past that neighbor who always had their door open; the one who liked to watch the hallway and get in everyone's business.

Brandon looked at the young people pressed against the metal barriers. "You'll get used to the fans, I promise. And they'll mostly ignore you."

"Yep, not a lot of teenage girls are too interested in checking me out."

Brandon turned his head quickly to look at her even as he was sliding her bag under the bus. "Where are you going with that comment? Fishing for compliments? Because you must know that there were plenty of people at the concert tonight who are probably dreaming that you're tucking them in. Teen or not."

"Ew."

"Right. That is pretty awful." He winced, stowed her bag under the bus, then gave it a flat-handed pat. "Before I forget, do you need anything from your bag? The bus won't stop until Portland, so it'll be a long night."

"No, I'm set."

He walked her to the front of the bus, then leaned in to speak to the man slouched in the driver's seat. "Feroz, this is Kyle's mom, Megan Gamble, but you'll probably hear the band calling her Mrs. M. She's joining the tour for a bit."

Feroz was a slim man, dwarfed by the club chair he sat in, who looked like he'd barely be taller than she was if he stood up. His smile was tired but his eyes were alert. "Welcome aboard."

"Nice to meet you."

Brandon led her past a couple of bench-like couches. "Okay, so here's the big tour." He waved his hand from left to right.

"Front lounge, obviously. There's a bit of a kitchen." He pointed further back to a small fridge and sink, with cupboards above and below. Walking past the kitchen into a narrow corridor, he said, "These are the bunks. I think they've saved you one of the bottom ones."

She stepped past him and walked down the narrow aisle to the rear. The beds were stacked three high, and could be closed off with small curtains. Hers was almost at the back of the bus, just in front of a tiny bedroom with its own private sofa. The room had a door made out of something flimsy, about as substantial as the display board from a middle school science fair project. Brandon caught her glance. "Kyle's got that one. I'm sure if he'd known you were going to be joining the tour he would have let you have it."

"Well, I'm not. He's the star, and I'm guessing he likes the perks. I'll be fine here." She tucked her purse on the little shelf at the head of the space. She didn't want to get in the way.

A bus tour. She thought suddenly of driving Kyle and Li-Fang to middle school dances, where she'd have to pretend not to hear them talking from where they sat in the backseat.

Back in the main cabin, Brandon sat down, gesturing Megan to the seat across from him. "So what's your story? You must have performed before. You certainly handle being on stage like a pro, and your sense of pitch is immaculate. I don't think I heard you sing a note out of tune all night, and usually I'm the one cringing like Simon Cowell. Impressive. So do tell, garage band in your past?"

He really didn't have to compliment her, which meant he probably meant what he said. His praise gave her the sudden image of her self-confidence in a tiny box, now swelling like the Grinch's heart and pushing at the boundaries that had kept her life so small for so long. Maybe if she'd had more confidence in herself she wouldn't have ended up doing so many things she hated over the years. Maybe she would have had the fortitude to turn down Jaimie and his propositions.

"Thanks," she said. "That's really kind of you."

"Don't dodge my question," he said with a smile. "You've done this before, and I'm curious. Where? When?"

She wiggled her outstretched hand in an ambivalent gesture. "Kinda? Mostly it was chorus, a few solos back in high school, that sort of thing. Later on, when I was still enrolled at San Jose State, I sang with a couple of bands, just backup stuff like I'm doing here."

"And?" He twisted just a bit to face her.

They certainly had some time to kill. Why not tell him more? He seemed eager to just hang out and chat. Maybe he missed that fiancée of his.

Well, no harm in talking, as long as she kept reminding herself that he was taken. And who was she to say no to spending a little bit of time talking to a good-looking guy with a voice as rich and smooth as the best red wine she'd ever tried?

Where to start? "Back in college, Kyle's dad, Jason, had some roommates with a band. We went to catch one of their gigs, and the guys pulled me on stage; made me sing a cover or two. Stevie Nicks. Heart. More recent stuff like Annie Lennox and Sheryl Crow. Music where they needed a woman's voice."

She thought back, remembering a little bar not far from the San Jose State campus. She and Jason had been listening to his roommates piece together a pretty decent set when she'd realized she'd needed to hit the restroom. When she'd stepped back out into the grimy little hallway, Jason was waiting, pulling her further away from the bar. Her hormones had been pretty damn sure he'd been looking for a private corner for a quick make-out session, but instead he'd led her past the roped off staircase and onto the tiny stage that was wedged between an amp and the banister.

The band had introduced her as soon as she'd stepped up,

applauding (along with Jason, the rat, who had clearly been part of the plot to get her to sing). They'd promised the crowd that she'd do "Never Break the Chain," but first had asked everyone to cheer her on for one number so she could sing backup and get comfortable. She remembered she'd had to lean way over to reach the backup mic, because the cord hadn't been long enough to reach into her nook. When it had come time for the promised solo, she'd threaded her way past the amp to get to the central mic.

The space was so cramped she could've sworn at one point the lead guitarist had ended up with his hands up her skirt—and he'd been gay and clearly not interested. But the people had *danced*.

She'd sung with that group on three, maybe four different gigs, and had a blast. Jason had been pretty into it. "My girl-friend, the star," he would say, pulling her up the creaky stairs to his room in the house he'd rented with those four other guys. And in the morning, she'd wake up alone to a note saying the surf was up and there was OJ in the fridge with his name on it. He'd told her she'd be wise to avoid touching any of the other drinks.

He'd been a charmer, her surfing Jason, with a body to die for and a face that she remembered every time she looked at Kyle onstage.

And kind. So very kind.

"That's a lot of thinking about a couple of times on stage singing covers." Brandon was watching her, and she realized she'd been silent for far too long.

Megan ran her fingers along the edge of the bench seat, the prickly spikes of the dated velour rough under her hands. There was a stain a few inches away from her—spilled beer, she guessed; maybe something stronger—something that all the steam cleaning in the world couldn't remove. At least it didn't smell like booze at the moment. More like stale potato chips and recycled air.

"Yeah," she told Brandon. "I sang a few times with that first band, just for a lark, and then Jason must have mentioned something to his brothers. There were four Marshall boys. Jason was the baby, and the only one without an ounce of musical talent. But the brothers had a band and needed a new singer, and kind of gave me the full court press, you know? After a while I told them sure, I would sing. I figured, why not? I didn't even know that it was a praise band. I'd been to church maybe twice in my life, so to say I wasn't a natural fit would be a huge understatement. But I sang with 2 Samuel 6 for about six months, until I started to show." A woman with a baby bump certainly doesn't fit in with an evangelical band praising God and preaching abstinence; not as an unwed mother-to-be.

But she'd been looking for an excuse to get away from that group months before the time they'd cut her loose.

"Where did the name come from? Two Samuel something?"

"Yeah, 2 Samuel 6. Apparently it's this verse where David danced before the Lord. I guess Christians get it. The guys thought they were going to hit the big time, made me sign a contract and everything. And they kicked me out for good as soon as they thought anyone would notice my baby bump." She'd been so eager to get away from them—especially David Marshall, the creepy oldest brother. "The family sure as hell wasn't around when Jason died and left me alone to raise our kid. Not much Christian forgiveness in that clan, no matter what they sang about."

And that was only the part of the story she could tell in polite company.

Brandon gave her another inscrutable look.

He held her gaze until she realized she'd been staring for too long. Here in the dim light of the bus, the green of his eyes was like the needles of a redwood tree high overhead on a foggy day.

Off limits, Megan. Off limits.

She tore her eyes away.

He was the only man who'd been interested in what she had to say for the longest time. Maybe someday she'd find a relationship with someone who listened like Brandon, though probably not someone as attractive or successful. But at least someone who asked her how she was doing; who cared about the answers, and about who she really was.

He swallowed. "You'll have to tell me more one of these days."

"One of these days? Aren't you on the bus? Too sticky for you or something?" She gestured at the stain beside her.

He quirked a small smile, crinkling the corners of his eyes the tiniest bit. "No. It's not just the stickiness. I head back to Tennessee tonight. I've got a meeting to take back home."

She said the name of the first city that came to mind. "Memphis? You're a Southern boy?"

"Yes, ma'am," he said, bobbing his head in a hint of a bow.

It felt like he was teasing her, so she gave his forearm a backhanded swat, connecting lightly with the solid warmth of his flesh.

"Ouch!" he said, mock-nursing his arm. "That's what I get for trying to remember my manners, is it?"

"Maybe."

She tried not to smile at him. "So," she said, just as Brandon chimed in with his own comment.

They did a little "You first"; "No, you," until Brandon spoke. "I'll be off. But I'll check on you when we meet up again in Seattle, okay? I'm picking up Greta when I get in from Memphis—she's the woman I'm hoping can replace you in a few weeks."

Maybe he was far enough away that he couldn't see the

blush she could feel in her cheeks. Right, the fiancée's sister. She wanted to ask about that, but didn't. "Okay."

He turned and walked back toward the door, then gave a final wave before disappearing down the steps.

And now she needed to figure out if the bus had Wi-Fi, and how to download her final, and just how she was going to study for an online exam while she was on this bus with the band. No parties for Megan, no sir. She had to just grind away, hoping to finally get to the point where she felt proud of herself. And maybe even make a place for herself in the world of music.

7

From the empty bus, Megan couldn't quite keep her eyes off of Brandon as he headed back to the venue. Eventually, he rounded the corner of the second bus and disappeared from view, and she shook herself to clear her brain. He'd been very kind to show her around; Kyle had made a good choice hiring him.

She looked at her tiny bunk, wondering if she could find the energy to start studying. It didn't look very comfortable, but needs must. Should she take off her shoes?

Yeah, for sure. Shoes off. It was a bed, after all. She sat and wriggled her feet out of her flats, slipped them into the tiny space under the bunk, swung her legs up into the bed, and closed the curtain. Once she turned on the reading light, it was cramped but cozy.

It didn't take long for the bunk to get uncomfortable. She had to hold her book up, which meant either a crick in her neck or an aching back. And with the lighting, she'd probably end up with eyestrain, too. But she had to study; she really wanted to pass this exam. It was for herself, of course, but it would be incredibly satisfying to show Jaimie that she was more than just a stupid side piece. She was going to do things with her life. And the irony was that while she was thinking about showing up Jaimie and proving to him that she was smarter than he gave her credit for, she was reading about the Bill Clinton/Monica Lewinsky scandals for class. She was almost the same age as Monica, so she remembered it well, but most of her classmates thought of the affair as ancient history. Right now, reading about the consequences of an affair between a boss and and intern struck a little too close to her relationship with her own boss.

She got back to her notes.

Twenty minutes later, the band thudded their way up the steps, the bus rocking with the weight of four more people climbing aboard and growing noisy with exuberant voices.

"Hey, hey, hey, Mrs. M! Where are you? You hiding?" Theo was clearly pretty drunk, but he sounded so damn cheerful that it was hard to resist just throwing down her book.

"Sh!" Li-Fang said. "She might be trying to sleep."

"No way!" Theo was practically shouting now. "We're just getting this party started! Mrs. M! Get yourself out here!" A heavy bottle hit the table.

She cracked open her curtain, finding herself looking at Zane's feet. He smiled down at her, the expression oddly kind; not what she'd expected, based on that shaved head and body-building physique.

He bent and reached out a hand. "Come on outta there."

"I'm studying for an exam." And she sounded like a total killjoy, some horrible combination of bookworm and mom, rolled into one unappealing package.

"Well, Theo's not gonna give it a rest until you join us, at least for a bit. Might as well have some fun and call it a study break?" Zane waited, more patient than she would have expected, hand still outstretched.

Instead of taking his hand to stand, she made a fist; he

closed his hand for a bump. "Seriously," she said, "I can't. I really want to do well on this test. It's the last exam between me and my degree."

Li-Fang was on the couch, leaning forward so he could just see her when she peeked out of her bunk. "Good for you, Mrs. M. Guys, leave her alone, 'kay?"

Zane stood. "Okay, then. But anytime you get sick of the books, you come hang with us. You're part of the band now."

She leaned back but left the curtain open, so she had a clear view when Kyle walked onto the bus pulling a young woman along behind him. "Night all," he said.

The rest of the band got silent. It was like two strangers had paraded past, not one.

She knew that this was the band's private time, when they could finally shed their stage personas and just be themselves. Relax. But Kyle had just brought a completely random groupie into the band's private space. Apparently he thought it was okay to do whatever the hell he wanted with random women, and these amazing musicians around her—the people he *needed* in order to be successful—were just supposed to put up with it?

Was this the way he treated his band? The way he treated Li-Fang, his lifelong best friend?

The bus pulled out almost as soon as Kyle clattered past with his woman *du jour*—*du nuit*? No, that was wrong, because *nuit* was feminine, right? *De la nuit?* Okay, high school French had been a long time ago.

She sighed and concentrated on her books as the bus maneuvered its way through city streets toward the freeway. The music and loud chatter drifting down the aisle from the front seating area masked most of the sounds coming from Kyle's bunk, so she got some work done, at least for a time.

But after a while, it got harder to ignore the sounds coming from behind the thin door. Her stomach churned when activities reached their literal climax, because she'd never be able to un-hear the rhythmic thumping overlaid with the woman's voice chanting, "Close, close, close."

Then there was a man's low grunt, and that was how Megan learned exactly what her son sounded like when he came.

What the hell had she been thinking getting on this bus?

Feeling pretty disgusted, she shut the book, shoved her feet into her shoes, and rolled out of her bed, nearly hitting her head on the bunk above hers.

"Mrs. M!" shouted Theo. "About time you got yourself down here. Make room, ladies and gents."

Theo settled a shot in front of her. "Here," he said. "You might want this."

Damn right she wanted a shot. Hangover and stupid online exam be damned.

How could Kyle flaunt a woman like this?

She slammed back her shot, felt the burn oozing down her throat, and settled in. Dropping the glass to the table with a satisfying thud, she said, "And to think I brought photo albums with me so I could bond with him. What the hell was I thinking?"

She looked down the aisle to the closed door at the back of the bus, catching Li-Fang's sunny smile. "You brought what?"

She buried her head in her hands. "You heard me. Photos." She looked up at the amused faces swaying on the couches next to her and across the aisle, behind the skinny table. "I thought maybe I could go through them with Kyle, and maybe that would thaw out our relationship. You may have noticed he's not exactly my biggest fan these days."

"Photos?" said Theo. "I've *got* to see these!"

"Can you even imagine baby Kyle?" asked Charlotte.

And then Li-Fang said, "Wait till you see the cowboy boots he rocked in the first grade."

"You guys are serious? You want to see these?"

The answer was so enthusiastic that she retrieved the albums from her bunk.

For an hour or so, the band—unlike her son—made her feel like one of them. Like maybe she belonged on this bus, even if it was just for now. They laughed and cooed over the old photos, some of them with Li-Fang and Kyle together. They played truly stupid drinking and trivia games, and she was incredibly bad at all of them but laughed until her sides ached. Zane got her a bottle of water after her second shot. "Drink this. Hangover prevention." She had to admit, it was rather sweet of him to look out for her.

She was still on a law-firm schedule, used to early bedtimes and obnoxiously early alarms. After having sung three shows in three nights with adrenaline levels through the roof, her body shut down hard and without much warning around one in the morning.

Megan stood, swaying with both the moving bus and the buzz of alcohol.

"Night all," she said, hitting the tiny bathroom and then rolling into her bunk.

And then she was out, sound asleep, dreaming of strange noises, swinging hammocks hanging in the branches of enormous trees, demanding music teachers, and being discovered naked in the shower.

When she woke she thought maybe it was still nighttime, because everything was dark. At home, the light poured through her thin drapes, but here the blackout curtains made her bunk pitch black, except for a line of light crossing her face. The bed rocked, she heard and felt the rumble of an engine, and everything came back to her.

She was on the bus. With the band.

Megan rolled over to face the aisle but couldn't deal with opening her curtain just yet. She was not in good shape. This touring life was not going to be easy on her body, especially after a night that involved four shots of—what had Theo been pouring? And why the hell had she had four shots? Or was it five?

She let her head drop back into the thin pillow. Had hangovers been this miserable when she'd been in her twenties? God, she needed water and caffeine and Advil.

The air smelled like men who hadn't showered well and laundry waiting to be done, but her next inhalation brought the blessedly strong scent of brewing coffee.

Outside the curtain, a pair of feet hit the floor of the aisle hard, and a voice echoed the thoughts in her head. "Coffee. I need coffee."

That would be Zane.

Well, at least she had the chance to get to know the band better—and not just when they were all getting plastered. Even if her personal to-do list included chewing Kyle out as soon as possible. Had he really had sex with some random woman less than three feet away from her bunk? What was going on with him?

Sounds and voices came from the lounge area down the passage, and then Charlotte said, "Get your own, you lazy bastard." From the next set of noises, it sounded like two bodies collapsed onto the padded benches.

Zane grumbled, clearly not awake.

Megan suddenly wished she'd chosen something less revealing than a tank top and shorts to sleep in. But she needed the coffee really, really badly, so she adjusted her top and pulled back the curtain.

Zane, Charlotte, and Theo slumped in the main lounge. Each one of them looked worse for the wear. They were so damned young that she wouldn't have thought it would hit them this hard, especially this early in the tour. They still had something like forty stops to go, and she didn't want to think about how rough they'd look by the end.

Charlotte sprawled up near the driver wearing fuzzy slippers and a pink flannel pajama set. She just needed an old teddy bear to look like a ten-year-old, with her scrubbed-clean face and unbrushed hair. She thumbed at her phone, taking sips from a mug. A half-eaten muffin rested on a paper towel balanced on her knee. Zane had his hands folded and head buried in his arms. His shoulders poked out of an old sleeveless shirt and looked big enough to crush the table where he was draped. Theo was a bit more awake, also on his phone, but his hair was an excellent example of why it was a good idea to shampoo out any hair gel before going to sleep. The right side stuck up, and when he turned his head to look down out the windshield, the patch above his ear had been so flattened that she could see his scalp through the dyed-black hair.

Li-Fang's feet appeared next to her bunk, then his face as he bent over. "Mrs. M! Good morning to you!"

He sounded way too chipper. Ah, to be twenty-something again. She pulled the pillow out from under her head and threw it at Li-Fang, who danced away.

"Hey," he said. "I was going to make you coffee, welcome you to my world, but for that, you can get your own."

"You dirty, rotten little scoundrel," she said, sitting up and banging her head hard against the bunk above her. "Ouch!"

Li-Fang was back to her bunk in a second, holding out a hand for her in the same way Zane had last night. "Easy, partner. You've gotta roll and then rise."

She rubbed at the new bump on her scalp, then stuck out her tongue. "Thanks for the hand. At least I'm not dead yet. I think." She put her hand into Li-Fang's, careful to tuck her chin before rolling out and putting her feet on the floor.

Slippers. She'd want slippers by tomorrow. This floor had that gritty feel which made her arches cringe upward.

"Just don't be doing that head-banging thing every day. We're not that kind of band." He scanned her, taking in the Ripped Bodice tank top from her favorite bookstore and the 49ers logo shorts. "Nice getup!"

She ignored him and took the three steps toward the kitchen area, holding on to the counter against the swaying of the bus. "Coffee. Need coffee."

Last night, Charlotte had shown her where they stashed various kinds of snacks, but she didn't remember seeing anything breakfast-y. Megan pulled open a drawer and found the stash of coffee pods and creamers; then another which was filled with a single enormous bag of Chex mix, about half deflated. Well, cereal might do in a pinch, but it wasn't her first choice.

"Up high," Zane said.

"What's up high?"

Zane stood and took two steps to reach the tiny kitchen. "Breakfast stuff. But I guess up high isn't going to do you much good, is it?"

She yawned. Hurry, coffee. "Nope. Five-two is too short for this bus."

Zane's smile under his buzzed head was basically seven-year-old glee. "And that's why they keep me around. Here," he said, easily reaching above her head to open the compartments. "We've got blueberry muffins, if you don't mind things in plastic; instant oatmeal packets; and plenty of Cocoa Puffs." He pulled a box of cereal halfway out just as she was getting ready to ask who on earth still ate Cocoa Puffs. Reading her mind, Zane said, "Believe it or not, Theo and Li-Fang fight over these things."

"How's a woman to choose, with a selection like this. Um, maybe a few of the oatmeal things?"

He brought down a basket. "Tell you what. Why don't you stash these in one of the bottom drawers. Then you'll be able to reach."

"Great."

"And if you need anything more, just ask. I don't like touring with hungry women. Doesn't make for a good day."

Charlotte heard that and threw a paper napkin his direction.

"What?" asked Zane. "I was being nice."

"And dissing me at the same time."

"Naw," Zane said, settling next to Charlotte and using his enormous shoulders to move her along the bench seat. "I'd never do that."

Charlotte shoved at his shoulder with one hand, and Zane didn't budge an inch. After a moment, Charlotte sighed and put her feet in his lap.

Megan slipped behind the table with her food, waking Theo, who draped an arm around her shoulder and muttered, "Snuggle time, 'kay?" He stayed tucked up against her, warm and sleepy, as she ate. She couldn't figure out if his snuggling was endearing, or a follow-up to the flirting he'd done on stage during each of the five shows she'd now performed. Whichever it was, it felt nice for the moment.

Everyone settled in for a quiet morning. Kyle and guest were still noticeably absent.

At the other end of the lounge area, Charlotte started a phone conversation, her feet still in Zane's lap. From the questions and exclamations ("Really?" "You've got to be kidding!") it seemed like she was getting some dirt from an old friend.

Megan returned a missed call from Keiko. "Morning, you," Megan said into her phone. Theo didn't even budge.

"Morning to you, too. So, is that hot manager there on the bus with you?"

"Keiko! Stop! And no, he's not."

Good lord, she really cut to the chase, didn't she? Megan was really glad the call wasn't on speaker. Theo dropped his head into her lap. The bus turned slightly, making the sun strike his face, and he threw an arm over his eyes.

"You there?"

"Yep. Just trying to figure out how to kill you from the middle of Oregon."

Theo rolled over, groping at her leg until Megan swatted his hand. "Watch it, bud. You can use me as a pillow, but none of that now. Little pervert."

On her lap, Theo grinned widely, but moved his hand away. "Comfortable," he said.

"You calling me a pervert?" asked Keiko.

"God, no. But this bus? This is going to be a very interesting few weeks. And that's an understatement."

"What's that supposed to mean?"

Megan looked down at Theo's head and decided maybe this wasn't time to give Keiko the full details. "Let's just say that sometimes band members, including my son, bring guests on the bus. And things can get noisy."

"You mean they have sex where everyone can hear them?"

Megan covered the phone with her hand. "Shh! Not so loud."

Theo mumbled, "You can make noise with me if you want. Just not on the bus. Not cool."

Megan stared down at him, and Keiko said, "What? Who are you talking to?"

"That's just Theo, being obnoxious."

"He's, what? Twenty years younger than you are?"

Megan took a shuddering breath, because that was exactly right. Megan was forty-two; the other band members ranged in age from Kyle and Li-Fang at twenty-three, to Zane, the "old man" at twenty-seven. "Okay. Enough. You've pretty much convinced me I need to talk to Kyle."

"Good luck with that," Keiko said, while Theo said much the same thing.

"Later, 'kay?"

"Sure. Bye now," Keiko said.

Theo snuggled back into her side until she pushed him away. "I sure as hell wouldn't say anything to Kyle, but make your own choices, Mama Bear."

"What, don't you think he's being obnoxious? None of you should have to deal with this. I mean, sex is awesome, but it should be private, and this bus is anything but. I'm going to talk to him."

"Your funeral," Theo said. "But if you can talk him out of bringing groupies on the bus, the rest of us would love you forever. I'd rather not share my down time with randoms whose names even Kyle can't remember. Go on, then, oh brave one."

She stood, and the movement of the bus threw her against Theo, who steadied her by the shoulders. He gave her a spin and pushed her down the hall. When she looked up, Kyle had appeared in his doorway, the girl in tow.

"Hey, guys," he said. "Um, say good morning to—uh, Alley? Sorry, bad with names." At least he looked a tiny bit embarrassed.

The girl barely looked at him, huge rings of mascara under her eyes. "Ashley. Hey, guys."

A very lackluster response came back. "Hey."

Megan ignored the woman and grabbed Kyle by the elbow. "Can I talk to you?" She jerked her head toward the rear of the bus.

"Now? Jeez, Mom. Let a man get some coffee."

She could sense that the band was dying to tease him. "*Ooh, Kyle's in trouble now,*" but no one said a word. She took it as a measure of how much they wanted her to have this conversation, and how much they wanted the behavior to stop as long as someone else took on the job of talking to Kyle.

"No, now. This won't take long." Hell, he hadn't let her get dressed after that first show; he could wait for coffee.

Still, Megan was rather surprised when he followed her back to his tiny room.

There was one pillow on the bed; the rest were on the floor, along with most of the top sheet and the blanket tangled into it. The fitted sheet was wrinkled, and clearly showed where two bodies had been spooning. She supposed she should be grateful there wasn't a wet spot in view, and that she wasn't the one who had to wash his sheets.

"How can you do this to the band?" Megan waved a hand at the bunk and turned to face Kyle, who promptly sat on the couch across from the bed.

Giving him a dressing-down had been easier when he was younger and shorter and actually felt like he had to do what she said, or lose privileges.

"Who I sleep with is none of their business. And certainly none of yours."

"Normally I'd agree with you, but not when you just had sex three feet away from me. There's barely even a wall in between us!" She slapped the quarter inch of corrugated what-ever-it-was carefully, not wanting to poke a hole straight through into her bunk. "I'm not trying to get in your business, and I'm certainly not interested in making our relationship even worse than it already is, but I have to stand up for your friends out there. You have no right to drag a stranger onto this bus. The band works their tails off for you and this music. Give them a break and let them decompress here on the bus, and don't parade around your sex partners for the rest of us to deal with. Not to mention the risk you're taking for yourself and for all of the band. These groupies? They could post anything at all, and it's not just you who'd pay the price for that. Theo and Charlotte and Li-Fang and Zane would have to deal, too. So keep your hook-ups off the bus, young man."

If anything, he looked even more pissed off, his furrowed eyebrows almost touching. "I'm not fourteen and living in your house any longer, so I'm pretty sure you have no right to tell me what to do. And, what the hell do you want from me, anyway? I live on a bus, Mom. Privacy isn't something I really have anymore, not when I'm working. So, I'm sorry, but if I want a sex life—news flash, I do—then the bus is one of my *better* options. If I were working some ordinary job, I sure as hell wouldn't be having sex where my mother could hear me. I love music and I tour. This life isn't easy, so if one of my perks is women who want to say they've fucked a rock star, I'm not always gonna pretend I'm a saint and give that a pass."

She sat on the bed, used sheets be damned. She couldn't really take this much longer. "Didn't I teach you any better?"

"Teach me better than what? I like sex! I like women, and they seem to like me. We're all consenting adults, looking to have a very good time."

She changed tacks. "I'm on this bus as a favor to you and the rest of the band, and apparently I'm solving a problem created by the fact that there's a little too much of this consenting sex going on around here. So maybe try to tone it down a bit."

"God, you sound like those Marshall brothers you were always complaining about when I was a kid, with their churchy, preachy attitudes about sex. Which strikes me as really odd, given that you seemed to hate everything they stood for, and never let me even meet them, even though they're basically my only family." Her own father had passed years ago, and her mom might as well be a stranger now, living in Idaho with relatives Megan had never liked.

The Marshall brothers, Jason's family, had always been pretty wacky about religion, but she hadn't let their brand of Christianity shape the way she'd raised Kyle. Sure, she'd preached moderation and consent and birth control and protection, but that was more because of the way her life had utterly changed when she'd gotten pregnant.

And she didn't want to think about the Marshall brothers and all that baggage now. "I'm not telling you to stop having sex"—here she was, blushing now just thinking about last night—"I'm just asking you to dial it back a notch, especially when it affects everyone on this bus. Again, I got on this bus to *help* you. I've got photo albums out there that your bandmates think are hilarious, photos I brought along to try to remind you that we used to have some good times, you and me. But now, what? You're pissed because I never let that god-awful Marshall family near you? And to get back at me and them and I don't know what else—you invade the band's privacy and bring random women on the bus with you to punish me because you wanted to meet your grandparents? That doesn't even begin to make sense."

He huffed a moment, just staring at her. "Maybe meeting my grandparents would have been nice, but that's not why I'm mad at you. If you don't know what I'm talking about, then you're just going to have to figure out what you *possibly* could have done that made me feel so jaded about sex. And when did you get your counseling degree, huh, Mom? Did I miss that somewhere between you bailing on college and working some crappy job you hate?"

Ouch. Again, he seemed to be talking about her and Jaimie. And that last bit was a dig about her dropping out, which hurt. "Hey, I'm almost finished with my degree, okay? You saw me studying for my exam backstage the other night. And after we get to Portland and I get a nap, I'm gonna to take my final online before the show. If I pass, I'll be done, and then I'm going to apply to law school. But right now I won't be working on applications, because I'll be too busy singing for you and your band. So, fine, be pissed if you want to be about the Marshall family, but don't dig at me for missing out on college, okay? Because that actually hurts, you know? It's not like I wanted to be a failure."

He reached out and grabbed her hand, forcing her to look him in the eye. "Hey, I'm sorry. That wasn't fair." His Adam's apple bobbed as he swallowed.

The apology didn't feel like nearly enough, but it was pretty clear he wasn't going to say any more. Alright, then. Time to meet him halfway. "I'm sorry, too," Megan said. "You know how prickly I get about college. I shouldn't have yelled." She didn't say anything more about the Marshalls. That was a step too far.

"No, I get it," Kyle said.

And because she was a mom, and because she always felt like it was her job to make this work, because she sure as hell wanted her son in her life, one way or another, she looked for some other way to make this better.

After a moment, what she came up with was, "I've been meaning to say thank you, by the way, for asking me to join the tour. I'm super flattered. I've always known my voice was decent, but not exactly a chart-topper, you know? So it means a lot to me that you're letting me sing with you and that lot." She jerked her head toward the front of the bus, where the rest of the band was entertaining Ashley from last night.

The bus slowed. They were in city traffic now, presumably threading their way toward the venue. "Well, you're actually damn good at music. So feel good about that."

After a moment, he spoke again, this time in a more conciliatory tone. "And, that woman last night? I wouldn't normally bring someone on a long-haul trip, but she has cousins in Portland, said she wanted to visit them. It's not something I do every night or anything."

"Yeah, just maybe keep it down, if you can? You're right, you never really do have any privacy. So I was out of line. Again, I apologize."

His face was relaxed, but the corners of his mouth tilted up.

It wasn't much, but that hint of a smile said enough. Right now he was okay, and he was okay with her, too.

But then he seemed to remember something, and the smile was gone. He stood. "We're pulling in now. I've gotta put my game face on. Brandon has me and Li-Fang doing press."

He looked cold again, shut down. Not letting her in. But she'd felt that flash of connection, and she was still the mom, still the cheerleader. "You've got this," she said.

"And you've got a couple hours off. Rest up. We've got a show to do."

8

The bus rolled into their Portland venue around ten in the morning, and Megan could have used the grit in her eyes to sand down a backyard deck. Like the rest of the band, she caught a catnap in the greenroom, and then somehow managed to work her way through her final exam for a class called "Sex, Power, and Politics." While she wrote, she kept thinking that if the class had added the word "music" to its title, she would have felt better about her chances of passing.

She mailed it off to her professor. She was supposed to feel excited about being so close to finishing her degree, but she was so tired she only felt relief at being done. And then guilt for being relieved. On some level, shouldn't a degree be about learning things that were useful or interesting? Most of her classes weren't.

Should she feel guilty for being on tour? She didn't think so; but then again, she was bailing out her adult son when he was in trouble, and paying the price by sacrificing her own goals. Which felt a lot like being enabling in a very unhealthy way, if she really was sacrificing something she truly wanted.

But was getting her degree the right goal? Because touring

didn't feel like a sacrifice. It felt like living out her wildest fantasies of a perfect life. And between her soon-to-come degree, possibly going to law school, and this tour, she could have a better chance than most at working in the music industry. She could represent musicians, and at least be close to the action. She could stand backstage like Brandon did, representing all kinds of bands and groups. And she could work to make sure they were getting a fair deal from their labels and the venues and Amazon and anyone else skimming money off the top, taking it away from the artists who actually did the work.

She didn't see much of Kyle before the show, but she did joke around with Hannah and Kryssa from makeup and wardrobe. They gave her grief for worrying about passing a class that had the word "Sex" in its title, and then begged for the chance to see the photo albums they'd heard about. Apparently the band had been hooting about how funny some of the shots were, especially a third-grade Halloween parade where Li-Fang, all gangly legs and missing teeth had dressed as Spider-Man; and Kyle had been a pirate, wearing all the jewelry and makeup of a wanna-be Johnny Depp.

Megan promised to bring the album by sometime soon, and wondered if she was ever going to get the chance to look at it with Kyle. She also picked up some good gossip from Hannah and Kryssa, mainly how Charlotte was finally getting over her last relationship, which had been with a woman who had been more interested in Charlotte's place in the band than Charlotte herself. "So maybe now Zane will actually have a chance," said Hannah. She gave Megan one last touch of lipstick, looked at her work in the mirror, and then said, "Perfect."

Hannah and Kryssa waved Megan off, telling her to break a leg for the show.

She kicked some ass that night. There was one awkward moment, where the set list taped to the floor in front of her was wrong; or maybe it was just that Kyle didn't follow it. She was taking a breath for her entrance when Zane kicked in an entirely different beat. She held her breath—literally—and didn't make a sound. Kyle had cued up a song from an earlier album: one the whole band had performed countless times, but not the one she had been expecting. She had glanced at Li-Fang, who gave her an encouraging nod, mouthing the words, "Roll with it."

After the show, Charlotte explained that it was just something Kyle did. He changed up the set list onstage to keep things fresh. "Better a fresh show than a dead show," Charlotte said. "That's what Kyle thinks, at least." Thank God Megan knew their song list as well as anyone, because she knew every word and every harmony.

After the set and load out, they hopped back on the bus, exhausted. Seattle was only a few hours away, so instead of spending the night on the road, the band rolled into a hotel parking lot around three in the morning, suffered through check in, and slept in unmoving beds.

Heaven.

Load in was earlier than usual, so they could do sound check and Greta's audition in one go. Megan wanted to nap in the greenroom, but Kyle told her no. "I want your opinion on the new chick," he said.

They sat around on the stage, waiting for Brandon to get back from the airport, where he was picking up Greta. Megan had found herself a perch on one of the amp cases off to the side. Zane was at his drum kit, and Charlotte rested on the tall stool between her three keyboards. Li-Fang, Theo, and Kyle sat on the ground, legs splayed, instruments nearby on their stands. Theo asked, "So, what do we know about this Greta woman?"

"She's on tour with Lara right now," Kyle said, which wasn't news, because Brandon had told them all. It still bore repeating, though, because all of them respected that one-name star. "Lara's playing across town tomorrow night, and her tour wraps in about four weeks. This chick, Greta, she's free after that. So we could pick her up then, assuming we like what we hear."

That covered the musical part of things, but Megan was more curious about the other tidbit Brandon had dropped back in LA. That this Greta was his fiancée's sister.

Focus. Audition.

Voices approached, and then Brandon was on stage with them, a tiny woman clinging to his arm. If she got any closer to Brandon, she'd be hanging from him like a stuffed monkey. If this was the sister, she didn't really want to imagine how the fiancée treated him. She barely came to Brandon's shoulder, and stared up at him like he was the most fascinating man she'd ever met.

"Really?" the girl said, responding to some story Brandon had finished telling as they stepped onto the stage.

Wow. That was one incredibly nasal and piercing voice. And this girl was a singer?

It got worse.

The woman laughed, a high-pitched squeak, and grabbed at Brandon with her other hand, pretending to stumble on overly high heels. At least Megan assumed she was pretending, because she used the move to press her boobs into his arm and feel up his bicep with both hands. In a caricature of the dumb blonde, she raised her eyes, framed by long false eyelashes, to his face. "That is about the best story I've ever heard. You are. Just. Fascinating." She punctuated each of her last two words with a touch of a long fingernail on Brandon's arm, and she drawled. Wonderful. Bring on the Southern charm.

Brandon smiled down at her like it was completely normal for women to fawn over him. Which struck Megan as seriously messed up, because—what about his fiancée? Where was she?

And why would a guy as decent as Brandon be letting his fiancée's little sister hang onto him like that?

But Megan couldn't blame the girl for the look she gave Brandon. It was unfair how handsome he looked every single day. How many suits did he own? And how did he keep that beard so perfectly trimmed? Greta was going to start running her hands over it in a minute, wasn't she?

"Everyone," Brandon said. "This is Greta. Now, she can't join us for several weeks, even if you all like her audition. Which I'm sure you will."

Greta gave a wave, still holding Brandon's arm. "Hello, everyone. I am the biggest fan of all y'all's music! Brandon here didn't have to twist my arm the tiniest bit to convince me to audition. When my agent told me y'all needed a new backup singer, I told her to sign me up quick, quick, quick." She pressed a hand to her chest and looked up at Brandon again. "And when Brandon told us we could make it happen today, I was just so excited!"

Greta didn't stop for breath, which probably boded well for her ability to sustain notes on stage. She just gave Brandon's arm a squeeze, making sure to flatten her boobs against his arm one last time before turning her eyes to the lead singer, who had to be a more exciting conquest than a lowly band manager. Not to mention the fact that Kyle wasn't engaged to her sister. "And you must be Kyle." She pranced away from Brandon, hand outstretched, her leggings showing off curves that Theo and Li-Fang were having a hard time ignoring.

"Hey," Kyle said, ignoring the hand. "So, you've done some recording, Brandon tells us?"

She nodded. "Yeah. I'm on a few tracks for Glowstix and the Red Licorice. I think Sweetie Pye likes my sound, the way it adds to the mix. It's so great to work with her! I swear, there need to be more women producing, am I right? And ya'll have heard I'm touring with Lara now, doing her backup vocals.

She's so amazing!" Her voice was still grating and high-pitched. How did this woman lay down the sort of power alto tracks most rock bands needed?

Greta edged closer to Kyle, looking up at him from under her incredible lashes and probably giving him a good view down her shirt. Kyle's mouth twitched, and she knew he must be enjoying this.

But Kyle got a hold of himself quickly. "Greta," Kyle said, "you'll be back here. We live on these mics?" He leaned into his with the question, then waved at the sound guy stationed at the main board, back among the seats. "Check your level, okay, Greta?"

Greta couldn't possibly walk that way normally, with her hips moving that much, could she? Maybe she was showing off the way she'd behave on stage, because sex appeal sure made the crowds happy. Megan thought it was more likely that Greta was just trying to entice the guys in the band, looking to notch her bedpost. Sure enough, Theo and Li-Fang watched her progress across the stage; and who could blame them, really? It was pretty hard to take your eyes off of a fit twenty-year-old wearing emerald-green leggings and a matching sports bra. To be fair, she'd covered the bra with a boxy tee; but the shirt was crocheted out of gold yarn, more holes than coverage. Her boobs and her butt jiggled.

Great. Even Charlotte was watching. Brandon, though, ignored it, which earned him a few points in Megan's book. He came over to sit next to Megan on her amp, then spoke into her ear. "Kyle's gonna run this pretty tight, but keep your ears open. We're meeting after to discuss the hire. I'd value your opinion."

She could have sworn she didn't actually will her body to move, but the compliment made her face twist toward Brandon. She caught a hint of sandalwood and citrus, just like she remembered from the night he'd first settled her onto the tour bus.

Brandon focused on the woman across the room, not looking at Megan at all, so Megan let her eyes linger on his profile, the slightly weathered skin with the barest hint of lines around his eyes. Smile lines.

She liked a man who smiled enough that those were the first lines that formed; not that wicked crease between the eyebrows from too much frowning. It would be nice to see more of his smile.

She mentally kicked herself for noticing how much she liked how this man looked, and those lethal smile lines. The guy was engaged, and his face put him way out of her league. Not to mention those shoulders. Sleeping with her boss back at the law firm, as disgusting as that was, was probably as high as she should aspire.

Sitting rigidly, Megan was careful to keep her shoulder and her leg from touching any part of Brandon's body. Then she tried to focus as Kyle started the audition. "First up, 'Running to the End.' You ready?"

Greta nodded, and on Zane's count, the band launched into the crowd-pleaser that usually closed the first half of their show. Theo laid down his throbbing bassline and Li-Fang took the lead on the electric guitar.

The girl closed her eyes and swayed, one hand wrapped around her mic as Kyle let loose the vocals for the song's opening. At that point, it was his voice over a spare drum and Theo's bass, but when they hit the chorus, Kyle laid into his own guitar. During a show, they would up the mix here, let the chorus take on the overpowering thickness that *Nirvana* had been so fond of.

Greta opened her mouth. "Oh, why?" she sang, layering her voice under Kyle's.

Jeez. That was eye-opening.

Greta's singing voice was nothing like her spoken one, which made Megan wonder if she used that annoying whine intentionally. Everyone would expect her singing voice to be awful, and then when she actually wailed away on a vocal power line, she'd surprise the hell out of a crowd. Or the people running her audition.

And it was a pretty damn good sound. She held the sustained notes easily, without wobbling on the pitch. Her voice was strong, and brassy enough to cut through the sonic layers; a good rock-n-roll sound.

Okay, then. Maybe Brandon did know a thing or two about managing a rock band. The girl talked like a whiny teenager, but her singing voice was raspy and powerful, a great match for the kind of music the band made.

Megan kept her eyes on Kyle, the band, and the girl. Next to her, the long fingers of Brandon's left hand ghosted the beat with his fingertips.

Brandon turned toward Megan and lifted his eyebrows, asking silently if she heard what he did. She nodded at him, acknowledging that Greta certainly had some chops.

Megan kept her ears on high alert. After a time, though, she realized something rather amazing. As good as Greta was, her own voice was just as good. It wasn't just braggadocio, either; Megan had so many insecurities she would wear out a therapist, if she could ever afford one. But Megan knew music, and she knew her own pitch was as stable than Greta's. And she certainly had more of an ear for improvised harmonies. Greta was strictly by the book.

Beside her, Brandon was clearly enjoying Greta's voice, which was probably for the best. Megan shouldn't join the Sutter Boys permanently. It would be a stupid move for the band's image. So this was a win. The sooner they found a reasonable solution to the band's problem, the better off the band would be.

Even if that meant that Megan would have to go home, actually apply to law school, and go back to that office and the prospect of Jaimie coming on to her again—at least until she could find a new job.

Well, she was done with feeling worse than dirt. Jaimie could take his puppy dog eyes home to his wife. Because Megan Gamble was better than that.

At the end of the song, Greta bent over to adjust the strap on her boots. She stuck her butt high in the air while she worked those straps, while Theo and Li-Fang practically drooled. Still bent double, Greta tossed her electric blue hair out of her eyes so she could stare at Brandon. "What did you think, Brandon?"

"Sounded great. But let's give you a chance to sing a few different numbers with the group. Kyle, what do you want next?"

He named a song from their first album.

"Ooh, I've always loved that one!" Greta screeched.

Megan winced, and Greta turned to face Zane, one hand on her hip and chest thrust forward. No one could take their eyes off her boobs. "So, big boy," Greta asked Zane. "Are we ready?"

Zane nodded. Megan watched Zane's gaze shift to Charlotte. *Hmm*, Megan thought, *maybe Zane does have a thing for Charlotte.* Interesting.

Charlotte, however, was looking back at Megan, and mouthed the words, "big boy?"to her. The two women tried not to laugh.

Despite the temptation to laugh, Megan paid close attention as the audition unfolded. She wasn't entirely sure the band would actually ask her opinion, but she wanted them to get this right. Yes, they should hire Greta, but maybe Megan could point out a few ways to make the fit work even better.

When the audition finally wrapped up, Brandon hooked Greta's arm through his. She turned toward the band as they walked, waving and blowing kisses like a little Dolly Parton wanna-be. "Buh-bye, y'all! So great to meet you. Can't wait to hear what you thought. But we'll hang out again, okay? It's a small business, am I right?"

"Theo, Li-Fang!" Megan said once they were out of earshot. "Get your jaws off the floor."

Li-Fang shook his head. "Damn, that woman...." He trailed off. "Sorry, Mrs. M. My bad."

9

Twenty minutes later, Brandon met them in the greenroom after seeing Greta to her waiting car. Even this early on tour, these rooms were all starting to look the same to Megan. A few couches around a large coffee table, a craft table to one side with snacks and drinks. Not much in the way of decor except the occasional poster for past events and tours.

"Her car service show up okay?" asked Kyle from the catering table, his hand hovering over a bland-looking sandwich.

"Yeah, no problem," Brandon said. "So, what did you all think?"

Megan slouched deeper into her corner of one of the couches, more exhausted than she had the right to be. The rest of them were wrung out, too. Maybe it was the audition itself that had done it, because it felt like they'd been performing for Greta as much as she'd been auditioning for them. Normally a performance meant the feedback of the crowd, which amped these guys up like nothing else. But the audition had been all about putting out energy without the usual payoff.

And they'd all be on stage in just a few hours. She wasn't looking forward to trying to rally. Extra caffeine would definitely be required.

It didn't help that Megan was low on blood sugar as well. How Kyle and Li-Fang did these shows and also all the radio and promo appearances was beyond her.

Kyle spoke first. "I thought she had a decent sound. Her credits are amazing, and I think her voice works with mine, better than Katya did. What do you guys think?" Kyle threw himself into the air to land on the couch, intentionally jostling Li-Fang.

"Watch it!" Li-Fang said, holding a can of soda over his head. He'd just cracked it open, so it took some fancy moves to keep it from bubbling over onto Kyle, Li-Fang, and Charlotte.

Megan put her own diet soda on the end table next to her, then reached to grab one of the bags of chips off the coffee table. She ripped it open and scooped up a large handful. Without a word, Theo took the bag, fisted his own helping of chips, then passed it down the line.

She hated barbecue chips. Why hadn't she looked before ripping the chip bag open like a starving woman?

She rubbed her fingers clean on her jeans, since of course no one had thrown anything resembling a napkin on the table. Then she checked the rest of the chip selection in front of them. She would kill for some veggies and hummus, but that wasn't on offer.

"Her sound was good," Megan said, agreeing with Kyle. "Pretty well supported on the sustains, but I caught one or two moments when her pitch wavered. And did she strike you as a little stiff out there?"

Theo said, "Not where it counts," then curved his hands in the air in front of him, clearly remembering Greta's impressive chest.

"Watch it," Brandon said, cutting Theo a glare, and then

taking in Li-Fang as well. He went to the craft table, grabbed Megan a bag of plain chips and a napkin, then threw a pile of napkins onto the table in front of the couches. "I really don't need to hire a new singer just to have her quit on us like the last one. And I don't want a harassment suit. All of you need to learn to take these issues a lot more seriously."

Hmm. That was interesting. And how had Brandon known she liked plain chips?

"What exactly did you mean, a little stiff?" Li-Fang caught Megan's eye, then tossed back a handful of the dreaded barbecue chips as soon as the words were out of his mouth.

Megan shrank back into her corner, wondering if she should have spoken up at all. Well, she'd already opened her big mouth, so that choice was behind her. "I just meant that it seems like she's going to sing note for note what she's heard on the albums, or whatever you all teach her, but I don't know if she'll be able to loosen up on stage. Vocally, I mean. Use her voice to play off what the rest of the band is doing. And did anyone else hear that slight pitchiness, or was that just me?"

Kyle actually looked at her. "She did say she was a fan, and anyone can have nerves, which would explain pitch issues. Her demo tapes were clean, and I know they didn't autotune those. So she stuck to the recorded harmonies, isn't that pretty much to be expected? I mean, most singers auditioning for a backup gig don't walk in thinking it's completely fine to riff like they're already a member of the band. And I'd rather have her singing by rote than getting crazy on us and screwing up the music. So, assuming we're going to replace Mom, I think she's a good hire. Anyone backing up Lara has got to be solid."

Brandon sat again and worked at his cuff, pulling it from the bottom of his jacket sleeve. "So, the rest of you, do you mostly agree with Kyle? That Greta can sing, and can hold her part for the rest of tour?"

Brandon looked around, getting nods and brief responses

from the band; but oddly, he didn't seem happy. "I heard the same pitchiness Megan did, but I'll agree with Kyle that it was probably nerves. Her tapes were solid, and Lara's people give her good reviews, say they'd hire her again. My main concern is the way you guys were responding to Greta's flirting."

"Hey," Theo said. "What were we supposed to do, just ignore her?"

Brandon sighed. "No. But I don't need all you guys lusting after the new girl, and then pissing her off. It's exploitative when it's in the context of a working relationship, and that's exactly what this will be. You guys will have all the power. We're literally sitting around this table talking about whether to hire her or not, so no matter how cozy you all get on that bus, or how badly she seems to be into any of you idiots, it's got huge potential to be an abusive relationship. She was flirting to get the job, and it worked, and you all need to realize there are plenty of women available who aren't on your payroll. Don't mess with her. That's wrong, and has always been wrong, even if lots of bands and celebs got away with stuff like that in the past. Not to mention the way it burned this band before."

Kyle stood up. "Nice talk. Don't hit on the new girl. Got it. I say we hire her." He ignored the napkins Brandon had added to the table and wiped his hands on his jeans (like mother, like son), then looked at his bandmates.

"I'm cool," said Charlotte, tucking her hair behind her ears. "You guys in?"

And pretty much like that, the rest of them were nodding and standing.

"When will she start?" Megan wanted to know, since it would impact her own life just a wee bit. Kyle turned to look at Brandon as well.

Brandon answered, "She can't join us until the show in Virginia Beach. I know that's a long ways off, but Megan's doing a great job, so I'm sure things will work well until then."

That was weeks from now. At least it would give her more time to work on her relationship with Kyle. And maybe even think about law school applications, if she was serious about the idea of starting a career with musicians.

Oh, and it would give her more time to enjoy the heck out of being on stage.

Wait a second. Had Brandon just said she was doing a great job? She looked his way, and the corners of his eyes wrinkled. His lips hadn't really moved, but that was a smile. Huh.

The band tromped out to do a quick photo shoot, but they didn't need her; so she found herself alone with Brandon on the couches, with a rare chance to just unwind.

Time to breathe. What a luxury.

Megan pulled out her phone and Googled law schools. Brandon took out his own phone, and for a time they sat in silence. After a few minutes, though, Brandon looked over at her.

How did he do that? Just look at her and somehow make her feel like she was interesting and worth listening to?

"You seem to be settling in okay," Brandon said. "Is there anything you need, anything I can do to make your job easier?"

"Other than a few more hours of sleep on a surface that isn't moving? I'm doing okay, actually. Even having some fun." She noticed the scar on his lip again, then moved her gaze away. She shouldn't be staring at the man's lips.

"That's good to hear." He leaned back, flipped his phone face-down on the sofa cushions between them, then said, "We've got time to kill, and I could use a little down time. Talk to me? Anything. Like, what's the story about you and Kyle's dad? How did you and Jason meet?"

"Friends in common back in high school. We met at a party, started hanging out pretty much right away."

"Was Jason already a surfer?"

She took another slug from her soda. "Yeah, he was. Jason's

brothers were all older than he was, and totally into the beach scene in Santa Cruz. As far as I could tell, when Jason was little, the Marshall boys spent most of their free time at the beach, and they let him tag along. There were plenty of hand-me-down wetsuits, which you absolutely need in that water, especially in the winter, so Jason started surfing when he was around ten. And you can't grow up surfing Santa Cruz without paying attention to Mavericks. You've heard of it, right?"

Brandon nodded, sipping at his water.

Megan continued. "That competition brings in surfers from all over the world. Big wave stuff, and it pretty much fascinated Jason, got him involved in the competition scene. His family was pretty supportive, which might seem weird, because the rest of the Marshalls were already part of some super evangelical church. I don't know, I guess I never thought church people and bathing suits went together really well, but there was a sort of surfers-for-Jesus thing going at the time, all these Christian kids riding waves together. Jason caught the surfing bug, but not so much the Jesus bit. That whole family used to get along pretty well, at least until Jason got me pregnant."

Brandon said, "Must have been rough, even without the whole judgmental family thing. Unwed mom trying to finish college? That couldn't have been easy."

"And I'm finally almost finished," she said, wondering when her grade was going to be posted. "But Jason was amazing, even if we were more "friends" than "boyfriend/girlfriend" by the time Kyle was a few months old. Jason was there for me and Kyle, even though his family cut him off because of the baby."

"And what about your family? Did they help?"

"No," said Megan. "Mom and Dad had moved up to Idaho by then, to be closer to Mom's family. I didn't see much of them, and they certainly couldn't help financially." Her dad's heart attack had been only a few years later. Megan hadn't been as close to her mom, even before she'd moved a thousand miles away. At this point, she and her mom only spoke on the phone a handful of times each year. Megan had never gotten along with her mom's family.

But she had her friends. And she had always had Kyle; at least until these last few years, when their relationship had gotten so sour.

"So," said Megan, changing the subject back to Jason, because that was easier to talk about than the benign estrangement from her own mother. "The best way for Jason to earn a living was to surf, so that's what he did. He got some nice sponsorships, but he was a big wave surfer, and those competitions mean flying around the world to wherever the waves are breaking. They give people a few days' notice, and competitors are expected to drop everything and fly in. So Jason did just that, even on days when I was counting on him to take Kyle. But Jason paid some of our bills, like childcare, and he spent a ton of time with Kyle when he was in town. Honestly, if he hadn't really stepped up, I would have had to drop out of school a lot sooner. Jason didn't have a musical bone in his body, but he's the one who first noticed that Kyle was into music."

Brandon cut another look her way, and she had a moment where she felt very self-conscious under his gaze, like she wanted to adjust the shoulder of the scoop-neck T-shirt she was wearing. The moment stretched, and she worked hard to keep her hands still.

He couldn't be checking her out. He was too polished to be interested in anyone other than someone gorgeous and young. Someone like Greta. Or her sister, surely. It had been a long time since she'd felt like she was young and attractive, so maybe she was just making up the way his eyes seemed to press on hers, almost a physical weight against her body.

After a long moment, he gave the tiniest shake of his head, like he was trying to refocus on the conversation. "This isn't in the bio."

What had they been talking about? Oh, yeah. Jason noticing that Kyle was musical. She tried to concentrate on her story. This might actually be interesting to Brandon as the band's manager. And that was probably the only reason he was hanging out with her. Professional interest. Right?

"Kyle was at Jason's one afternoon while I was working on a group project for a class. I got back to Jason's around dinner time. I think Kyle was almost three. The house was kinda dark, like the guys hadn't gotten around to turning on the lights after the sun started going down. Most of the housemates were sitting around the living room—two of them were part of that first band I sang with. Kyle was wearing his favorite shirt, with this green dinosaur on it, sitting on the floor in the middle of their tiny living room. There was a guitar in front of him, in an open case on the floor, and music playing over the speakers. Kyle was clearly listening, and he was also playing the guitar. I mean, he was plucking the strings one at a time, but when I walked in a new song came on and Kyle got really upset, like little kids do when they can't express themselves.

"None of us knew why he was freaking out, and the guy who'd left his guitar in the living room was nervous that Kyle was going to hurt the instrument—rational, right? But Kyle wouldn't let go of the guitar. Jason was the one who said that the guitar didn't 'sound right,' and the guys and I immediately understood. The song playing over the speakers wasn't in the same key as open guitar strings, at least when no one was working the fretboard. The guitar's owner was closest—he had been about to grab the guitar away—but he started to hold down the strings to the fretboard, so when Kyle ran his fingers across the strings the notes fit the chord progression of the song playing on the speakers. Kyle looked like he'd discovered that magic was alive in the world. And after a little while, he pushed the dude's hands away so he could work the strings with both hands, one on the fret board and the other strumming. We just sat there, kind of stunned, and watched Kyle basically teach himself to play, all in about ten minutes. It was the most incredible thing I've ever seen."

"That's quite the story."

"I know. He's got real talent. I mean, I can carry a tune, but he's far more talented than I am."

He looked straight at her again, and this time she didn't have the urge to fidget. "Don't sell yourself short."

God, did he think she was talented? Wow. She wanted to sit with that thought for a while.

"If Kyle was three, then Jason wasn't around much longer, am I right?"

It still hurt to think about it. Jason hadn't been her lover anymore, but he'd been Kyle's dad and one of her best friends. "Yeah, the accident happened just a few months later. Sort of bad luck, but also the sort of thing that happens to professional surfers. A bad fall in really rough water knocked him on the head, and by the time anyone was able to get to him, he was gone."

They sat quietly for a while. It isn't easy to restart a conversation after talking about a death, but eventually she got thirsty and realized her can of soda was empty. She reached a hand toward his water. "Anything left in that bottle?"

He stood, "Yeah, there's plenty, but let me get you your own drink. Want another soda?"

"No, but sparkling water would be great."

He made a trip to the craft table and then returned, cracking the cap off the plastic bottle and handing it to her.

"And that's when you dropped out of school?" he asked, sitting back on the couch. A little closer this time.

"Pretty much. I was sort of cobbling life together with Jason's help, but after that, I literally couldn't make it work. I know it probably sounds awful, but the fact that we were friends at that point and not boyfriend and girlfriend made it easier. If I'd still been head-over-heels in love, I would have been completely overwhelmed. As it was, I was just—what's one step down from overwhelmed? A basket case? Desperate. Anyway, there I was: twenty-two, single mom of a toddler. Yeah. Tough years."

"But you kept yourself going? Both of you, I mean."

"I had to work to pay rent and buy food, but working meant I had to pay for childcare. And that meant I had to work more hours. Life really sucks when you're trying to scrape by. Luckily Keiko's family had some connections, so I started as a word processor in a little law firm, and eventually became a paralegal. When Keiko graduated from law school, she joined the same firm. We've been working together ever since."

But that wouldn't last much longer. Megan only planned to stick around until she could find a new job away from Jaimie.

Brandon turned to her and spent a long moment looking into her eyes. She loved feeling seen like that, but it made her depressed to realize how long it had been since any man had looked at her like he saw something to admire. "You've done remarkably well, you know. You raised a superstar on your own, and you've made an honest living for yourself, not to mention that you're a disgustingly talented musician yourself. And you're touring with this bunch of idiots, putting up with these crazy hours and life on the road. A pretty big sacrifice. So, thank you. I'm sure the band doesn't say that a lot."

"Not really," she said. "But I just did what I had to do."

"Still, you didn't have to drop your life and join the band."

"I guess not, but here I am."

"Here you are," he agreed. "Damned lucky for all of us, I'd say."

Maybe he did like her, at least a little bit.

10

"Oh no you don't! Those are my Goldfish!"

Kyle lunged across the table in the center aisle of the bus and tried to rip the bag of crackers from Megan, but she grabbed a fistful, then lifted the bag behind Theo's head to pass it down to Li-Fang. If the table hadn't been in the way, then Kyle would have snagged her prize.

The fight over the snacks intensified, until everyone but Zane was hassling everyone else at full volume. But Brandon was trying to make calls. Megan hated acting like the mom in the room, but apparently someone needed to do it. "Keep it down, guys. Brandon's trying to work."

This was the first time Brandon had ridden with them since Megan had joined the tour, but Charlotte had told her he did that every now and then. And none of the band had blinked when the dressed-down manager had climbed onto the bus with them back in Salt Lake for the eight-hour ride to Denver. Then again, they'd spent the night in Salt Lake, so this was a day trip, not an overnighter. Maybe that was the difference.

Brandon's first words on the bus had been, "I hear there's a photo album floating around somewhere." Which had led to the whole band, even Kyle, sitting around in the front lounge, looking at photos and giving Kyle and Li-Fang grief.

It had been wonderful, and Megan wondered if Brandon had done that intentionally in order to help her really spend some time with Kyle. Intentional or not, it had worked.

Brandon had spent a good thirty minutes with them before asking if he could use Kyle's room to make some calls. But even after Brandon had left, Kyle had been—happier? Looser?

At any rate, he wasn't glaring at her every time he caught her eye, so that was progress. By the time she left this tour, she was going to make sure that young man not only talked to her, but wanted to. She'd give him reasons to actually call, and they'd be able to get their relationship back on track.

Megan didn't think her goals were unrealistic. She couldn't imagine that most grown man spent a ton of time checking in with their moms, especially not a touring musicians, but hopefully they could be in touch at least once a week. That wasn't too needy, was it?

Kyle brushed past her, laser focused on Li-Fang and the coveted bag of crackers as he stalked around the table. "Don't worry about Brandon, Mom. He probably just wanted to hide, give us some space to get our own work done."

If tickle fights over snack food were what Kyle thought of as work, then she'd clearly been living the wrong life.

Megan's phone buzzed. Speak of the devil. It was a text from her boss, Jaimie. *Wondering if you have any updates on when you'll be back to the office.* She'd been in such a good mood, and there it went.

There was only one reason Jaimie was anxious to have her back. The paralegal workload could easily be divided up, and the firm used a regular temp agency when things got really crazy. So this was just a man wondering when his booty call would be available again.

Nope. Nope. Nope. Not happening, not ever again.

She glanced back at her phone, realizing that even his text messages were careful. This message looked so damned innocuous. Anyone could read it and not suspect a thing. What a lawyer.

It looks like four more weeks, she responded.

Kyle stood up and reached unsuccessfully for the snacks, making a mime's pouty face. "Not fair. Why is everyone so mean to me?"

"Poor widdle baby," Li-Fang said, standing with one hand braced on the window as the tour bus swayed. With his other hand, he held the bag out of Kyle's reach. It helped that Li-Fang had more than two inches on Kyle. He waved the bag over his head. "Our sad little front man never, ever gets his way."

Eight hours on the bus was a long time, and the group was punchier than she'd ever seen it, even with Brandon there to keep them a bit more in line. Certainly a far cry from a law office, especially one with a boss she alternately avoided and slept with. But, enough. It was hard to feel sorry for herself with this crowd around her. Especially when the band was in a great mood.

Aw, to hell with it. She might as well enjoy herself. She'd forgotten what it was like to spend time with people who were in their twenties, with energy that seemed boundless and this group's penchant for turning every afternoon into a party.

Kyle stepped onto the cushioned bench of the couch. He hung on to the overhead storage unit with one hand and stretched across the aisle toward the bag of crackers, which Li-Fang held behind him. The two of them had grown up pulling this kind of stuff, playing keep away and running around constantly, even at the public pool deck in the summer with lifeguards yelling at them. But she hadn't seen Kyle like this in years, loose and relaxed. It was certainly better than fighting with him over his right to live his sex life out loud and practically in public.

"Catch," Li-Fang said, pitching the bag under Kyle's arm to Charlotte. Charlotte snagged it one-handed from where she sat wedged against the kitchen area.

Kyle whipped around, his foot almost knocking his guitar off the seat.

"Watch it, doofus," Zane said, moving the acoustic aside so Kyle wouldn't wreck his own instrument, then shaking his head as he looked from Kyle to Li-Fang. "How old are you two?" Zane calmly took the bag from Li-Fang and handed it to Megan.

Right. She'd been trying to grab a snack before that text message had come in.

Megan took the bag and let out a very inelegant snort at Zane's question. "If you think he's bad now, you should have seen him when he was actually a kid. Thanks, Zane."

"Just looking after my people," he said, glancing from Megan to Charlotte and back again.

Charlotte's cheeks might have pinked up the tiniest bit.

Megan took a large handful of crackers, then handed the bag to Kyle.

"Finally," he said as dramatically as if he had been on the brink of starvation.

Theo snuggled up into Megan, and Megan shoved him away for about the fortieth time in ten minutes. He said, "A man's gotta try, right? But do tell, Mommy Megan, what was Kyle like when he was young and foolish?"

Li-Fang raised his eyebrows in two quick beats. "You mean, as opposed to right now?"

"Har, har," Megan said. "He was an absolute terror. I almost lost the security deposit on the apartment we were renting when he was two. He used to have this train thing he could sit on, and one day he almost crunched a hole in the wall. Even without the hole, there were scuff marks *everywhere*."

Beside her, Theo laughed and sat up for a moment. "No way! I had one of those trains. I totally loved it." Then Theo lay back again, stretched out his legs out along the bench seat, and settled his head into Megan's lap.

She pushed him off and popped a few of the crackers into her mouth. "I bet you were as bad as Kyle was. I'm gonna bond with your mom one of these days over 'my kid was more of a handful than yours was' stories."

Theo tilted his head back to look at her upside-down from where he was now prone. "Nah. Can't see it. She's like twenty years older than you are and thinks my career is a total waste of time. She also believes I'm hiding an unacknowledged fondness for spreadsheets, and that soon I'm going to be begging her for a job at her accounting firm." He scooted back and rested his head on her lap, and this time she let him stay.

Megan shook her head, looking at Kyle. He'd been holding the bag of Goldfish out to Charlotte, letting her take handfuls of crackers, but now he took one final helping for himself, closed the bag, and wiped the crumbs onto his pants. He took his guitar back from Zane, then sat down across from Megan and began to pluck at the strings. Megan kept her eyes on his fingers and her ears on the alert. He was very, very good at what he did. At the moment, Kyle's seemingly random fingers on the strings perfectly replicated the energy of the past few moments, and then transformed it into something a crowd could dance to.

Li-Fang picked up the bag and ate one last handful, but soon tossed it aside to wipe his own hands and seek out his violin. "Now that Mr. Lead Singer isn't having a low-blood sugar hissy fit, it seems like maybe it's time for some song-writing." He sat to pull out his case, and then lifted it onto his lap. Li-Fang narrowed his eyes slightly, listening for potential harmonies and instrumental lines.

Kyle let one corner of his mouth lift. "Damn straight it is. But I don't see your lazy ass doing anything useful. Get that case open and give me some help here." With at least another two hours left on the road, it was as good a time as any to work on new material.

Megan's phone buzzed again. *Hurry back. We all miss you. And remember, officially you only get three weeks off a year, so if I weren't so anxious to have you in the office, I'd have every right to fire you.*

Her stomach churned. That bastard. Sweet-talking her and threatening her all at once. A prince among men, for sure. At least now she knew there were guys like Brandon in the world, decent men who paid attention and cared and did the right thing.

And then the music pulled her back out of her head. Kyle drove through a chord progression on his acoustic, pulling hard at the strings and shifting the key from major to minor. It settled there, energetic and danceable while still carrying something dark.

Interesting.

She sat back and observed. Onstage she had to be on her game and in the moment. Off the bus, Kyle was usually on his own, or with one of the women he picked up. Almost ten days into her time with the tour, she hadn't realized she'd been waiting for this: a chance to really look at Kyle and judge for herself how he was doing.

When Kyle bent over his guitar, he was so clearly the grown version of the boy he had been. She had seen this exact set of his spine, this exact tilt of the head before. She'd seen it on a scrawny kid in a T-shirt that said, *I make seven look good*. She'd seen it again back when Kyle had been fighting his first outbreak of acne at the age of fourteen. How odd to look at this grown man, this famous star, and see her own little boy, the kid she'd raised.

The sound of the violin drew her back again.

Li-Fang stood, his violin tucked under his chin. The riff he played would go to the lead guitar in most bands, but not this one. He switched between violin and lead guitar depending on what the song needed. Li-Fang had stared music lessons when his parents had handed him a violin at age four. The time hadn't been wasted, because today he was both very well-trained and quite intuitive. His violin-playing was one of the things which gave the Sutter Boys their unique sound.

The line Li-Fang was playing around with now soared so freely on the violin that Megan couldn't imagine it on another instrument.

In the back of the bus, Brandon appeared just past the kitchen area, standing between the two bunks closest to the front lounge. He narrowed right in on Theo's head in Megan's lap for some reason, but that was the moment when Theo sat up and grabbed his bass from the case under the bench seat. Megan propped herself back into the corner, happy to listen, which seemed to be exactly what Brandon was doing from the other end of the lounge.

The band got to work. It was surprising and very cool to see just how quickly a song could come together when all the circumstances were right. There went Charlotte on a mini keyboard, which must have been stashed somewhere close, laying in some synth under the acoustic of the other instruments.

Kyle began to sing, mostly nonsense syllables, but there was already a distinct emotional energy to the song. As upbeat and driven as it had started, it seemed that Kyle wanted to lay a dance tune onto a more somber sense of longing. Why longing? What was it about?

She liked it. So often in a song things were spelled out. The singer didn't get the girl, or their dad died, or they were messed up from drugs or booze. But for this first draft, Kyle seemed to want to leave the reason behind the melancholy a mystery, and Megan approved. It certainly fit her mood.

She began to float a descant above Kyle's tenor, wondering

if maybe she was out of line. Was she supposed to contribute to this or not?

She dropped back out, even though she certainly wanted to get in on the action.

Zane, beating a drum line on the bench seat's baseboard, raised his head to look over at Megan. "Nuh, uh, Mrs. M. No stopping now, 'cuz that sounds good. Keep it coming."

Kyle, too, gave her the nod.

That was a great feeling. Kyle wanted her to sing. She joined the music, basking in this feeling. A group of incredibly successful, professional musicians *liked* it when she sang. Her ego perked up.

This wasn't just singing, it was creating. What a thrill, to pull music from the air! Even for Megan, just a few shows into her place on the tour, the normal setlist had begun to feel calcified, like music which had once been alive had now turned into a fossilized imitation of itself. When music was fresh like this, just being born, it was animated and vivid and somehow immense, poised to expand further and become something that could surprise even the people creating it.

At the back of the lounge, Brandon had his phone out, probably taking stills for their socials. Today she barely registered Brandon, which was certainly unusual. But songwriting blocked out almost everything else.

The music changed tone, getting bolder. Still melancholy, but even more insistently a dance tune.

Kyle abruptly stopped strumming and reached a hand toward Theo. "Give me your bass, man. Got an idea." When Theo passed his instrument across to Kyle, the angle was awkward for them to do a straight exchange, so Kyle just held the guitar out, waiting, until Megan grabbed it from Kyle's hand.

She thought again of when he'd been tiny, assuming she always had a hand available to carry whatever it was he wanted her to. Sometimes back then she'd felt like an octopus with the amount of crap she'd had to juggle.

Kyle bent over Theo's bass, and Megan cradled Kyle's guitar in her own lap, where a guitar belonged. Still singing along, feeling the magic of creating something out of thin air, her fingers found the fretboard and she picked up the line Kyle had been playing.

Soon Theo noticed, raised an eyebrow, and glanced at Li-Fang. "Would you look at that? How come you guys never told me Kyle's mom played the guitar. That's smooth!"

Li-Fang, picking out a lead's line on his violin, shook his head. "Couldn't have told you, because I've never heard her play before. Since when do you keep secrets from me and Kyle?" Li-Fang asked.

"I don't really play."

"Sure sounds like you're playing to me," Kyle said. "You always said you were no good, but that was clearly false modesty." His smile softened the words, nurturing her birthday candle-sized flame of confidence.

Megan glanced at her left hand on the neck of the guitar, but found that looking down distracted her. The chords lived under her fingertips in the same way as melody and harmony flowed from her mouth, and it was easier to play if she kept her brain out of the action. Shocking, the way her fingers remembered this from so long ago. "I was just a high schooler with a guitar, nothing to get excited about."

Charlotte took her hands off her little keyboard, leaving the sound a bit hollow. "You haven't touched a guitar since high school? I hate to think what my keyboard skills would be if I quit playing for that long. Shit, you're really good."

Her fingers might remember what to do, but playing guitar on re-virginized fingers meant the strings quickly started to bite. She'd have blisters and open sores pretty soon if she played for too long, not to mention she could already feel that the strength in her index finger was going to go in a hot minute. "I swear I haven't played since I was younger than you all. But I've got to stop. My fingers are way out of shape for this." She released her hands from the fretboard and held up the bright red tips. "I've gotta stop, or I'll leave blood all over Kyle's strings. Somebody take this."

Somebody turned out to be Theo, since he was right next to her and since Kyle was still mucking around on Theo's bass.

Without looking up Kyle said, "Mom, seriously, you should start practicing, build up some strength and calluses so you can play longer. As long as you need to, 'cuz I do know what it feels like when the music in your head won't shut up until it gets out into the world."

And how the hell was she supposed to do that without an instrument?

"News flash, I don't exactly own a guitar anymore. And stop flattering me. You all are the pros, not me. I'm just along for the ride. It's not like the world is missing a great talent with me sitting on the sidelines. Tell him, Li-Fang!"

"No can do, Mrs. M. I'm gonna have to watch my back so you don't take over my spot. That said, I am better on the violin than she is, so Kyle, you'll keep me around for that at least, won't you?"

"I'll have to sleep on it, but yeah, I guess we'll keep you in the band. Even if mom is better looking than your sorry old ass."

Li-Fang looked over his shoulder and down to his backside. "Hey, lots of girls like my butt."

They got back to the music, and soon had the outlines of a song about loss and the longing for good, rowdy fun. Kyle made up a bunch of lyrics on the fly, and Li-Fang started recording so that tomorrow they would still remember what they had done. Megan contributed where she could, but after another hour or so of work, the song wasn't finished. It needed a twist.

She'd only been singing, not playing, but the guitar had ended up back in her lap, and now she had an idea. She coaxed out the chord progression they'd been using, pursuing an idea. "Let me try something. I kinda think all it needs is a different voice in the bridge."

Kyle nodded. "Okay. Can't hurt. What are you thinking of?"

Megan took the melody.

You know I've
Spent
Too
Long sittin' all alone
When the world stopped its spinning,
Left me wanting to moan
For the
Days
Of
Dancing that had just disappeared
Now I'm dancing again
And I've dried all my tears!

The band had started backing her up, the instruments driving a dance beat to her words. She kept singing.

Because the light's come back on
The music's started again.
And we're stronger and brighter
And we're dancing again.
They can't take away our freedom,
They can't take away our fun.
Yeah we're back at the party
And the party's
Just
Begun.

When they were done, everyone was moving to the music.

God, that was amazing. It was a blast to sing and invent on the fly, but also so damn satisfying. They'd just pulled music out of thin air! How cool was that?

Zane clapped her on the back. "Sweet! Wait till I get on my kit with this one. No one is gonna be sitting down when we play this for a crowd."

"Mom, I think you just got yourself a solo. We can totally pull this into the set."

She wasn't going to hold her breath waiting for that to happen. But it would be fun to get a guitar in her hands again.

"Brandon, did you get it?" Kyle directed the question to the back of the bus, where Brandon still stood thumbing at his phone.

"Sure did. I'll get this to the label. It'll be gold for the social media team."

Megan patted her hair. Charlotte had persuaded her to put braids in her pigtails. She looked like a complete idiot. "God, well I hope I wasn't in it."

"Oh, you're in it all right." Brandon looked very satisfied. "And I think a lot of people are going to love seeing Kyle's Mom in these things. Good way to broaden the band's reach."

She scowled, and Li-Fang patted her knee. "Don't stress, Mrs. M. Everyone's gonna love it. Trust me, the label doesn't put up anything that takes away from what the band's doing. So if you stay in there, it'll be good."

It still sounded like a great way to be publicly embarrassed.

The bus turned off the freeway, and she stood to stretch. Theo put his bass away, and Kyle carried his guitar past Brandon to his suite in the rear of the bus, so no one was paying attention to what Li-Fang said to her next. "I've got an extra guitar floating around on one of the crew buses. I'll dig it out. You need something to practice on if you want those fingers of yours back in shape."

"Li-Fang, I couldn't take one of your guitars! I know how much those things cost." She'd Googled it once, and the guitars he'd played sold for four thousand dollars!

"Yes, you can. I don't know why Kyle won't just give you one himself, but you need to get playing again. I saw the way you perked up during that session. Mrs. M, you've always been one of my favorite people, but there've been a lot of times when it was like you were just going through the motions. You've been coming alive on stage, but this here...." He gestured at the trashed lounge where they'd just been jamming. "Seeing you in songwriting mode made me see how much you need this. I think you might need music even more than Kyle does. Totally sucks that you gave it up for so long."

"Maybe I just needed to get some confidence back."

"I'll say."

He gave her a brief squeeze on the shoulder, then walked down the aisle to stow his violin.

There was a new text message from Jaimie. *I miss you.*

Her stomach churned. God, she just wanted to text the man, tell him to stop bothering her, that there were no more *benefits* in the "co-workers with benefits" thing they had going. But that was too much like a breakup to do over text. And he probably wouldn't even take it seriously. He'd just plan on charming her again, and complaining about how sad and unfulfilled he was in his marriage.

Just like that, her good mood was gone, along with the confidence she'd been reclaiming. Writing music was one thing, but she'd never be able to live a musician's life until she really believed in herself. And right now, she was only taking baby steps in that direction.

11

They played Boulder the next night.

Onstage, it was pretty hard not to pump up the energy; what with the crowd sending waves of noisy affection washing over Kyle and Li-Fang, the small splashes of adoration that those two didn't capture left her damp and exhilarated.

Deep into the show, maybe two-thirds of the way through the set list, Megan lifted a hand high overhead at the end of one of their songs. She couldn't keep the joy off of her face, because —damn! This life! How would she ever go back to a job in a law office, and a tiny interior cubicle, and spend her days poring over immigration cases and adoption proceedings and estate plans?

She was not looking forward to that, but she did need to earn a living, which meant she was stuck with Jaimie, at least until she found a new job. And if she went back to that office, she needed to convince him that she was never, ever sleeping with him again. If she didn't, he'd just keep dogging her, hoping she'd relent one day.

And really, hadn't this whole mess started even earlier— before she'd even met Jaimie—back when she'd been pregnant with Kyle, not even showing yet, and part of that awful band, 2 Samuel 6? Back when she'd been singing with Jason's brothers.

On stage was not the place to rehash that in her mind.

"Thank you all very much," she called, her voice lost in the chorus of thanks from other band members. She got all the audience love she could ever want, but didn't have nearly a star's price to pay in terms of the hassle. No paparazzi following her, no obsessed fans stalking her. Just the rush of being on stage, singing into a mic like her soul could fly out of her mouth and grow into a vast and gorgeous being, independent of her body and created wholly from sound. She waved again, then ducked her head to brush her face against her bicep, trying to wipe away a lock of hair that was glued to her cheek with her sweat.

Yeah. She was worth more in the world than being the woman her boss banged every now and then.

Kyle stepped back to his mic, saying, "So, Boulder, Colorado! How's it going? You feeling lucky tonight?"

The crowd roared, and a lone woman's voice rose into a tiny gap of relative quiet. "You can get lucky with me!"

He laughed. "Let me go check with your boyfriend first, sweetheart. But I'm talking song-lucky, not," here he thrust his hips once, "plain old lucky-lucky."

At that point, Kyle dropped his voice down to a more conversational tone. "So, I'm gonna let you in on a little secret."

The crowd got even louder. Kyle was really good at this, working the audience. Maybe that was a skill worth learning. "As you might imagine, we have a lot of time to kill on the bus, and we've been using it wisely. At least that's what I think. I was wondering if you might like a sneak peek at some new music we've been playing around with."

The crowd clearly loved the idea.

He must mean the song they'd been working on yesterday. They'd certainly spent enough time on it on the bus—at least another hour even after they'd essentially finished writing. And Kyle did have his little quirk about mixing up their sets. But this still seemed pretty crazy. She hoped he knew the words to the bit she'd made up; she sure as hell didn't remember them all.

Megan wrapped her hands around the mic in front of her. Sometimes she didn't quite know what to do with them, so the mic stand gave her some security. It made a great prop.

Kyle gestured her way. "For those of you who don't know, that's my lovely mom standing back there. Say, 'Hello, Mom!'"

The crowd chanted, "Hello, Mom!"

Wait.

Was he going to expect her to sing?

No. He had to be kidding. Megan waved and forced out something she hoped came across as a laugh. What was Kyle doing?

"So, we were just getting a new number set, sort of jamming on the bus, when good old Mom, here, came up with a killer close. And I thought maybe we could test it out on you all. Since you've been such a great audience."

He kept talking, but she only heard her own internal voice saying, *No, no, no!*

Kyle wrapped up. "I take it that's a yes? You want us to show you what we've got?" Zane and Theo started in on the beat, driving the dance rhythm into her bones.

Normally she'd start moving, loosening up and getting ready to have a good time doing something she was figuring out was not only fun, but also something that she was pretty damn good at. But she couldn't just start dancing when he expected her to sing that stupid verse she'd ad-libbed on the bus. At least the beat and Theo's bassline were bringing back the shape of the tune. But now, with a crowd staring down at them, the joy she'd just felt gave way to pure panic, because she couldn't possibly remember the words.

Kyle brought in the guitar.

God, this was a nightmare, like finding herself naked in a college classroom about to take an exam for a class she'd forgotten to drop.

Now what?

She looked forward and just offstage to see Brandon staring at her again. Great. Someone whose opinion she valued was going to witness her humiliation.

Dammit! She was going to ruin this moment Kyle had set up with the crowd, and then Brandon would fire her and she'd go home to Cupertino and live a boring little life in a boring box and try to turn down Jaimie's next advance. And the one after that. And the one after that, too.

Li-Fang raised his bow arm and threw her a glance. He grinned at her like he expected her to be totally into it, but she made a frantic gesture with her hand that—thank God!—he understood.

Li-Fang lowered his bow and spoke into his mic. "Hey, Kyle." Li-Fang's voice was lighter than Kyle's higher, drifting up into counter-tenor ranges. He often took an upper harmony. "I think maybe we should have warned your mom. Look at her. Mrs. M wasn't expecting this."

Great. Now everyone was doing just that. Looking at her. She was already so flushed under the lights that they probably couldn't tell she was now blushing.

Her eyes drifted sideways, to Brandon standing in the wings. From his expression, it seemed like he could see the pink rising to her cheeks, and that he had no idea how to fix things for her from offstage.

She was going home. He wouldn't have to fire her, because she'd just dissolve into a puddle of embarrassed mush and slink away before anyone could track her down.

The crowd shouted, "Come on, Mom!" and "Please!" and

she started to feel like she'd eaten something slightly rotten just before the show.

Kyle looked back, waiting. "Well, if I'm gonna sing, I'm gonna need some help."

Li-Fang gave her a look so ludicrously suggestive that even the audience would be able to tell he was joking. "I've got something in my pants that could help," and the crowd, those perverts, went wild. Yes, they loved it, but what the hell was Li-Fang thinking, even talking that way about her? Wait until his mother got wind of this, because she sure as hell would.

The crowd kept shouting lewd suggestions, and she heard at least a few voices offering to take Li-Fang's place or asking her to meet them after the show. What? This was just unreal!

Li-Fang, the cheeky bastard, grinned at her, watching her flush rise. Over in the wings, Brandon started pacing. He looked ready to explode.

Li-Fang reached into his back pocket and pulled out a cell phone.

Oh.

My.

God.

She was going to kill him.

Thumbing open the screen, he strode toward her, throwing words over his shoulder to the audience. "You all are a bunch of pervs, thinking of Mrs. M that way. Though, she is a mighty fine-looking woman. She'd have to be, wouldn't she," he said as he continued his stroll to her corner of the stage, "to give birth to the idiot singing lead."

Women's voices screamed themselves hoarse in agreement, and Kyle waved at the crowd before turning to grin at her.

Li-Fang covered his body mic with one hand, then said, "The lyrics are right here. Just sing it like you did on the bus and you'll be fine."

She took the phone, looking at the words and then back at

Li-Fang. "Thanks," she said back, holding her hand over her own mic.

From the front of the stage, Kyle mouthed the words, "You okay?"

She nodded the tiniest bit, and he turned back to the audience. "She's in! Excellent. Honestly, Mom, I was almost afraid you were gonna mom-divorce me or something. But you've got this! Boulder, are you ready?"

There were enthusiastic calls from the crowd.

Zane and Theo had been vamping on the beat, and now Kyle came back in on the guitar. She held Li-Fang's phone in her hand, looking at a typed version of the words they had sung yesterday on the bus. With a pretty strong sense of disbelief, she listened to Kyle sing the first several verses, chiming in as usual on the backing lines. So far it felt pretty normal, almost like this song had been in the rep for months.

Then she focused again on the fact that in just a few moments she was going to have to sing lead on the final verses.

Deep breaths. She supposed she should be grateful that her voice was feeling pretty well warmed up tonight.

When her verse rolled around, she leaned into her stand mic, pulling it forward with one hand while the other kept a death grip on Li-Fang's phone.

And she survived. It wasn't perfect, but it was so much better than the crash and burn she'd been worried about. She actually held the crowd!

She'd had a lot of really great highs in her life. The high when she'd first met Jason. The moment she'd first held a screaming baby Kyle, already using the pipes he'd be famous for. Certainly the crowd energy during her first few shows. Each one of those highs on stage had felt like a once-in-a-lifetime experience, but this? There was nothing like this on the planet, even if her voice had been shakier than it should have been, and even if she'd been holding a damned phone to read the lyrics. She could do better, but for tonight, she'd take it. Because this? This was worth living for.

She kept catching Li-Fang and Kyle turning her way, nodding.

They knew.

They knew what it was like to hold a crowd like this, and they had just gifted her with this experience. They could have kept the number under wraps. Kyle could have done the entire song as lead. But they hadn't.

Even if the band recorded this with someone else on their new album, she'd still have this moment. No one could take it from her.

And this crazy idea tried to grow inside of her. What if she could actually perform? What if she tried to make a go of it as a musician, not just a lawyer or an agent or a manager or someone who supported musicians?

Li-Fang ripped off his final flourish, letting the high note whine until it was almost too much, and then the crowd exploded. Scattered here and there, and then stronger, she heard a growing chant. "Mrs. M! Mrs. M! Mrs. M!"

"That's right," Kyle said. "Give it up for Mrs. M, my amazingly talented mom." He turned back to look in her direction, but kept his voice pitched for the crowd. "Thanks, Mom. Maybe we can do that again sometime."

He didn't even let the noise level settle, just rode the energy straight back to their normal set, and the show finished the stronger for it. But after she stepped back to the rear of the stage, where the lights weren't quite as strong, she started to come back to earth.

It was okay. She could survive slipping back into the background.

On her way to her dressing room she passed Kyle and Brandon chatting in the hallway. Brandon stopped talking as soon as she got near, and focused on her. He shook shaking his head slowly, as if he couldn't believe what he'd just seen saw, but that he'd liked it a lot. "Well, well, well," he said. "I guess if I hadn't figured it out before, now I know for sure where Kyle got his talent. Great job out there. Congrats."

And just like that, an echo of the feeling she'd had on stage returned. It felt, pretty literally, like she was so buoyant that she would float higher in a pool of water; like her lungs were filled with stuff lighter than air.

"Brandon's right," said Kyle. "He just gave me an earful for throwing that at you onstage, and he's right. I should have said something before the show. But you were amazing, and I think they all got a great sense of the new song. And they sure liked it, didn't they?"

She couldn't hold back the smile that blossomed deep in her body and spread past her lips up to the corners of her eyes. "I guess they did. Thank you."

"Well," Brandon said. "You deserve it. I can't wait to hear more."

"Next time, Mom, it'll be even tighter. But it's good in your voice, you know?"

First Brandon, and now Kyle? "Thanks again," she said. "I'll look it over on the bus. It'll be better next time."

Brandon nodded. "It was already darned impressive. Not perfect, but very, very good. You've got talent, Megan."

Before she could say anything more, Theo and Zane clattered up behind her, exuberant in their own praise of her performance. Before she knew it, their moment had swept her past Kyle and Brandon toward the green room and the fans and the rest of the evening.

Not perfect, but very good? She'd take it any day of the week. Because she could get better. She knew it. And she rode her performance high for a long, long time.

12

In Minneapolis, at the meet and greet, Megan realized she was getting good at dealing with fans. She maintained a smile most of the time, even when her face muscles hurt, and developed a solid repertoire of comments for the (many) people who thought she was just a random woman sitting at the far end of the table. Every so often, though, someone would perk up when they realized she was Kyle's mom, and she'd get an enthusiastic greeting and the sort of questions every mom loves.

"Aw! Was he as cute as a baby as he is now?" This time, the question came from a girl who was probably still in high school; one whose own mother stood just behind her.

"Yeah. He was a pretty adorable kid." She and the mother exchanged smiles. It felt like she and the other woman were both thinking fondly of vivacious toddlers. The girl in front of her was bouncing on her toes; she was clearly as high energy as Kyle had been at her age. Megan posed for their selfie and the pair moved on, leaving Megan to plaster on a smile for the next fan.

It was easy to bask in the constant gushing from the die-hard fans. These people were awestruck at being in front of this band they worshiped, and even at Megan's end of the table the compliments were non-stop.

Still, her energy was starting to flag when someone called to her from down the table. "Megan, you need this?"

Zane reached around Charlotte to tap Megan's arm. Rolling her shoulders, Megan leaned back in her own chair to meet Zane's eye. The line of fans showed no sign of letting up, not yet. He was holding up a small bag of goldfish crackers, the size she used to pack into Kyle's lunches.

"Yeah, I'm starved. Probably gonna crash soon."

"Thought so," Zane said, tossing the bag her direction.

Even a single handful of the tiny crackers sent a welcome surge of energy into Megan's body. Her blood sugar must have been really, really low.

Charlotte, sitting between them, kept signing a poster, but Megan could see her grin.

"Zane's our mother hen; or, mine, at least," Charlotte said as she slid the poster to Megan. "He's the only one of these idiots" —Charlotte glanced toward the head of the table, where Kyle and Li-Fang were the star attractions—"who realizes how hard we gals can crash. And he doesn't like dealing with me when I'm hangry. I guess you're on his list of people to watch out for now. Not a bad place to be."

Charlotte grabbed a few of the crackers from the bag Megan had just opened and turned back to Zane. "Thanks, pal."

"Thanks from me, too," Megan said.

And then they were back to the fans, signing and posing for selfies and generally acting as one giant PR machine.

At the law firm, Megan had been lucky to get a half-hearted "good job" every couple of weeks. So signing autographs—they wanted her *autograph*? Really?—and smiling for selfies pushed her far over her normal annual allotment of kind words and enthusiastic praise. A stiff mouth from trying to smile for a solid hour was a price she was willing to pay.

With the rest of the band, Megan headed for the greenroom when they had signed their last posters and posed for their last photos. Load out always took time, and the band typically just hung out until it was time to board the bus. Tonight she was scarcely shocked that a few of the attractive women from the meet and greet made it back into the private space for the after-party. Even though she'd learned to expect it, she didn't really enjoy realizing that Kyle and Li-Fang and Theo would all disappear at one point or another. Did these guys never give it a rest?

And Kyle, despite their talk back on the bus, pretty pointedly looked her way when he sweet-talked his choice of the women into leaving the room with him. Like he wanted her to notice.

Here she was, surrounded by testosterone and sex, and she certainly wasn't getting any. She'd cut Jaimie out of her life; and even if he had been an awful person, he'd been the one she'd looked to for that kind of release. It hadn't been good sex, but at least it had been something.

No, that wasn't the right way to think of it, because this was better, dry spell notwithstanding. Now she could hold her head up again.

But still, this environment didn't exactly make her appreciate celibacy for its own sake. And while there were plenty of women around for the guys--and both men and women for Charlotte, should she choose to indulge—it made Megan's skin crawl to think of hooking up with some random man. If she deserved more than being her cheating boss's mistress, she deserved more than being a notch on some guy's bedpost, even if the physical release would have been more than welcome.

Why, she wondered, was it so difficult to deal with the fact that a new generation was having sex? Or for younger people to face that fact that a woman not even twenty years older than they were still wanted it? What did they think, that their own sex drives would just melt away when they hit the ripe old age of—what number would they even plug in, thirty-seven? Forty? Fifty? Seventy? The rest of the band was so much younger than she was that they probably dealt with a huge ick factor in thinking about her as a sexual being (except for Theo, with those come-on that were his warped way of expressing affection).

Looking around at all the attractive women and men in the greenroom, at Zane and Charlotte cozied up on their own, still not willing to admit an attraction but also not hitting on the groupies like the others, Megan just wanted out of there.

She grabbed a diet soda from an ice bucket and headed out through the maze of corridors toward the exit.

Pressing open the outside door with her back, she popped the can of soda and stepped onto the metal balcony that over-looked the loading dock. After a moment to just breathe the evening air she sat, letting her legs dangle and threading her arms through the bars of the railing. She'd managed to grab a shower before the meet-and-greet, and her still-wet hair dripped chilly drops onto the thin fabric of her old T-shirt in the cooler air outside.

The door opened and shut, and then someone sat beside her, polished shoes dangling next to the worn off-brand canvas sneakers she'd changed into after the set.

There was no need to look up to see whose shoes those could be. Why was the only age-appropriate man associated with this tour apparently taken?

That was easy. Because in her life, the only men ever interested in her were the ones likely to cause her heartache, the long-gone Jason being the possible exception.

Well, Brandon being taken wasn't any reason to be less than welcoming. She looked over and said, "Brandon, hi. When did you get in?"

"Just before the show. But during the meet and greet I…"

She chimed in with him before he finished, "Had some calls to make."

They shared a grin. Mind meld.

Taken man. Figures.

"Yeah," Brandon said. "I guess you're used to being around lawyers. I may never have practiced, but I kinda can't put down my phone either."

"I noticed. But back in my office, calling anyone after six at night was bad form. Your contacts don't seem to mind, do they?"

He nodded. "No, they don't. Office hours in the music business aren't really the same as in most other industries." He made the air quotes around the words "office hours."

Brandon's voice was so warm. The timbre was amazing. Megan was used to the voices on the bus. There, she keyed into Kyle's—a light tenor with a big range on the low end, a voice that soared and then darkened to a growl on stage—and Li-Fang's—his voice even higher and smoother than Kyle's, and a good addition to the band's vocals. So when Brandon spoke, she immediately noticed the man was a bass, with depth and power and resonance.

And it fit her image of him as someone who had his act together, who had slowly accumulated professional expertise, who had real-world power that seemed to match his timbre. Obviously, that made no logical sense, but there it was.

When she looked over again, Brandon took a pull from the beer bottle dangling from his fingertips, staring at her like he was trying to figure something out. Meanwhile, she tried to reconcile his wardrobe choices, which screamed Scotch in fancy crystal glasses, with the sweating Coors actually in his hands.

She reminded herself that he was taken, and tried to get her heart to stop daydreaming about something that wouldn't ever happen.

"So," Megan said. "Tell me about this fiancée of yours. She's a sister of Greta, right, the one who's going to take my slot?"

When Megan looked at Brandon, expecting a shy smile or a look of pride or some expression on the happy side of the equation, she knew she'd said something wrong.

Because the guy was basically frozen, his lips a hard line, throwing that scar further into relief against his lips and the softness of his beard.

"What?" she asked, then shook her head. "Did I miss something? I swear I'm not usually an idiot, but back in California, when you were first telling Kyle and the band you had a lead on a singer, you called Greta your fiancée's sister? She didn't give you back the ring or anything?"

The corners of his nose quivered with tiny little breaths that told her he was trying hard to keep it together. Finally he looked away, setting the bottle beside him and wiping his palms along his thighs. "Yeah, I still call Katrine my fiancée, because I don't know what other word to use. The thing is, she's dead."

The moment she'd heard of Jason's accident flashed to mind, and Megan reached out her hand for Brandon but stopped short of touching his arm. That wouldn't be right.

She withdrew her hand and placed it over her beating heart. "Oh, God. I feel like an idiot. I'm so sorry to hear that. I had no idea."

"Obviously. And I'm sorry, too. I know it's misleading when I talk that way, but I just don't know how to talk about it. I only met Greta when Katrine was in the hospital. It was early Covid, so none of us could visit or anything. She went quickly. And we were all pretty desperate, sometimes, to talk about stuff other than that damn disease, so Greta and I started talking shop.

And, yeah, I thought of her when the band needed a new singer."

"Makes sense."

What she wanted to ask was why Greta had been hanging all over him at her audition, and then why he had warned the band not to hit on her. Either Brandon had a thing for Greta, or Greta had a reputation that Brandon didn't like.

But she couldn't ask that.

He kept talking. "Greta's five years younger than Katrine was, but she reminds me a lot of her sister. That sense of fun, and that crazy confidence Southern women get when they do their hair and makeup and it's like their appearance is this armor that makes them invincible."

Well, Megan certainly didn't have that Southern charm or confidence—or any confidence at all, basically. She fought off disappointment. Well, at least she knew the type of woman he was attracted to. "So, you gonna ask her out?"

He picked at the label of his beer bottle. "I've thought about it, but it just never happened, I guess."

God, this was going to kill her. Was he available or not? She elbowed him gently, hoping that wasn't too pushy. Argh. She should pretend that she was his friend, encourage him to ask Greta out, if that was what he wanted. Since he apparently liked Southern girls, not women who lived in yoga pants and barely threw on eyeliner and mascara for a day at the office. "Why not? You have her number, right?"

"I'm not going to ask someone out by text message, okay?"

"Why not? Isn't that what most dating apps are about?"

He sighed, and then his voice became teasing. "Not relevant. And how on earth did we end up talking about my lack of love life, anyway? Okay, your turn. Fair's fair. Got a boyfriend back home?"

She shook her head. Jaimie had never been her boyfriend. "Not even close. And I'm not done asking questions, yet! I've told you some of my stories, but I haven't heard any of yours. You some rich kid with a mommy and daddy who always paid for everything?"

Megan raised her eyes and found Brandon looking rather intensely at her. After a moment he seemed to remember that he'd been asked a question. "Not exactly. I grew up outside Nashville."

"You still have family there?"

"Yep. But we're not in touch. I've got a big brother in prison, a dad dead from drinking too much, and my mom is married to another SOB who hits her as much as my daddy did. I'm lucky I'm not in prison, too."

That wasn't at all what she'd expected. "You sure pretend to be a guy who came from money, though, barely getting around to rolling up your sleeves even though it's after midnight."

"Or maybe I'm just compensating, d'ya think of that? Trying to prove I'm better than that now." The scar on his lip stood out white.

She glanced at the thin line, which led her to think briefly of other things lips were good for. She closed her eyes. When she opened them again, he lifted his eyes to hers, as if he'd been thinking about her lips, too.

"How'd you get the scar?" She kept her voice quiet, afraid of pushing into business that she had no right to ask about. Because, that story about his family? That was a pretty big reveal about his past, and she was almost afraid to hear the story behind the scar.

"Well, it wasn't my dad, at least. Compared to what he used to do, the story's almost funny, even if the cops were involved."

His voice was lighter now, so it couldn't be that bad, could it? "The cops, huh?"

"Yep, and it all starts with a girl," he said.

"Aw," Megan said. "Look at you, still thinking about the girl back home." She hoped she didn't sound heartless, especially after what he'd said about his family, but she desperately wanted him to have something cheerier to think about.

He waved his drink in her direction. "Not really, but *anyway*, back in high school I had a terrible crush on this girl named Alexa Griffiths. There was a teacher everyone hated, Mr. Perkins, and he gave Alexa a D-minus on an essay or something. So my two best friends and I decided it would be a great idea for me to show my love to Alexa by toilet papering Mr. Perkins' house. We loaded up the rolls with rocks so we could throw them farther, and of course one of the rocks broke a window. Then his alarm went off and scared the shit out of us. My friends and I hopped the wall from his yard back onto the sidewalk, or tried to. I got snagged up on the top of the wall and came down really hard, face first on a slab of sidewalk that a tree-root had broken. Cut my lip open badly enough I probably should've gotten stitches. I was bleeding all over the place, and I must also have bonked my head pretty good, because I staggered around for a while; probably had a minor concussion. By the time I was thinking straight, my friends were long gone and the cops were there."

"Not good. Did they just take you home to your folks? Or was it worse?"

"I never figured out whether they were going to warn me or arrest me or what, but I was pretty much shaking in my proverbial boots. And I really didn't want the cops to deliver me home to my daddy. I don't even want to think about how much trouble I'd have been in. But the cops let me go. This old guy who lived across the street came over and talked to them. He'd seen the whole thing, and told the cops that he'd make sure I learned my lesson. Could they forget the incident if he paid to repair the neighbor's window and then made me work it off? The cops said yes, never even wrote down my name. These days, they would've run a million background checks before leaving a teenager with some random dude, but I guess back then people weren't quite as paranoid. Today they would never leave a teenager with someone who hadn't gone through sixteen background checks."

"Did you ever figure out why he did it? The guy who stuck up for you? Was he some old pervert or what?"

Brandon leaned forward, letting his bottle dangle between his fingers. "No, not a pervert at all." He stopped for a beat, then continued. "I think he just wanted to do something nice. But he was like that. Decent and hardworking. More than decent, actually."

She waited for him to say more, but he seemed to think he was finished. She reached down to pull up the heel of her sneaker. It was rubbing against a patch of skin that was threatening to blister. "Well, I guess that's one thing we lose with all our background checks and waivers and bureaucracy. The casual good Samaritan can't just step in and do a good thing anymore. Can you even imagine it? 'I know it's the road to Emmaus, sir, but do you have any ID?' Jesus would have sat there for a heck of a long time if he'd been checking everyone's background."

The corners of his mouth quirked up. "Never pegged you or Kyle for the type to know their Bible stories."

"I don't." She drained her can of soda dry, then gave it a little shake. "But that stupid-ass band I was in? Those guys quoted the Bible like it was...the Bible or something." Lame way to finish that sentence. "But I want to hear the end of your story. So, the police let you off and hand you over to some random guy. Then what?"

"Ever hear of Sidecar Productions?"

She looked at Brandon and raised her eyebrows, like, *Do you take me for an idiot?* Everyone knew that label. "Sidecar? The label that found REM, the one that Malcolm Reynolds ran with that other guy, what was his name?"

"The other guy's name was Richard Elmwood. Which

happened to be the name of the guy who saved my butt. And the job he wanted me to do was sweeping floors and cleaning up in the studio."

Her eyes got wide. "Wow. Now that's a way more exciting job than I had when I was a teenager. I waited tables at one of those family restaurants that rang a bell when anyone ordered the super sundae."

He laughed. "I remember those. Didn't they make the girls wear those short skirts and frilly white blouses?"

"Can't forget the wonderful red choker to really tie the look together."

His eyes crinkled at the corners in a really wholesome way when he laughed. "Sure wish I'd seen you in that!"

"Stop," she said. "You're just humoring me now."

He opened his mouth to say something, then shut it and cocked his head to the side. "I don't know what you think you look like, but if I hear you imply you're old or ugly or out of shape one more time, I swear to God I'm going to get T-shirts made with the words 'Hot Mama' over the tour logo and a photo of you onstage. No one—and I mean *no* one—would ever look at you onstage and see anything other than a ridiculously gorgeous woman who can make a damn backup line sound like it should be pulled out to the top of the mix."

At first Megan wanted to cringe. He sounded almost angry. But as the meaning of his words settled in, she began to sit up straighter. He couldn't be entirely serious, of course, but if Brandon Thatch was willing to say that after all the disgustingly attractive women he must have worked with over the years, well then, maybe she didn't have to feel like a complete has-been every time she got on stage.

But she just said, "T-shirts, huh? Can I at least help choose the colors?"

"No problem."

"Fine, then. T-shirts it is." She held his eyes for a moment and the heat there made her wonder if there was something starting to happen between them. Maybe he actually thought she was attractive. Maybe.

Or maybe she was reading him wrong, because just then he looked away.

Awkward.

After a few beats of silence, things felt more comfortable again, somehow, until Brandon said, "Hey, speaking of that band you were in, d'ya know I've actually heard of them?"

"2 Samuel 6? Really?"

Brandon swallowed a bit more of his beer and said, "Well, I *am* from Memphis, you know, and the city's Southern enough that we get a few of the Christian rock acts coming through, not just rockabilly and blues. They probably came through at some point, and I guess now that I'm spending time with you, I got reminded of the name. Didn't that band get some bad press for preying on young girls?"

She took a sip of her cola, staring into the darkened parking lot. "Yup," she said, popping the last letter loudly between her lips.

"So, they kicked you out because Jason got you pregnant, and then it turns out they were doing the same thing? Charming."

"Yup." And that wasn't even the whole story.

She kicked her legs a few times. The night was getting colder. It felt good against her bare legs after a hot and sweaty show.

"So, I know this will sound random," said Brandon, "But was there a guy named David Marshall in the band?"

Her stomach turned. Talking about the band was bad enough, but talking about David Marshall? That made her truly ill. She tried to keep her voice even. "How on earth would you know that? David was their lead singer and Jason's oldest brother."

Brandon lowered the bottle. "He emailed me earlier today, completely out of the blue, and asked if I was in contact with you."

"Why? How?"

"I'm guessing it's because of our social media. Especially since we've added the new duet to the show, your name is getting some traction."

"Well that's ridiculous."

"Why?" He looked genuinely curious.

She made a teenager's *duh* expression. "Because I'm a forty-year-old backup singer, that's why. My name shouldn't be getting traction."

"Nevertheless, this random dude from your past got in touch with me about you. Or maybe not so random. He's Kyle's uncle, right?"

Now that was another horrible thought. And one that Kyle had reminded her of that night on the bus when they'd argued. "Right. But what did he want?"

"He didn't really say, just that he wanted to be in touch with you about something to do with his band, and asking if the new backup singer was really Kyle's mother."

This couldn't be any good. "I can't say I like this, but there's not much I can do, right?"

"I won't give him your contact info, that's for sure."

It was easier to breathe, but her heart was still beating frantically, just thinking about David Marshall. "Thank you." She swung her feet again, feeling the harsh patterns in the metal balcony imprinting themselves on her rear end.

Brandon leaned over, gently bumping his firm and very warm shoulder against hers. Like magic, her heart rate slowed. It was as if calm and confidence flowed from his body straight into hers. She enjoyed his shoulder's heat for a moment. It felt like it would be too obvious to move away; and besides, she liked touching him.

He nudged her a tiny bit, then spoke. "Can I take you out to dinner sometime?"

That was unexpected. "What, you going to spring for a place with fancy silverware and everything?"

"Probably not. But if you need a fifty-dollar steak, I can try to make that happen."

"Cheapskate. A good steak can be seventy-five a plate."

He stifled a smile. "Cheapskate. That's me. I'll own it."

She shoved his shoulder back, laughing. "Stop it."

Brandon turned, looked straight at her.

"What's that look for?" she asked.

His expression was open and his eyes somehow relaxed, as if he didn't often find people he would just sit with. Be comfortable with. Maybe he was used to being always on, always looking for a break for his clients or the possibility that someone was trying to pull a fast one, and couldn't believe the relief that came from simply existing.

And she wondered why she would inspire that kind of comfort. A college drop-out. A barely-making-ends-meet single mom, at least until Kyle started sending her ridiculously large checks.

He lifted his hand and used one finger to lift a strand of hair away from her face and tuck it behind her ear.

She held her breath for a moment. That was the kind of move guys did to women they were interested in. It had been a long, long time since she'd had a chance to do something crazy like turn her cheek into a man's hand and feel its warmth melting into the bones of her face. So when he rested his open palm against her cheek, she didn't move; she couldn't.

"I guess I don't like the thought of men back home overlooking you. You're massively talented, you raised an incredible musician, and you're so damned easy to talk to."

"Well," she said. Brilliant repartee, that. "Thank you."

Something connected their eyes: something she didn't want

to think about, not with this dead fiancée and his maybe being interested in Greta anyway. But he'd just asked her, Megan, out to dinner. Not Greta. He wouldn't do that if he wasn't interested, right?

The door behind them banged open, and he jerked his hand away from her face.

"Whoops!" said a girl's voice, and she and Brandon were suddenly about six inches further apart than they'd been.

Kyle and the girl tucked under his arm looked down at them, and more voices carried from down the hall. "Sorry, man," Kyle said. "Didn't know you were out here. Mom, we're pulling out in a second, so I'm just going to walk Zoe here to her car. Catch you on the bus?"

She huffed out a breath in half of a chuckle. At least he was taking this one to her car, so she wouldn't end up moaning in bliss inches away from Megan's head.

Somehow Brandon had managed to get to his feet in one smooth movement that left her feeling uncoordinated. She looked up at the three of them towering above her, then at Li-Fang as he, too, came outside. "Sounds good," she said to Kyle.

Megan needed to get up, but her skirt was far too short. She was trying to figure out how to get back to her feet without flashing everyone when Brandon held out his hand. "May I?"

He was back to his formal self, not the man who had been relaxing next to her. Maybe seeing Kyle had reminded Brandon just how old she really was.

She took Brandon's hand in one of her own and held onto her skirt with the other. "Thanks," she said, and let him haul her to her feet, hyper-aware of the strength in his hand and arm.

Brandon watched Kyle leading Zoe by the hand, and then the two girls tromping down the steps after Li-Fang. She really, really didn't want to know how Li-Fang generally seemed to have two women in tow at any given time. Just not an image she needed to dwell on.

Time to excuse herself before Brandon felt trapped into a pity date with the old lady. "Nice chatting, but really, you don't owe me dinner." She looked again at the women with Li-Fang and Kyle, at the other young things in their carefully selected clothes and artful makeup coming out the doorway with the rest of the band. "It's nice of you to offer, but I'm sure you've got better things to do with your time than babysit me."

It was a shame, though. Dinner would have been something to look forward to. Once Brandon let his guard down, he was a good listener. He was certainly easy on the eyes. And time was ticking by so damned fast. She'd be off this tour and out of his life so soon. Her eight weeks on tour were almost half over. How was that possible?

"You're blowing me off?" he asked.

"No, not at all. I just don't want to impose."

He shoved his hands into his pockets, his posture straightening as it had a few minutes ago when he'd dodged the question about his scar. "Okay." He nodded slowly. "I can take a hint. And I wouldn't want to make you uncomfortable." He started to turn away.

All on its own, her hand reached for his arm. She found her fingers resting on the fabric of his shirt. It might look starched and pressed, but under her fingers it felt as soft as an old T-shirt mellowed after countless trips through the wash.

"You didn't make me uncomfortable," she said, all in a rush, then stood taller. "I just didn't want you to feel obligated."

"I didn't, and I don't."

He was so tall. She remembered to drop her hand away from his arm. His eyes followed the path of her hand when she wrapped it across her belly, suddenly feeling the chill of the high desert air.

"Do you need my coat?"

She met his eye and shook her head. "It's not far to the bus. I'll survive."

He chuckled, just one quick burst of sound. "I believe that. Life's thrown you too many curves for something like a chilly night to stop you. I'll say it again, you're a pretty remarkable woman, Megan Gamble."

She was absurdly pleased that he'd used her real name and not called her Mrs. M. It made her feel like maybe he saw her for herself, not just as Kyle's mom. Maybe he had been serious about the dinner.

"Thank you. And thanks for the dinner idea. I appreciate that you'd even think to ask."

"Well, I'm serious. I'd love to take you out."

She had the sense that he was waiting for her to breathe, and her voice went dry. "If you're sure, then yeah. Why not? When you get back from LA, that is."

God, this man had a lovely smile. It reached his eyes.

He looped her hand through the crook of his arm, and led her down the iron steps and across the parking lot toward the tour bus. "Well, then, I'll have to make this a quick trip."

13

Kyle kept the new duet in their set, and now ended every show with "Hey, Look, Ma! I've Made It!" It made her laugh for joy every single time, and the crowds loved it, too.

It got to everyone in the band, actually, leaving them hyped and crazy with the energy flowing through their bodies. After every show, Megan wanted to go dancing, to splash in the surf, to ride a roller coaster, to move, move, move!

She knew she should focus on researching and applying to law schools, and finding a realistic path to representing musicians; but as much as her head told her it was the logical path forward, her heart told her something different. And she couldn't possibly focus right after a show, not high on endorphins from being on stage.

Sometimes it helped to grab the guitar Li-Fang had loaned her, and to let songs find their way into the world, birthed through her fingers. She kept a notebook now, scratching out lyrics on the bus or in the greenrooms or whenever her eyes peeled themselves open in a hotel room. It was one way to work off the performance buzz.

The guys kept finding other ways to work off their energy. Especially Kyle.

In Chicago, Megan was looking for a bathroom after the set and walked into a room to face a young woman bent over, her bare breasts hidden by her son's hands and his head bent to kiss the side of the woman's neck. Megan and the woman both screeched, and Megan backed out of the room much faster than she'd entered, bladder still full. Kyle's legs had been spread wide to bring his hips exactly in line with the woman's.

In Indianapolis, she was heading for the bus when she heard moaning coming from a large storage area off of the main backstage corridor. She walked by and had a side-on view of a pair of hands gripping an amp case, the green nail polish of the visible hand glowing in the dark. The figure was partially obscured by Kyle's body, pumping away from behind, the lower curve of his butt visible under the edge of his T-shirt, jeans bunched between his rear and his knees.

Kyle turned around and locked eyes with Megan in probably the worst moment of her life. She would give almost anything to unsee that image. He shouted something which she couldn't make out, she was in such a hurry to get the hell out of there.

Honestly, she didn't have a problem with Kyle's sex life. Her problem was that she hated having him shove that sex life of his right up in her face.

That, and the fact that the only sex she'd had for years had been more poisonous than fulfilling.

So, maybe not that different from Kyle's?

At their stop in Detroit Megan needed to charge her phone, but her charger was in a bag that the staff had locked away somewhere. She was opening random doors looking for her bag when she'd found Kyle on his knees, his head between the legs of a woman who was nude from the waist up. Her flowing skirt did little to disguise exactly what was going on.

Megan backed away, again, and decided the phone could wait.

This was getting old.

With the number of times Megan had walked in on those scenes, she wondered if she was doing something wrong, misreading some obvious signals. Or maybe Kyle was just staging these things so she would stumble across them? It was like a curse, show after show, dealing with Kyle and his women. She'd hoped that their talk on the bus way back on their way to Portland might have calmed things down. He hadn't brought women onto the bus again, but this wasn't any better.

Three nights after the Chicago incident, the bus rolled east across the farmland of western Pennsylvania. These days, things on the bus were quieter. Charlotte lay in her bunk pretending to read. Zane and Li-Fang scrolled through their phones in two different corners of the front lounge, and Theo sat on the floor, resting his back on the mini-fridge and watching something on his laptop, the charger cord threading over his head to the outlet in the kitchen. Brandon was meeting them in New York rather than taking the bus, so it was just the band.

She steeled herself. If she was ever going to talk to Kyle about his sex life and why she didn't want to see quite as much of it, this was as good a time as any.

Megan rolled out of her bunk (she hadn't bumped her head in ages) and looked through the open door to Kyle's room, where he sat on his couch picking at his guitar as if the strings helped him set his thoughts free.

That's the way it worked for her, at least. Megan had been playing Li-Fang's loaner guitar daily. The pads of her fingers bore witness to that. When she played, sometimes there was literally nothing going on in her mind, just music making her breathing steady and even.

"You got a minute?" she asked.

He glanced up, seeming hung over and sleepy, and gave her an uneasy look. "Sure."

Megan sat on Kyle's bed, across from his spot on the bench sofa. It was pushing midnight, and she needed to crawl back into her bunk soon if she wanted to give a good show tomorrow night. "I'm gonna try to say this like I'm not an evil, judgmental person, but why am I always walking in on you when you're with a groupie?"

He stared at her, then looked back down at the guitar. "Not your kink, huh? Watching people?"

"Kyle! Why do you think you can talk to me that way? Why? I truly don't understand what I've done that makes it seem remotely okay for you to set me up for this kind of stuff. It's like you're trying to get caught."

"No, I'm not trying to get caught. We've already gone over this, and I don't need to rehash this argument." And then his eyes narrowed, not in the sexy glower he threw at audiences, but in calculation of his advantage. "I sure as hell didn't invite you on this tour to lecture me. We both know you're no saint. Don't throw stones in glass houses and stuff, okay? Mom." The last word was filled with contempt so strong it almost sounded like disgust.

"What is that supposed to mean?"

"Pretending you're all innocent isn't going to work."

"I'm still not sure I understand what you're talking about." Well, that was a lie, because she suspected he was talking about Jaimie. But she could hope he was in the dark, couldn't she?

"Oh, I think you understand me perfectly. You're the woman who's been sleeping with her boss since my sophomore year. Or maybe it started before that, I don't know. So don't give me shit about my sex life."

If she hadn't been sitting down, her legs would have buckled. It was like he had kicked her straight in the gut. Sure, she'd suspected that he knew, but hearing him confirm that he knew about Jaimie hit her even harder than she'd expected.

"How?" She only got one word out.

"How? I saw you, that's how."

"You what?" This was truly a nightmare. "What exactly do you think you saw?"

He put an elbow on the table and rested his forehead on the heel of his hand. Then he looked up at her, the bags under his eyes dark against his pale skin. "Not that I want to think about this ever again, but you were sitting on the kitchen table facing away from the door. Your boss was rutting into you, still with his damn suit jacket on." Suddenly, Kyle looked like he wanted to strangle her. "I mean, the man is flat out disgusting, always has been, and you're always complaining about him. You don't even like the guy—he sounds like a pompous ass, he never respected you—and there you were, legs open."

She wanted to throw up. "What were you even doing home?"

"That's your question? Mine is, 'What were you thinking?' And you want to give me grief about banging girls in front of the band? In front of you? I'm not sure you get to judge me when I'm not exactly getting reamed by my boss or anything, let alone doing some girl that I *know* is married!"

"It isn't what you think."

"Like fuck it isn't. You slept with your married boss. Class act, Mom." Then Kyle's eyes widened. It was like he could read what was going on in her head. He collapsed further back onto the little couch. "Jesus, Mom. You're still doing it with him, aren't you? You think he's going to leave his wife and kid and, what, move in with you?"

"No. And as soon as I get back, I'm going to talk to him, tell him that I am never sleeping with him again. Ever. And I'm going to look for a new job."

He stared her down until she realized she should just tell

him the whole story. The affair with Jaimie made Megan look like a caricature of an office slut, but at this point, it would be hard to fall further in Kyle's eyes.

She squared her shoulders and faced him across the narrow aisle. "It started at a Christmas party a long time ago. We were drunk, which I know is about as cliché as it gets, and he'd been really down. His wife had just kicked him out of the house, and he was lonely, and I made a bad choice, okay? I told him right away that it could never happen again. But somehow it did. I mean, not a ton of times, but more than once, you know?"

"Does the guy even respect you the tiniest bit?"

She hid her head in her hands, then tried to look up again. "Looking back, no, I don't think so. Because he kept yo-yoing back and forth, moving out and hitting me up, then moving back home a few months later. So basically, he always had someone, either me or his wife. God, it's pretty messed up, isn't it?"

"Sounds like." He leaned forward, trying to look her in the eye. "You know, I really don't give a shit about your sex life. My problem is that sex is supposed to make things better, not worse, and that boss of yours does nothing but cut you down. You deserve so much better than that. I'm sorry if I've basically been pissed at you for years, but that is really messed up."

"But if you've known all this time, why are you acting this way now?" She truly didn't get it. Shouldn't he have taken this out on her years ago, back when he'd seen her with Jaimie? And what an awful thing she'd done, having sex in a place where her teenaged son could walk in on her. Were there other ways to win the worst mother ever award? Probably none as effective as her method.

Kyle thought for a minute. "Yeah, that was a long time ago. I kinda buried the memory for a while, because I really didn't want to think about it. But then, after our second tour, when things were really starting for the band, do you remember how

I tried to get you to take some damned money from me and quit your job?"

She nodded. "You know I can stand on my own two feet!"

He wiped a hand down his face. "Of course you can. But I wanted to get you away from him, and I thought some money would help. He poisons how you think about yourself, makes you think you're good for nothing but scut work in the office, and that's how he keeps you fragile enough that you'll keep letting him dick you around. Literally. He's an evil guy, Mom, even if he maybe pretends not to be."

That took a second to sink in. And the problem was, Kyle was right. She worked hard at her firm, but Jaimie did have a way of belittling her work. She'd miss something small in a document, and he'd tell her not to worry, that next time she'd get it right. Negative, backhanded compliments—the kind that actually felt like praise until she stopped to think, and realized were condescending. They were always the sort of words that kept her scared and convinced that she only had a job because he was taking pity on her.

She slumped back into her seat, feeling like an idiot. "So, you're mad at me because you think that I'm rejecting your help?"

"That's part of it, I guess." He leaned forward in the tiny space and took her hands while the bus swayed. "But I hate thinking that you're going back to that. Because I think he'll just tear you down again, make you feel like you're not worth the air you breathe, and I just can't stand him doing that to you. And if you won't let me help, then I just get so pissed off!"

She sat back. "You really have been pretty awful to me on tour."

"Okay, so maybe it isn't the healthiest behavior, and maybe I've been trying to get back at you. I don't know! I get that you hate seeing me with groupies, but then I think about how you're still with Jaimie, and I just get so steamed. You've worked so damned hard, and you were always there for me, letting me mess around with my music, just being a good mom. You were what I needed, and then suddenly there you were, banging your boss, and while you were doing that, he was getting in your brain and making you feel worthless. And you won't treat me like a grown man, someone you can rely on now, someone who could possibly help you out for a change."

"Okay," she said. "Maybe I have been too proud. But having made it on my own, it's like the one thing I can actually be proud of. And it hasn't been easy."

"I know."

The bus swayed, the wheels rolling over a bad patch of pavement, and she let the motion rock her. Yeah, her sex life had been way too unhealthy. What she wanted now was a relationship—one where the sex was great, sure—but that relationship part was what she longed for. Someone to talk to, and someone who valued her as a person. But what about Kyle? "Don't you ever want it to be more than sex? Maybe find a relationship someday?" She didn't know if she was asking about what she wanted for herself or for him.

He blew a puff of air out of his nose, a half-laugh that didn't reach his eyes. "Mom, I'm twenty-three, and a touring musician. Not being in a relationship is fine for now, at least for me. Maybe that'll change, but for now, this suits me just fine. So the sex isn't going to stop, because I happen to like it. But I will try to keep it more discreet, okay?"

"Yeah, I'd appreciate that." She paused for a second, looking down. "You know, I am planning to get out of that office. I'm on leave now, and I'm going back, but only till I find something new. And I passed my last class, so I'm officially done with my undergrad."

"No way! That's amazing, Mom. I'm really proud of you."

That sunk in, soaking deep into her heart. "Thank you. And now I'll be able to apply to law school. Jaimie's firm was going to pay for it, but it's more important that I get out of there. I'll figure out tuition on my own."

"I'd totally help with that."

"You would?"

Kyle nodded. "Absolutely."

"Thank you." She hesitated a moment. "I was thinking, if I get my JD, I'll be able to represent music acts, you know? Work in the industry."

He gave her that full smile of his, the one that could be seen from the back of an arena. "That's great, Mom! Really great. Or you could even try to get a few singing gigs. You're pretty kick-ass on that stage, you know."

"Thank you." She remembered what he'd told her at the start of the conversation, and hid her face in her hands again. "I still can't believe you walked in on me when Jaimie was there. That's totally humiliating. What were you doing home that day, anyway?"

He put a finger in a hole at the knee of the gray sweatpants he was wearing. "I think I was supposed to be at Li-Fang's for dinner or something, because you had some conference thing you went to down in Gilroy, I think? But Li-Fang was at a violin lesson, and I didn't want to hang out with his little sister, so I figured I'd come home and then just head over there later. I walked home and saw what I saw through the sliding-glass door. I got out of there pretty damn fast, I'll tell you."

"Ah," she said. She remembered now. Jaimie had planned to drive her to a conference, but they had decided to drop her car off first. And, as she recalled, it had been a while since they'd last hooked up. So his "needs," as he liked to call them, matched up pretty well with how sex-starved she had been at that point.

Note to self, she thought: *never get into a situation where the best way to get any sort of sex is to let your boss under your skirt.* Just not a good plan.

Kyle leaned forward and touched her knee. "I truly don't get it, though. You never dated. Why didn't you try to meet someone decent, and not just let a guy like your boss use you as his hook-up? I keep telling you, you're so much better than that."

Megan thought back to David Marshall and 2 Samuel 6. Was that the root of all of this? She sighed. "I'm not certain I know myself. Something pretty disgusting happened to me, once."

She thought about saying more, but couldn't. The memory came, so wrong it hurt. A small mirror. The noise of people outside the closed room. Three men inside the room with her.

The next thing she knew, Kyle was by her side, an arm wrapped warm around her shoulders. She leaned into him and let him rock her while she blinked fast to keep her eyes from watering.

"Hush. Stop that, now. I've got you. It's gonna be okay. I'll do better. Shh. Hey, shh. It's gonna be okay."

She rocked under the weight of his arm, eyes closed against the tears. "Sorry. Something really ugly happened to me a long time ago, and it messed me up. Sometimes I think it's why I could never say no to Jaimie. I guess I thought no man would ever want me for anything more than just sex. I mean, there was no one who asked me about myself, or seemed to care about who I was as a person." She wiped the snot leaking from her nose onto the back of her wrist. "I'm such a damn mess."

"Shh," he said again, rocking her gently with the motion of the bus. He wrapped his other arm around her and rested his chin on the top of her head. "I've got you. You'll be okay. You are the best, baddest-ass mom on the planet, okay? I mean, you're on a major tour, and you bring down the house with your duet, and no one should ever make you feel like you're less than they are, not ever again. Okay?"

She couldn't really speak, so she nodded.

Kyle kept talking, wiping at her teary face with his thumbs. "You move forward with your life, okay? You've got this. Hey, dry off this pretty face of yours."

She pulled back and wiped at her eyes, snuffling to clear her dripping nose. "I bet you tell all the girls they're pretty."

"Damn straight. Too bad none of them hold a candle to my mom."

"Stop." She put a hand to his cheek. "You're a good man, Kyle Marshall." She might be a mess right now, thinking about Jaimie and what had gone down with the Marshall brothers, but she had Kyle back again.

They'd probably manage to screw things up again, but this was better. Even if it took crying her eyes out and thinking about parts of her past that she shied away from as hard as she could, if it made things closer to right with Kyle, she'd do it again. Healing this relationship meant so much to her.

And it was none too soon. Time was ticking down on the tour, at least for Megan.

14

After Megan's conversation with Kyle, the band played two shows in New York, with the luxury of a free day in between to do whatever they wanted. Like, sleep. Go shopping. Binge-watch something.

Daydream about Brandon.

Which led directly to Megan doing something she should have done years ago.

Sitting in the middle of her king-sized bed, she opened her laptop and sent Jaimie her resignation. She could find a new job after she got back, even if money would be tight for a while. She'd never been good at telling him "no," even when she'd intended to; so the best way to get out from that messed-up situation was to rip off the bandage and leave.

Quit.

It was worth giving up a stable job, and worth giving up a free trip to law school. When she pressed send, it was like fresh oxygen flooded the room, making everything lighter and easier.

She picked up the phone lying next to her on the bedsheets and sent a message to her group chat with Keiko and Li-Fang's mom, Jiao. *Just quit my job. Should have done it years ago and feel amazing right now. Details over coffee once I'm back in CA. Feeling awesome.*

Her phone chimed with a text from Jaimie. *I don't accept your resignation. Let's chat when you get back. You're too valuable to me and to this office for me to just let you go.*

She hit "mark as read" without replying, and prepared to ignore Jaimie's messages. This was fun!

Now, what should she do with all this extra energy? She thought about writing, working on a new song that had been tickling the back of her brain; but first, she wanted to tell Kyle she was done with that office and done with her boss, no matter how many times Jaimie might beg for her to come back. She knew Kyle would feel better about her if he knew she was out of that toxic environment.

Shoving her room key into the sports bra she'd slept in, Megan threw on a T-shirt and found a pair of flip flops. She checked her butt in the mirror to make sure these were the leggings without the hole in the rear end, then stepped into the hallway.

Something about Megan's brain had always locked onto numbers. Every time the band pulled into a hotel, the tour manager checked in for the group, then called out rooms and handed out key cards. And every time that happened, Megan would remember exactly who had been assigned which room. She didn't mean to, but it was the way her brain worked.

So she knew Kyle was in 418, just down the hall. And it was eleven-thirty in the morning, so Kyle probably wasn't "entertaining." Anyhow, she didn't have a key to his room, so it wasn't like she could interrupt anything, or even like she could see anything much more graphic than she already had.

It turned out that his door was propped open, with the sounds of two guitars coming from inside. He was singing something new, maybe working with Li-Fang or Theo.

"Hey," she called, knocking on the door frame. "Okay if I come in?"

"Yeah, that'd be great, Mom."

So she pushed open the door to Kyle's suite and came face to face with Kyle and—

Shit!

David Marshall sat kitty-corner from Kyle on one of the room's two sofas, and each of them was holding a guitar, their identical hands stilled over the strings.

Why was it surprising that their hands looked so much alike? They were related, after all.

Kyle's face looked hopeful.

Her own froze in shock. A moment ago she'd been eager to tell Kyle about quitting her job, but the pride she felt in getting away from Jaimie disappeared like it had never existed.

She could barely breathe.

This was the first time she'd been face-to-face with David Marshall since months before Kyle was born. David had aged. He had Kyle's eyes, but a heavier build, bulky with too much enthusiastic eating: a man who looked far older than she did, but who would probably still be considered attractive. Again it struck her as so damned sexist and unfair, that men were allowed to age and still be considered desirable, but women weren't.

She stood there, frozen, the ghostly feeling of David Marshall's hand on her wrist burning and vivid, though he'd only held her there once, all those years ago.

Kyle's face changed from hopeful to confused and guilty.

"Mom, do you remember my uncle David? He got in touch when he saw posts about you on our socials."

The email to Brandon? But Brandon would never have handed out Kyle's info, so David must have poked around on social media until he got Kyle's attention. And Kyle, eager to be in touch with his family, must have actually reached out in return. That was the only way this could have happened.

Kyle was still talking. "Uncle David was going to be in New York, and I thought it might be a great opportunity to mend fences. So we decided to meet up, make some music."

Kyle used the neck of his guitar to gesture, which prompted David to rise slowly to say hello. He was tall, like Kyle. Like Jason. Like she hated to remember. David had always been bulky, but now he was downright frightening, even from across the room.

"Mom? You okay? Come, sit down." Kyle rose too, looking between Megan and the couch he'd just vacated.

She backed a step toward the open door behind her. "Sorry. I didn't mean to interrupt." Her voice was fainter than it should have been, and her whole body started to shake, tiny waves of panic on the inside that she hoped didn't show in the way her muscles moved under her skin.

"Sorry," she said again, backing up, reaching for the door-frame behind her. "Bad time. I'll catch you later."

Kyle and David exchanged glances, and part of her mind registered David saying, "I'll go."

Kyle stayed put, and David crossed the room toward her, those long steps moving so much faster than her own feet could have, even if she hadn't felt like she'd lost control of her entire body.

Once, she'd found a tiny bird just after a cat had gotten to it. It had been alive, but with a tear across its throat. The little breast had vibrated with rapid breaths, too fast to be normal. The bird hadn't lasted long.

That was what Megan's breathing was like now.

Megan reached the hallway, but David was right behind her. He caught her by the right wrist. When she jerked away, he held up his hands like he was trying to calm a skittish animal. "Hey, Megan. It's okay. I just wanted to meet Kyle."

She cradled her arm like the bone was broken. Her voice wasn't working, and David took that as a sign that he could keep talking.

He jerked his head behind him. "He seems like a pretty great guy. Normal, even with all the fame that follows him around, trying to warp his head. You did a good job, but I wish you'd let us help. The family, I mean. And you're looking good."

She felt his eyes travel up and down.

She swallowed.

"So," he said, lowering his voice. "While I'm really glad to meet Kyle and all, I had a little something I wanted to talk to you about, too. I'm real glad you stopped by."

He had to know she would never in her life "stop by" anywhere he was. Didn't he? She finally found her voice. "Tell me what you want to say. But then I never want to speak with you again. And I'd appreciate it if you'd stay away from my son."

"Now, now, now. No need to get all protective. He seems to like me. Fun playing guitar with him." David jerked his head toward Kyle's room, as if they were just normal acquaintances shooting the breeze. Catching up again.

"So," he said. "I don't know if you've been following me and my band?"

He tipped his hands open, questioning, and she shook her head, no.

"Ah. Well. Okay, then. So, we're still touring, doing really good work for the Lord, but ever since the Covid shutdowns, it's been harder to keep our finances straight. And, well, with your work for Kyle here and his band..."

"The Sutter Boys." She didn't need to tell him the name of the band. Everyone knew it. But she said it anyway, her voice rasping against her dry throat.

"Well, I thought it was about time that you started to pay what you owe us."

Her head tipped forward in confusion. His words didn't even make sense. "What I owe you? Why do I owe you anything?"

He got a nasty smile on his face. "Because of your contract."

She shook her head as if she was trying to get water out of her ears. "What on earth are you even talking about?"

He looked at her like she was a little girl who just needed someone big and strong and male to explain simple facts to her. "You do remember you had a contract with 2 Samuel 6, right?"

"Yeah, kinda."

"Well, part of our agreement was that 2 Samuel 6 owns the rights to any songs you create."

"So?" She was still confused.

"So," he said. "That duet you're singing with the Sutter Boys? Social media makes it pretty clear that you were one of the co-writers. And I'm guessing, if you helped write that one, you're probably writing other stuff with them for their next album. And our band owns rights to what you create."

She was still very confused.

It must have shown on her face, because David sighed, like it was some kind of burden to talk to a woman as stupid as she was. "You need to pay us royalties, because those songs you write are our property. And while I would never take advantage, it does seem fair that you maybe start sending some of that money our way."

There was no way that made any sense. "You've got to be kidding. Over my dead body will I tell Kyle anything like that."

He grew taller, his powerful chest and growing belly imposing. "No, no, no! You don't have to tell Kyle anything. You can just pay me out of what you get from him. That should cover what you owe us."

"You have got to be crazy. What leverage do you possibly think you have?"

"Well, your boy seems awfully happy to finally meet me. No

offense, but a single mom isn't the same thing as having a real family. And while my dad may have passed, Mom's still around, and the boys and our kids and stuff. I think Kyle would really like them all. I'd hate to have you disappoint him again, keep him away from knowing a family that loves him."

What she heard, somehow, was that if she were truly a loving mother, she'd encourage Kyle to see the Marshalls. Even worse, she heard the implication that her love had never been enough.

David patted her on the shoulder. She was surprised her body didn't explode or sink into the ground or crumble to dust with the poison of his touch. "Why don't you think on it? I'm getting along real good with Kyle. I'm sure I'll be seeing more of you."

He opened the door and disappeared back into Kyle's room, leaving her standing in the hallway.

She tried to remember which way her room was, if it was even on this planet; and wandered down the hallway, feeling lost. Suddenly, Brandon was there outside a different doorway, looking from her to Kyle's door and back again.

That's right. Brandon's room was across the hall from hers.

"Who was that?" Brandon asked. "And what was that about? Are you okay?"

She swallowed again, her mouth having gone from dry to flooded with bile, and Brandon moved to her quickly.

"Never mind. Don't worry about it. Let's get you back to your room, find you some water, okay?"

He wrapped a wonderful arm around her shoulders and led her to her room.

15

Megan fished her key out of her bra, so rattled by having seen David Marshall again that it didn't even occur to her to be embarrassed about where she had stashed it.

She tried and failed to open her room, her hands shaking badly, until Brandon said, "May I?"

She handed Brandon the plastic key and waited until he got the door open for them, then ducked inside.

He followed her in and let the door close. "I want to know what happened back there, but first, let's sit you down and get you some water or something."

Megan ended up in one of the arm chairs by the windows, with Brandon at the mini-fridge. Looking inside he said, "Water, cranberry juice, soda, and a bunch of booze."

She realized she was supposed to answer. "Juice, maybe?"

"Coming right up." He grabbed one, along with bags of chips and pretzels from the basket on top of the fridge.

"Here you go," he said, laying the snacks on the table and placing the opened can of juice directly in her hand.

He sat in the chair across from her, the light from the window hitting his leg. The crease of his dress pants cut a shadow as sharply defined as one of the cliffs in Yosemite. Why was she noticing that? Likely because it made it easier not to think about the man in Kyle's room.

"Do you want to talk about it?"

Of course she didn't. She had broken down talking to Kyle on the bus, and that had been from just *thinking* about David Marshall. And look how well that had worked out—letting herself think for a moment about that awful experience, and then trying her best to bury it again. Yeah, that's right. She'd been totally prepared for that encounter back there. Totally in control. No problem.

"No, I don't want to talk about it. Not at all. But I think I need to anyway. Do you know who that was?"

Brandon shook his head.

"David Marshall, the guy who emailed you. Apparently he also reached out to Kyle—I don't know how he got Kyle's contact information, but somehow he did, and Kyle—shit, this feels like my fault." And what was she going to do about paying this guy money? It wasn't as if she'd accumulated vast amounts of wealth. Ha! It was more like she was finally close to paying off her car.

"What's your fault?"

Should she even tell Brandon? He was the band's manager, and this could be a huge problem for them, if somehow something Megan had signed back when she was nineteen could bite the band in the butt. "Maybe nothing. Maybe something kinda huge."

"Oh-kay-ee," he said, leaning back and drawing out the word into three long syllables. "Talk to me. Whatever it is, I'll try to help you figure this out."

"But what if it hurts the band?"

"It's my job to protect the band, so don't worry about that. And whatever is going on has clearly freaked you out."

She still couldn't quite bring herself to say anything.

Eventually he leaned forward. "I know you're kind of isolated on this tour. The band is great, don't get me wrong, but they're not exactly your support group. And I'm sorry that it's just me, and not someone from back home, but for now, can you trust me enough to tell me what's going on? I'd like to help."

Her wrist still burned where David had touched her. She rubbed it with her other hand, trying to wipe away the sensation of David's hand on her skin.

She could do this. She could trust Brandon. But she needed to start with the easier stuff. As if possibly compromising the earnings of your son's livelihood was easy. "So, you remember that ages ago I sang with David's band, the band he and his brothers run, 2 Samuel 6?"

Brandon nodded.

"Well, I guess I signed some sort of contract with them. They always had big dreams, so they tried to do things right. Lock stuff down, you know? David claims my old contract with his band somehow gives him rights to everything I write—any songs, at least. So, now that I'm singing the new duet with Kyle, and with the photos and tags on the Sutter Boys' social media, and the way the PR team has made it look like we're sitting on the bus every day writing music for the next album—anyway, David's convinced that I'm co-writing with the Sutter Boys now, and—ta da! That means that I'm supposed to pay David royalties or something, like I'm earning tons of money from being this ace songwriter." Her voice had gotten faster and faster as she'd tried to get out the words. Her mouth was dry, so she sipped at her juice, which was probably a mistake. It was way too acidic.

"Whoa. Hold on. He's claiming royalties based on a twenty-year-old contract? Do you have a copy of it?"

"No. Why would I? But he must have it somewhere."

Brandon nodded, like this was just a business problem to be

solved. "Okay, so the first step is getting a copy of that agreement. I'm gonna guess that everything is going to be just fine, and that nobody's gonna be paying that joker any money, but we need to see that old contract."

She nodded, and then realized exactly what that meant. She was going to have to talk to David again, wasn't she?

At that point, everything hit her. The man who had mistreated her back when she was a pregnant teenager was just down the hall. That same evil guy was making nice with her son, which meant she might have to deal with him over and over again. She could end up being on the line for a lot of money, if he was calculating his payout based on streams and downloads for the Sutter Boys. Or she could cost Kyle and the band a ton of money. And given her luck, instead of blaming David for being an extortionist, Kyle would blame Megan for keeping him away from his family just when he was starting to get to know them, and just when she and Kyle were finally on speaking terms again.

Megan burst into tears.

And then Brandon was next to her, sitting on the rounded arm of the chair, his arm around her shoulders as she sobbed. "Hey, Megan. It's gonna be okay. It's just a contract. We can sort this out."

She had curled forward into a ball, her hands catching the tears as they boiled over, her elbows digging into her thighs. Her breathing was so ragged and deep that she could feel her back pushing Brandon's arm up and down as he tried to comfort her. She thought she felt his hand gently touching her hair, but maybe she only imagined it.

She said, "There's more than just the contract. It's something far worse, at least for me. Something I haven't ever told anyone. I tried to talk to Kyle a few days ago, but I just couldn't." She took a very deep breath. "You see, David and his brothers sort of tried to rape me."

Brandon's arm went completely still. Then his hand pressed firmly into her back and then floated away.

Before he said anything he moved back to his chair, like he would spook her if he stayed too close. "I don't even know what to say. Kyle's uncle? The Christian band guy? I know this has to be impossibly painful for you, but what happened? Shit. You shouldn't have to talk to me. Can I call anyone for you? Do you want to talk to one of your friends? That woman who came with you to the San Jose show, what's her name? Or Li-Fang's mom—you're friends with her, right?"

But now that she'd started the story, she just wanted to spit it out. "No. That's okay. I need to get this out now, I think." She curled in on herself, trying to gather her nerve.

Brandon's right leg started into a rapid up-and-down, sewing-machine twitch. She hadn't realized tension could actually roll off of anyone, but that's what was coming off of Brandon. Tension. A tiny corner of her brain realized how difficult this must be for him, to listen to some woman he was still getting to know talk about an attempted assault from years and years ago.

But this wasn't about Brandon.

Despite his tension, he was patient; and his silence gave her the space she needed to clear her mind and distance herself from the horror that had happened so long ago. After a while, she finally said, "Maybe you need to know, so you can understand just how screwed up this really is."

She uncurled a bit, but kept her eyes down on the edge of her T-shirt. Part of the hem was coming undone, and she worried the hanging thread as she spoke. "The guys in my old band were always this weird mix between super polite and sort of—lecherous? They were polite because I was their little brother's girlfriend, and all women should be on pedestals, and stuff like that. But they also pretty much knew that Jason had left the church, and sort of assumed that we were having sex, because they knew that 'non-Christians' sort of just did that. That's how they thought of us. 'Non-Christians,' like we were heathens or something. There were categories of people, the 'saved'—those were the people they went to church with —and the rest of us, the unclean. So there was this weird shaming stuff they did, making me feel guilty about myself and my body, that I wasn't a good girl because I wasn't saving myself for marriage, and that I was this huge wicked temptress because I had convinced their baby brother to 'lie with me in sin.' Like somehow it was all my fault, like I was supposed to have worn a damn burka around so he wouldn't have strayed due to my wicked ways. Somehow it's always the woman's fault, and the guy is totally blameless. But Jason wasn't like that. Kyle's dad was a good guy, and we had a pretty normal relationship, even if his family was super messed up. I didn't realize just how rotten they were until I got pregnant.

"After they heard I was expecting, the politeness vanished. I was officially a slut, as far as Jason's brothers were concerned. All of them, but especially David, started to really look me over hard before shows, so I could practically feel their hands on me —even when it was just their eyes. I knew they were imagining me and Jason having sex, imagining what my body looked like, or maybe even what it felt like to touch me for themselves. You know the way some guys undress women with their eyes, and picture every little detail of a woman's body under her clothes? That's what they were like, and they kept getting more and more blatant about it. David was the worst.

"One night after our set, we were in this stupid little church library. It was just off of the multipurpose room at this church where we'd been performing. David..."

She broke off and swallowed, then stole a quick glance at Brandon, who was leaning forward to listen.

He was really, really good at this listening thing. He didn't look like he pitied her or blamed her or wanted to fix her. He just looked like he ached for what she had gone through.

"I was brushing out my hair in this little mirror, and David came up right behind me and grabbed me by the hips. He pulled me back and rubbed my butt against his erection. I mean, I could still hear all these church people talking in the other room, and David was literally grinding against me. I couldn't believe it, so I looked over at Matt and Paul, the other brothers, hoping they would help me, I guess, but they were staring at us, just looking sort of hungry. I mean, I don't think any of those guys were getting any action, not with all the sweet Christian girls who were into the stuff their band played, so Jason's brothers were probably horny, like, all the time. David rubbed himself against me and leaned over next to my ear and said, 'You do know that guys have needs, right? And we know that you're already giving it up for Jason. So we figured, maybe you could help all of us out. Take care of this little problem for me, then help out Matt and Paul over there.' He took my hand and held it between us, so my knuckles were on my ass, and my hand was palming him through his pants. They thought that because I was clearly a slut, then some little gang bang wouldn't be a problem for me. Since I wasn't a nice Christian girl, like the girls they planned to marry."

Brandon said, "They wanted a gang bang? And they thought you'd be into it because you were already sleeping with their younger brother? That's just so wrong." Every ounce of his disgust was in his voice.

"No shit."

He looked like he was going to be sick. "Did you ever report it?"

"How? Report what? That some guys propositioned me? That wasn't exactly an actionable crime as far as I knew. I just never even thought in those terms."

Brandon's shoulders were rigid under his jacket, like he was afraid how she would answer the next question. "But you got away from them, right?"

She nodded, and Brandon's shoulders relaxed the tiniest amount. "I did get away, but I have no memory of how. I mean, I didn't want to piss them off, even if they were acting like wanna-be rapists or something. The worst thing was, it was a real job, you know, kinda like I'm working for the Sutter Boys now. These guys were paying me to show up at their gigs; and not only that, they were going to be Kyle's uncles, so they were gonna be family. And Jason's family was sort of getting powerful in those Christian circles, preaching the word of the Lord like they didn't understand the meaning of hypocrisy. So maybe I said something sort of benign, like a good little girl, like I was minding my manners. 'No, thank you.' God, I might even have said, 'maybe another time.' I just don't know. Later on, I remember finding bruises on my wrists, so David must have been holding me even though I was telling them no. But those assholes probably never believed me, or never thought I had a real right to refuse them, especially since I was already a fallen woman. They probably held out hope for weeks, maybe even months, that I would give in and 'take care of their needs,' as David put it. I never even told Jason, but after that, I made him come with me to every single show. It just felt safer, you know.

"They made me feel like such a slut, and for what? Because I slept with my boyfriend! But in their world, having sex with anyone at all, even someone you loved, was apparently enough to put you in God's bad books for eternity, so they shamed me and they tried to play it to their own advantage and basically tried to rape me; at least that's what I know it is now, now that I've got a few years under my belt and understand exactly how wrong they were. Needs, my ass. Those guys were just creeps."

"God, you've been living with that memory all these years? That is seriously messed up."

"Well, it's taken me a very long time to get past it. I probably haven't, actually. It messed with my mind. I've felt like maybe all I was worth was being some random woman a man could use to make himself feel better. And when I was talking to Kyle on the bus a couple of nights ago, I just sort of wondered if that's why I haven't had a healthy relationship since Jason." It was like her mouth-to-mind connection was broken, or stuck on full-speed-ahead, because she blurted out the next thing on her mind. "Did you know that since Jason, my only long term relationship has been with my boss?—or my old boss, I should say, since I finally quit that job. I tried dating a bit when Kyle was really little, but I kept getting dumped, just one guy after another, like as soon as we'd had sex they'd miraculously realize that their old girlfriend was the one for them, or they'd meet someone new, and just have that instant spark. I was convinced it was me, that I was just super unlovable. So when my boss started hitting on me, my self-confidence was gone. And I was pretty damned exhausted from raising Kyle. I started sleeping with Jaimie, who happens to be married, but somehow a drunken one-night stand after the Christmas party —I'm such a damned cliché—turned into almost ten years of me every now and then sort of giving in when he just 'needed a little relief' or something. Which is why I quit my job, but God, I feel like such a terrible person!"

She started bawling again, and this time Brandon kept his distance.

Part of her was really glad, because right now she might just vomit if any man touched her, but partly—of course!—him keeping his distance just made her feel unclean. Like she was really and truly damaged goods, and that no one would ever want to be in a real, caring relationship with her ever again. And certainly not Brandon, who had had enough pain in his own past, and needed to find someone uncomplicated and better. Purer. Less contaminated.

"You're not contaminated."

Had she said that part out loud?

He reached his hand toward her, and after a moment she put her hand into his. Its warmth was heaven.

He said, "You're not contaminated. What they did to you?—what they suggested, that doesn't touch who you are inside. Those other guys you dated? They were idiots for not sticking around long enough to appreciate the things I see. Even the thing with your boss? It sounds like he was very good at manipulating you into doing what he wanted. Don't you dare blame yourself, not for that. You're amazing, Megan; please know that. You're a damn good mom, and an incredible musician, and a gorgeous woman who's bubbling over with fun and energy. Please don't let that past shape how you feel about yourself. Please."

God, it felt wonderful to have him holding her hand. Just warm and alive and flooding her with confidence.

"Thank you. I needed to hear that."

After a time, he squeezed her hand and released it, though for a moment she imagined that his thumb had given the back of her hand the smallest of caresses.

"Just speaking the truth."

She gathered herself and wiped her eyes with the corner of her T-shirt. "Now what? I mean, what do we do about this contract?"

Brandon asked, "Do you want me to get in touch with him? I don't want you to have to deal with him, not if I can prevent it. I mean, I don't want to be all white knight, 'just let me take care of you,' but if I can make this easier for you, I'd really be touched if you'd let me."

She thought for a moment, because it was a really generous offer. She'd love to just pass this problem off to Brandon, and not have to deal with David ever again. But part of the problem was the way David had taken her power and her confidence in herself, so it would be better if she could find the strength to deal with things herself. She shook her head. "I appreciate that, truly, but I want to do this. And whatever happens, I don't want Kyle getting near this mess. Those men were lunatics."

"Try criminal."

"Maybe. But they are Kyle's family, and I think you understand why I've kept them out of our lives. David told me that his dad passed away, and I guess their mom has dementia now. And you should have seen Kyle with David. He looked so damned happy just to meet someone from his family. It's not like he got much time with my family; Mom and Dad retired to Idaho ages ago, and then my dad passed, and my mom spends all her time with her relatives back home. It's been hard for her to stay in touch, so Kyle never knew either of them super well. So it makes sense that he's looking for family anywhere he can find it. I'm worried that if I send you to go asking for the contract and David makes this even uglier, it'll spoil Kyle's chance of connecting with the Marshalls. They were truly vile to me, but people change, and Kyle deserves to figure it out for himself, if they're the kind of people he wants in his life."

"At some point, though, you need to tell Kyle what that man did. It's a pretty important bit of background information, and he might not want to have anything to do with them."

"Yeah, I should tell him. But not yet. I think it's right to give him a chance to form his own impressions, and then maybe I'll talk to him."

Brandon nodded. "I see the logic in that. I don't love it, but I get it. Just remember, though, if he decides he wants the Marshalls in his life, you'll have to deal with them, too."

She put her hands on her knees and stood. "Then I'll just have to figure out how to do that. But first I'm going to get in touch with David and get a copy of that contract."

"And then you're going to show it to me, and we'll figure out, together, how to cut this guy off at the knees. There's no way that kind of clause is enforceable. None at all." He stood and headed for the door of her room.

She followed. "Thank you. It means a lot to hear you'll have my back." She let herself reach out and put a hand on the warm muscles of his upper arm.

He covered her hand with his own. "Of course." When he looked at her, she had no idea what he was thinking. Poor woman, maybe. But she wanted to just hold his eyes, keep looking at the calming green.

She bit her lip, then waved behind her. "I should try to get myself together for the show."

"So I'll leave you to it?" She could hear the question, the way he was really asking if she was okay being alone.

"I'll be fine. I'll call Keiko, too, let her in on things."

"That sounds like a good idea. But you know how to reach me. Call me or text anytime. I mean it."

"Thanks."

He saw himself out, and she leaned her arms against the door, letting her forehead come to rest between her hands.

Once upon a time, when she'd been a whole woman, undamaged, she would have let herself dream about being with a man like Brandon. One who could listen and empathize, and one who could offer to help without making her feel like she was incapable.

Once upon a time.

16

After New York the band headed to Boston, and then back to Philadelphia. Jaimie was still texting a couple of times a week, reminding her that he was saving her job, and that they needed to talk when she got back home.

No thanks. Instead, while they bounced around on the bus, Megan gritted her teeth and sent an email to David Marshall asking for a copy of the contract she'd signed so long ago. She had bigger problems than Jaimie, now.

She was still thinking about David Marshall after they got onstage that night. That contract could be really, really bad, or basically nothing, and she just didn't know.

She shook off her worries as much as she could, and began grooving to Zane's drumbeat. The audience deserved the best she could bring, and she could only deliver a performance if she got her head back in the game.

Megan danced, and Theo caught the motion of her hips. He grinned and layered in that bass line that synced with her heartbeat. The crowd was already dancing, and they were only two numbers into the set. Everything told her it was going to be a terrific show.

"Philadelphia, we are glad to see you!" shouted Kyle, and the crowd roared back. These days, the cries from the audience had occasional shout-outs for Megan herself, which made her smile. She half thought they were complete idiots for cheering her on, and half reveled in the attention. A woman could get used to this.

After her duet with Kyle she blew a kiss out to the audience and pranced back to her place upstage. When she turned to wave to the crowd again, Brandon actually nodded his head and smiled from the wings. He was usually a complete stoic during the shows, so that nod meant more to her than the name drops from the audience.

She was really doing this.

Afterward, the band headed to the hotel before the crew even finished load out. Their next show was just down the road in Baltimore, so close that they were going to bus down the next day.

There was another message from Jaimie on Megan's phone. She was so done with that man. She'd already told him she'd quit. What else did he want?

Shaking her head at Jaimie's persistence, she headed to her room, one of the songs on their set list rattling around her brain like the reminder of something forgotten. Or maybe a hint of an idea trying to be born.

She grabbed the guitar that Li-Fang had loaned her, grateful again that he'd thought to loan her an instrument. She really needed to scratch this creative itch, just get the tune and words out of her system, because the rattling in her brain wasn't a tweak to the song they'd done on stage. It was something new. And it was demanding, whatever it was.

Well, she would find out soon.

Forty minutes after check in, still wired from the performance, and with the outlines of her new song down on paper, Megan was hungry enough to eat even the overpriced fusion food in the hotel. It was the only real eatery open at this hour, and that was just because Brandon had pulled some strings for them.

She headed downstairs and was crossing the lobby when the second elevator dinged open behind her.

"Hold up, Mom," Kyle said.

She turned to see his legs make quick work of the space between them. The movement brought back Jason's walk so clearly: his athletic, surfer DNA was blatantly evident in the body of her son.

Nature, not nurture, at least for that confident walk.

Kyle held his old acoustic guitar case, the one with a Red Hot Chili Peppers sticker on it from a concert she'd taken him to when he was fourteen, just before he'd started playing his own gigs.

He held it out to her. "Here," he said.

She almost laughed. "What? Are you five again? Need me to hold that for you while you do something more important?"

"No," he said, still holding out the guitar case. "I want you to have it. Thought you could keep my old guitar company for a while. I know Li-Fang loaned you one, but the more I think about it, the less I like that. You should be playing your own guitar, but until then, I'd be honored if you'd play mine."

He twisted the instrument onto its side, holding it like he was a butler presenting her with a stack of freshly-laundered towels.

Around them, the quiet bustle of a late-night hotel lobby pulsed.

Damn, Kyle was handsome. Sometimes it was hard to look at him without feeling something akin to deja vu. He looked just like this famous rock star whose photos she saw in magazines and plastered on social media, but he also looked like her own boy. And under the chiseled jaw, she could still see hints of that same from face years ago, when it had been rounded with childhood and still unknown to the world.

She kept her hands at her sides. "Sweetie, I can't take your guitar."

"I barely touch this one anymore. So you can and should take it, at least until you can find one of your own." He held the case out again.

It wasn't so much that she smiled; rather, something warm and wonderful grew inside her— something that absolutely showed on her face and made her feel such love for this kid she'd raised, this man he'd become.

Biting her lip, she held out her hand and took a grip on the handle. She was still glowing when they turned together in the direction of the restaurant off the lobby.

She caught the hint of a smile on Kyle's face as they walked, and felt like she could read his mind: that he was proud to loan her this particular guitar. It wasn't expensive. At the time he'd bought it, he hadn't been able to afford much with his lawn-mowing money, but it was precious. He'd used it to write some of his very earliest—and very terrible—songs. Come to think of it, this was probably a more meaningful gift than the first time he'd sent her a check from album royalties.

That check had come with the instructions that she should pay down the mortgage. She'd been so hurt by that, with her gnawing need to always stand on her own two feet; but she'd taken it, because living in Silicon Valley was too expensive for words. She couldn't afford to ignore a gift. She had probably been too quick to interpret that first check as proof of her own inadequacies, but there it was.

"Hey, hey, hey!" Theo shouted from the table as they approached. "Fearless leader," he said, nodding at Kyle. "The divine Ms. M." This with a nod to Megan.

"Hardly Bette Midler," she said, but the comment was lost in the mayhem. She settled into one of the vacant chairs, storing the guitar under the table for now, but caught Brandon's smile. Were they the only people who immediately thought of the one-time Broadway star?

They ordered and ate, the band only getting more raucous as the evening went on. Eventually the younger folk said their goodnights, and Kyle led them to the car waiting outside. Clubbing was on the agenda, it seemed.

The sudden quiet made the vacant seats around Megan and Brandon seem all the emptier. Their large round-top table was now crammed with half-finished beers, empty shot glasses, and a platter which had once held surprisingly delicious Indian-style nachos.

She shared another glance with Brandon. "Where do they get the energy?" she asked.

"They are really young, remember." Brandon stared after the band for a beat, then looked at the wreckage on their table. In a gentler voice he said, "Hey, I hate to remind you, but did you make any progress on getting that contract from Kyle's hideous uncle?"

The place between her shoulder blades that had finally been loosening up started to throb again. "I emailed yesterday. Let me check if he's responded."

She pulled out her phone and felt her stomach plummet. He'd replied. She wanted this to be done, and there was no way for things to get better with David and his demands until she actually, say, dealt with it. But that didn't make opening the response any easier.

"I take it you got something," Brandon said.

She'd been sitting there without moving. After a swallow of the watery stuff left in her glass, she said, "Yeah."

Then she opened the email and practically shouted, "That bastard!"

Megan, I made a copy of our old agreement, but I think I'd rather give it to you in person. Just so you know what I'm thinking, I believe

$200,000 would be a good start at covering what you owe us. I'm not an unreasonable guy, though, so I'll give you until the end of tour to get it together. See you then! David

She handed Brandon the phone, but he spoke before he could possibly have read the whole thing. "He wants to meet with you in person? That doesn't even sound safe. I could go with you, just be in the room to make sure he doesn't do anything really obnoxious. If I'm not overstepping."

"Would you?"

"Of course." And then he raised the phone again to finish reading. "Jeez, that's ballsy of him. Two hundred thou, and he hasn't even given you the agreement? Not exactly giving you a lot of chances to look it over."

"Nope," she said.

"Listen," Brandon said, leaning forward and looking her in the eye. "When we get it, give me a copy and let me forward it to the guy we use for our legal work. This isn't just on you. I can help. I want to help. Please?"

God, the way he looked at her when he asked. Like helping her was the only thing that he wanted. Like she mattered to him.

Still, it had been hard enough even confessing to Brandon. Could she really let another person in on this? "Do we have to pull the lawyer in? This whole thing makes me feel so slimy. I hate that I opened the band up to something like this."

"That's why we need to. And I do think we can make this go away, but I can't do it on my own." He put his hand onto the table, and then Megan's hand was in his, his warmth flooding not just her hand, but her heart. Brandon cared.

But this was her mess, wasn't it? Whatever happened, she wasn't going to take a dime from Kyle and the band. That wasn't fair to them, to make them pay for her mistake. But the lawyer was probably a good idea. David Marshall clearly had the morals of Machiavelli, and would do anything to raise money for his Christian outreach. So if he could tap into the Sutter Boys' earnings directly, no doubt he would try.

With a sigh she said, "Okay, then. When David gets me the contract, I'll get you a copy and you can call your guy. It'd be smart to pull in someone with entertainment experience, and the only lawyers I know are at my old firm. They're trusts and estates people; they don't deal with entertainment contracts. And I'll look at it, but if the lawyers at my firm aren't qualified, I'm sure not."

She pulled her hand out of Brandon's to sit back on her chair. How on earth was she going to come up with $200,000? The money she was making on tour was nowhere close to that amount, and she sure as hell didn't want to make Kyle and the band pay for her mistakes.

Brandon grabbed the bottle of scotch and two glasses off the table, and stood. His voice was cheerful, which she knew was intentional. "I don't want to look at this mess anymore, but I'm too wired to head upstairs. And I think both of us need to get the stink of that email out of our clothes. Wanna sit with me? We'll talk about anything and everything but David Marshall and his asinine claims. I promise." He motioned to a booth along the back wall.

Megan pushed to stand. "Why not? I mean, clubbing would work, but there's no way in hell I'd survive that at my age. God, between the show and that stupid email, I'm pretty damned wired. I won't be able to sleep for ages."

"Tell me about it," Brandon said. He looked back as she bent to pick up the instrument, then twitched up one corner of his mouth when he saw the case in her hand.

A busboy started to clear their old table.

Across the room, Megan slid into the booth, laid the case beside her, and stretched out her legs. Far better. She was still rather amazed by Kyle's gesture. She remembered when he'd bought this for himself, how proud he'd been of the case with its fake leather marbling, the plastic handle.

Brandon took the seat across from her, angling so his back was in the corner. The edge of his shoe was just visible from where she sat, and she imagined their legs crossing under the table, though they didn't touch. From a distance, the X their legs formed would create the illusion of strength.

"Good show tonight, by the way," he said, raising his glass in Megan's direction.

The show had been a good one. But as much fun as she was having, touring was definitely starting to catch up with her body. She hadn't had enough sleep since they'd started. "What city are we in, again?"

Brandon paused with the bottle of scotch over his glass, then poured a finger of alcohol into the bottom. The glasses were heavy, quality in the heft of them. "Philly."

"Kind of all blurs together." She held her own glass close for a moment, then thought *what the heck* and pushed it toward Brandon and the bottle he was still holding. She nodded for him to stop once she had her own finger of amber liquid. "I'm glad I don't have to remember where we are and where we're going. Thank God you're organized enough that we don't have to."

"It's good to be appreciated for my superior brain," he said, the corners of his eyes wrinkling with his gentle sarcasm, "but I'll share my secret if you ask nicely." He put the bottle back on the table and fidgeted with the cuffs on his shirt, finally unbuttoning them. What kind of man could wear a suit backstage at a rock concert, keep it on for the ride back to the hotel, ditch the jacket only after hitting the hotel bar with the entire band, and not roll up his sleeves until after midnight? Once upon a time she'd been intimidated by Brandon and his expensive suits, but not anymore. Some beautiful clothes hid ugly human beings, but with Brandon, the quality of his clothes just reflected the quality of the person underneath.

She looked at him fondly. "Your secret is safe with me."

Brandon's fingers fished under the rolled edge of his shirt-sleeves and retrieved a folded scrap of paper. "I know the cool kids keep everything on their phones, but I actually have a cheat sheet." He pushed the slip across the table.

In the process, his hand brushed against the outside of her ring and pinky fingers. She carried the feeling of his skin back across the table with the paper to see a list of cities with the top few lines crossed off. "That's actually kinda sweet. I hadn't figured you for a pencil-and-paper kind of guy. More of a 'Siri, where are we?' person."

"I learned the business old-school. Guess I kept some habits from those early days."

That's right, his years at Sidecar.

She reached under the table to pull the strap loose on her shoe, and then drew her knees up. She wriggled her bare feet on the bench. Bliss.

Brandon looked over at her feet, and she drew them closer to her body. He probably thought she was an unsophisticated idiot. "What?" she asked. "Never seen a woman's bare toes before?"

He rolled his eyes, but stiffened for a moment. "Not in a hotel bar I haven't. Bad memories, I guess. They used to say 'barefoot and pregnant,' where I'm from, and I knew a couple of really smart girls who got pregnant right out of high school, never left town, never lived the kind of lives I thought they should have."

Pretty much exactly like Megan.

She looked down, feeling small, and noticed she was still holding her untouched scotch. She took a sip, then put her glass back down. Yup. Scotch was awful.

"Don't like scotch much?"

"Not really," she said. "More of a white wine girl. Usually the cheap stuff, but a nice glass of Sauvignon Blanc is heaven when I can afford it." She played with the ice cube in her glass, scooting it around with her finger, fishing it out of the liquid, and popping it in her mouth. When she looked up again, she could have sworn Brandon was staring at her; but if he had been, his eyes had shifted away very, very fast.

Searching for something to say, Megan came up with, "So, how much trouble do you think they're getting into tonight?"

Brandon wasn't as relaxed as he had been. "Not too much, I hope. As bands go, these guys are pretty in control. The drugs aren't too hard, the hotel rooms aren't too trashed, and the one-night stands don't usually result in too much drama."

"Except for losing your backup singer."

He sighed. "Yep. Except for that. But I get the feeling you don't mind too much."

Nope. She didn't mind, not when it meant she got to be on stage, singing. "Hey, can I ask you something?"

"Of course." He took a sip, then slung his arm along the back of the bench seat, the glass dangling from his fingers.

He looked like a magazine ad, with that jawline, the white dress shirt still crisp despite the hour, and the rolled-up sleeves. And he'd just looked away from her, so she clearly needed to stop noticing stuff like that. She looked down again. "I'm a short-timer now, with Greta ready to start soon, and I know I'm too old to fit in, no matter how nice you are about it. But I feel like I've just figured out what I've been missing, having lived all these years without performing. I don't want to give up music again. Do you have any tips? Do you think I could stay in the business, at least at some level?"

Brandon kept his eyes on his scotch for a moment. Eventually he raised his eyes to look at her, but she was too embarrassed by her earlier thoughts to keep looking. And also, why had she asked that question the way she had, like she was begging? A cocky young man (someone like her son, for example) would have asked with an unshakable sense of entitlement. Was she insecure because she was older than the average age of a singer starting out, or just because she was a woman?

"Yeah, there's work for singers. It might be hard from the Bay Area, because there's not much of a scene, but in LA there's a fair amount of session work. Backup singing, which you obviously handle really well; commercials. You could start gigging if you wanted, throw out a set mostly of covers—maybe even write some of your own stuff, if that's something you wanted to try. You've got enough talent that you could put something together, even if most club owners would rather hire a hot twenty-something. And I could get you a few auditions, drop your name to some business contacts, that sort of thing."

She let a breath out, feeling almost light headed. "That's great. I mean, I know there's no guarantees— not in music, anyway—but you're more encouraging than I thought you'd be."

She let her mind drift. She could probably even pack up and move to LA, if she wanted to. Now that she'd quit her job, and with Kyle touring so much, she really didn't need to hang on to her house.

"So," he said, gesturing with his chin to where she'd set Kyle's guitar under the table. "*Are* you writing your own stuff? I saw that guitar Kyle gave you, and I know you've been borrowing Li-Fang's. Is there a songwriter sitting at this table with me?"

Why did that make her blush? "Maybe?"

"And why are you putting a question mark at the end of that word? Don't you know what you're doing with your time?"

"Okay, yeah, I'm writing. But it's difficult to own it, you know. It feels so risky to say, 'Yes, that's me. I'm writing music.'"

But it was worth it to fess up to her secret creativity, because Brandon broke into a fond smile, the corners of his eyes crinkling in that way she found more and more attractive. "Good. I'm glad you're writing. Don't let this asshole David Marshall slow you down. He can't possibly claim ownership in stuff you create now."

Her smile disappeared. She probably looked old, tired, and worried now.

Brandon laid a hand on the table, his palm open. "Hey. Don't do that. Really, we'll beat this."

She put her hand in his.

We.

He couldn't possibly mean anything by that, but she liked the sound of being part of Brandon's team, even if it was just for this one thing. Getting her out from under David Marshall's thumb once and for all.

Well, it wouldn't be easy, but she was going to get past that man and what he'd done. The way she'd already started to, by getting out of her old job and away from Jaimie. Because that whole situation was a result of David's actions so many years ago.

The corners of her mouth twitched up, just barely. She felt something like relief. "Why do I believe you?" she asked.

Brandon gave her hand a squeeze. His face had softened, and he was almost smiling. Almost.

Her own smile widened, until she thought of the man they were fighting. David Marshall. She shuddered, her hands suddenly lonely in her lap; and Brandon seemed unspeakably far away. Remote.

"Don't let the bastard get you down," he said. He tried to catch her eye again, but it was too much, somehow, so she looked away.

He stood, saying, "It's getting late. I should probably head upstairs."

"Yeah, me too."

Earlier, she'd almost wondered if maybe they were going to

hook up, but he was throwing off a very *don't touch me* vibe at the moment. She couldn't quite figure it out. He said she was good-looking and talented, and then he shut down like he didn't want anything to do with her.

Well, he knew what kind of damaged goods she was. And besides, wasn't he interested in Greta?

She had to ask. "So, how's Greta? I kinda thought you were interested in her."

The smile lines at the corners of his eyes disappeared. "Did I say that? Well, she's certainly attractive, and you know how much I love a woman with a great voice."

Argh. Damn. So he *was* interested in Greta. He was pretty free with the compliments about Megan's singing, so it figured that would be high on his list of things he found attractive.

She edged away from him in the elevator, needing to give him some space just for her own sanity. Then she was disappointed when he did the same. Now they were basically in opposite corners of the elevator, and she couldn't figure out why. Downstairs, it had felt like they were connecting, but now she'd gone and reminded him of Greta, and there went her chance.

He spoke, just before they reached their floor. "I'm at the point in my life where I'm not going to tell any woman that I'm interested in her unless I feel like there's a real chance at a relationship. And I sure as hell wouldn't lead anyone on. You know that, right?"

She nodded, reading his meaning loud and clear. He *hadn't* said he was interested, so he *wasn't* interested in Megan.

Was that pity she saw on his face? God, she hoped not.

The only other words they spoke were, "Good night," and then they parted in the hallway.

She got to her room, placed Kyle's loaner guitar next to her roller bag, and threw herself onto the bed.

Despite all the ugliness of David's email and that awful

history, Brandon had turned her evening around, at least until that awkwardness on their way up to the rooms. She hadn't felt like a failure during the last half of that conversation. She'd felt interesting and attractive, even.

She wanted to smack herself on the forehead, because she realized she had a crush on Brandon. A bad one. And he wasn't interested. Though, he had spent a lot of time with her. And he listened well. And she liked listening to him. But then, he'd basically warned her off, right?

Why was falling for someone so damned hard?

She opened the case to Kyle's old acoustic and tuned. There was a lot of good music rooted in in love and heartbreak and confusion. Maybe because people who wrote songs for a living needed the music to figure out what they were feeling.

And crushing on someone was damned confusing.

17

Brandon had commitments for some of his other bands during the week between their night in Philly and Megan's last show, which would be in Virginia Beach. She missed him, and she spent far too long rethinking that last conversation. The connection they'd seemed to have; the comments about Greta, and the way he'd pulled back. Or had he pulled back before then?

Okay, pep talk time. This was almost the end of Megan's tour, and she didn't want to waste her last opportunities to enjoy this kind of arena performance. Because that thrill was nowhere close to wearing off. Not by a long shot. She sang and she slept and she danced on stage and she guzzled water and she dozed on the bus and she mastered the art of turning on yet another unfamiliar hotel shower.

And she was better at music now; better than she'd ever been, even as a young singer. Her vocal control was better, as was her ability to anticipate and round out the music the audience heard. She'd learned when to stay quiet and let Kyle's voice shine alone, and when to add hers to build the excitement and tension. How to improvise the riffs and alternate harmonies—the kind that made live music so amazing.

And she waited until she could see Brandon again. Hoping. Not daring to hope. Hoping again.

Based on his steady stream of text messages and the way they cheered her up just when she was the most tired, he was either really good at leading her on, or she had misinterpreted his withdrawal back in Philadelphia. These texts? They had way more of a *relationship* feel than just texts between friends. So maybe he was interested. At least a little. And there was no way he'd intentionally lead Megan on if he was really interested in Greta. He was not that kind of man.

But with Megan leaving the tour and heading back to California, they were running out of time. And Brandon was the first man she'd truly had an interest in for years.

Maybe she should be hopeful about making something happen with him, just like she was planning to make something happen with her music. She spent bus rides Googling law schools and their reputations for turning out music lawyers, researching open mic nights, reading the blogs of entertainers just starting out and performing at smaller venues. Learning the practical stuff she'd need to know to turn this music dream of hers into reality.

And then it was time for her final show. Virginia Beach.

Her normal pre-show adrenaline rush was tempered by two things: the anticipation of time with Brandon after the show, and the knowledge that this was going to be her last time on stage with the Sutter Boys. After tonight, there would be a very big hole in her life. She didn't want to leave music. Not at all.

Not ever.

So she wasn't going to let that happen. Not again.

When they arrived at the venue she kept her eyes peeled for Brandon, but didn't catch a glimpse of him until just before sound check. He was glued to his phone, and stayed that way until the opening act had finished and the stage was set for the Sutter Boys.

Their opener tonight was *Always Got Your Back*, one of the cuts on the second album. Zane started this alone onstage, and one by one the other band members made their appearances on stage, strolling to their instruments.

Just before her turn to step into the lights, Brandon reached for her hand, then pulled her in for a sweet kiss on the cheek. "Sing pretty," he said.

Megan arrived on stage with a lot of color in her cheeks and a wide smile on her face. She threw the crowd an enthusiastic wave, and headed to her mic with even more of a strut to her step than usual, swaggering and moving her body so that no one would be able to take their eyes off of her. Including Brandon.

Taking a quick look over her shoulder, she confirmed that for herself. Excellent.

Last of all, Kyle took his long strides into the lights and the adulation. He grabbed his mic stand, and began roaring out his lyrics.

This was a story-song, based on what he and Li-Fang had been through as kids, how they'd bonded. Bullies had thrown out racist taunts about Li-Fang and his Chinese heritage, and Kyle had stood with him. And each of these men had relied on the other as they learned to figure out girls, survive school, and start chasing their dreams.

Kyle hit the chorus and Megan added her voice to the mix, belting into the arena.

Dream large, my brother.
I've got your back for good.
Dream large, my brother.
Don't give up, don't back down,
To the bigots around.

We will stand, we will rise,
And we won't shut our eyes
Till this 'hood
Stands for good
For our brothers
Black, white, and brown.

She leaned into the mic, feeling the power of the song one last time from the stage, reveling in the way the music moved her whole body.

Tonight Li-Fang caught her eye, and she danced with him, matching the motions of his head and his bow arm with her hips, her hair, her feet. Finally Kyle looked back at her, feeding off her energy for a moment. He took what she gave out and sent it to the thrilled crowd in the pit, the fans up in the rafters, and everyone in the arena.

God! These moments on stage when Kyle looked at her! She couldn't believe that the boy she'd raised now did *this*, throwing his soul on the line at every single show. Kyle had been the center of her life, and she had missed him as only a single mom could, even though it was abundantly clear that he'd found his calling on stage.

And now these were her last moments living in her son's crazy, amazing, glorious world.

By the next chorus, her voice was stronger, her connection with the crowd more electric than ever before.

She would have been thrilled to spend a day with her adult son, watching him do what he did best, no matter how he'd made a living. But she had a son who was a goddamned rock star with more than 500,000 followers on Twitter and whose official videos regularly claimed hundreds of thousands of views on YouTube. So for Kyle, a normal "day at the office" meant this: living his loudest, fullest life in front of more than ten thousand people.

At the end of the first number, Megan looked out into the amphitheater at the screaming and dancing crowd. Wiping at her forehead with a cloth they'd staged near her mic, she lifted an arm and waved.

It hurt to smile.

Dammit, she was going to enjoy this show like it was her last night on earth, not just on this tour. This was a night born for fun.

Theo sidled over between numbers. "On fire, Mrs. M. Sure as hell gonna miss you. You really need to leave, or can we sweet talk you into staying?"

"Get back over there, Zane's starting the count."

Theo, the brazen flirt, gave her a kiss right on the lips before zooming across the stage to his normal spot stage right. She pointed a finger at him, and he laughed at her even as he laid down the bass line for the next number.

She noted that in the wings, Brandon had folded his arms across his chest and was glaring at Theo. What? Brandon felt possessive of her?

Even though she and Brandon didn't have a chance in hell —not in this crazy music world that she and Brandon both inhabited—it still felt pretty damn good to clock that reaction. Would he stay in touch after she left the tour? Would he ever be interested in starting something?

The crowd chanted choruses, roared between numbers, held cell phones aloft to capture favorite moments on video, screamed against the barriers in front of the stage—it was like sunlight to a plant. On stage, the band absorbed the crowd's energy and let it amp up their performance.

Sweat pooled in the small of her back and dripped from the hollow between her clavicles. She rolled her hips, belted into her mic, fed energy back to the crowd.

At the end of the number, Kyle thanked the crowd, and Li-Fang chimed in. They loved Li-Fang almost as much as they loved her son. So when he took the mic, the crowd listened, quieting around the edges.

"Virginia Beach, you're a great audience. Thank you!" He waved an arm at the crowd, waiting for them to calm further. "We were hoping you could help us appreciate someone mighty special."

Zane and Theo laid down a thumping rhythm, one she recognized as another duet. After they'd debuted that song they'd written on the bus, she and Kyle had found their groove. This was an even newer piece of music, but it was ready. And she'd expected they'd start performing it; so this time, she didn't feel as blind-sided as she had for the debut performance of her first duet.

Li-Fang continued. "So, some of our die-hard fans recognize the amazing Mrs. M, Kyle's mom, back here on backup vocals."

Applause and catcalls rose. Megan waved at the crowd.

"Yeah, I know she's hot. Trust me, knowing Mrs. M meant the bar was set pretty damn high back when I was a kid and first discovering that girls were good for something other than doing the fancy lettering on group posters. But she's leaving us!"

Li-Fang clutched at his heart, and the crowd started calling up, "No!—Mrs. M!—Don't leave us!"

Megan laughed at their cries, while swaying to Zane and Theo's beating line. She leaned into her own mic. "You sure know how to make a lady feel welcome!"

More cheers.

"Well," Li-Fang said. "This is another song we've worked up during tour. This one isn't out yet, and tonight will actually be our first performance; that is, if you think it's a good idea."

More roaring.

"Great. At least a few of you know what I'm talking about. So you know that while we've still got Mrs. M here with us, there is no one on earth who would do a better job of landing these vocals and bringing you—Our. Brand. New. Song. It's called 'Dancing Again,' and we think you're gonna love it!"

Almost quivering with anticipation, Megan waited a beat for Kyle's cue. For a moment, she thought back to that first duet, when she'd been reading off of Li-Fang's phone. She'd come a long way since then, both in confidence and in actual performance chops.

And even her relationship with Kyle was way better. It wasn't like he confessed all his darkest thoughts to her, and he'd probably ghost her until tour was over, given how overworked they all were; but he trusted her when she was on the stage, he'd been kinder to her on the bus and at the hotels, and he'd been more discreet with most of his hookups. Not to mention the guitar he'd given her.

Kyle motioned her forward, and Megan strutted downstage until she was level with him, clapping her hands together overhead to tell the crowd to watch her, that she was gonna start this one off. She shouted, "This one's a party, people! Hell, after the shutdowns of 2020, I think we could all use a little more dancing in our lives, make up for lost time. So if you're not on your feet yet, get on up now! Let's do this." She counted in the electric guitar, and Li-Fang took her into the first verse.

Toward the end of the number, the band dropped out, leaving her voice bare, singing above the driving claps of the crowd. Megan found herself alone in a spotlight, singing the words:

We've always got a choice
We can choose to dance, choose to use our voice
We can choose freedom, we can choose to forgive
Bring the light to the party
Live the life we're meant to live!

The show lasted another hour and fifteen minutes, but

somehow it seemed like it was only seconds later that she was backstage, wiping sweat from the back of her neck.

It was over. Really over. That high of an arena crowd? She'd probably never feel that again, no matter how many small clubs she broke into back at home.

In the auditorium, the chants of the crowd were dying away, leaving the sounds of seats folding up, feet shuffling, groups calling out reminders of where they were meeting up.

The post-performance crash hit her body, leaving her feeling oddly hollow. For the last eight weeks, each time she'd come down from the high of a gig, she'd known that the next night, or at least the night after that, she'd have the love and energy of the crowd washing over her again. But not tonight.

Now there was just the dirt on the floor next to the stage, the equipment cases ready to roll forward and take on the gear, roadies in old T-shirts and arena-staff with clipboards and headphones.

And the next time she saw any of this, she'd need a backstage pass. She'd just be one of the masses.

This is what "over" felt like, and she didn't much like it.

And then Brandon held out a freshly uncapped water bottle for her.

After shows, Brandon always made a beeline for the lead singer, so Megan really wasn't expecting that he would be thinking of her before thinking of the band. His readiness to take care of her even before talking to Kyle was oddly touching.

It also made her heart leap, thinking of the implications. Maybe he hadn't pulled away in Philadelphia because he was interested in Greta; maybe there was another reason. Maybe she had a chance.

"Thanks," she said, even though Brandon only had time for a quick glance before he turned toward Kyle, somehow getting ready to do that post-show debrief even while he was taking care of her. The two men chatted, inches away from her: Kyle in his post-show, sweaty glory, all rock god and lean muscle and vibrating energy; Brandon with his back mostly to her, the suit jacket stretched across his broad shoulders.

She'd never see this conversation again, not as a performer: this moment when Kyle and Brandon strategized after a show, talked through what could be tweaked to make things even better for the audience.

And she loved performing so much.

It hit her again. Her last show. The last time. The crowds wouldn't scream her name again. Kyle wouldn't grin at her before launching into "Hey, Look, Ma! I Made It."

Even in the noise backstage, she was aware of the timbre of their voices: Kyle's tenor, that smooth baritone of Brandon's. She couldn't hear their words, not really; but she was still here.

She'd been living this incredible life, and now she was going home to an empty house and a job hunt and the prospect of Jaimie demanding a painful conversation about exactly why she'd quit—not that she was going to *tell* him that she just didn't want to deal with his entitled, whiny, needy attempts to sweet-talk her into sex just one more time. He didn't deserve that much of her time or energy.

To hell with that. She was strong. She really was. A strong woman didn't need to work with a harasser—and she needed to face it: that's what Jaimie was. Her harasser.

If Jaimie forced a conversation, she could honestly tell him that she had different goals now. She wanted to work with the music industry.

In front of her, Kyle and Brandon continued their conversation.

She was going to keep performing. She would write songs and set up gigs and find a way to pay her bills and keep going. In fact, there was an open mic night about six blocks from her house once a month, and she could certainly put together a short set before the next one. Because music was something she needed.

She turned slightly, her shoulder nudging Brandon's back, he was that close. In the VIP section a few feet away, women were crowding the rope-line as usual, decked out in their heels and makeup and form-fitting clothes, each eager to follow one of the guys into his bed—or even a closet.

David Marshall stood at the far right of the crowd.

Her body went stiff.

Fuck.

"Anything the matter?" asked Brandon, turning immediately and following her eyes to the backstage fans. Brandon hadn't been as focused on Kyle as she'd thought. If she hadn't been so worried about David and that damned contract, this kind of attention from Brandon would have made her feel so very good.

Kyle used the moment while Brandon was distracted to flash his photo-ready smile at the women in the crowd. Li-Fang and Theo were already back there, chatting up girls.

Megan leaned closer to Brandon. "He's here. David Marshall's here."

Brandon found David's face in the crowd and leaned closer. "There on the right?"

She nodded, having trouble swallowing. She should be as thirsty as sin after that set, but here she was, her untouched water bottle sweating away in her hand, with a knot in her throat because David Marshall had showed up.

Brandon touched her elbow with one hot finger. "Do you want me to come with you? I'm betting he's got that contract with him."

Megan shook her head. "No. I need to do this alone."

At that point Kyle, who was closer to the crowd, spotted David. Before Megan could reach either of them, Kyle headed toward that end of the crowd, a smile wide across his face. "Uncle David! You came!"

Kyle gave his uncle a back-slapping man-hug in greeting.

Megan drew closer, dreading this with her whole being. She hated David Marshall with such good reason, but he was Kyle's uncle, and Kyle had so little family. Should she let Kyle have a relationship with an awful man just to give him some connection with the family, or was it better to let Kyle know just why she found David so appalling?

Maybe the man had kids now. Was it fair to cut Kyle off from cousins—potentially nice cousins—he'd never met, all in order to keep him away from a man like David Marshall?

She wanted to throw up.

Brandon inched his way closer to the three of them.

"So," Kyle said to David. "What'd you think of the show?"

"Impressive," David replied. "It was great to hear your mom singing another new number. Doing lots of writing?"

Kyle nodded.

It was like watching Kyle dig a hole under both their feet. She exchanged a look with Brandon, who shook his head to say no, don't interrupt. Let it go for now. At least, that's what she read in Brandon's eyes. So she bit her tongue. When it came down to it, she trusted Brandon. She sure as hell wasn't thinking clearly.

"Well," David said, turning from Kyle to Megan as he spoke. "You all are sounding great. Can't wait to get into the studio with you and record something."

It was the first time Brandon had seen David, and the first time Megan had seen them side-by-side. Both of them were good-looking and well-groomed, but while Brandon came across as the polished business man, David was oilier. He was well-dressed, but with that air of plastic and makeup that a television news anchor might exude.

Or a televangelist.

"Yeah, man," Kyle said. "That'll be fun. I'm still up for that laying down a track for your next album. But hey, I've gotta go. Manager still needs me, and then I believe I owe these lovely women some attention."

Kyle turned his smile back on the women backstage, shaking hands with a few squealing girls. Then he said, "Give me a minute, ladies. Then I'm all yours." He excused himself so he and Brandon could finish their post-show debrief.

Brandon gave Megan's hand a squeeze as Kyle wrapped up. He said, "Catch you later?"

"Absolutely." On an impulse, she stretched up to kiss Brandon's cheek.

The planes of his face softened, and a smile creased the corners of his eyes. He tightened his fingers around hers.

Well.

When he released his grip, she took a deep breath and squared her shoulders. Now that it was just the two of them at this corner of the rope line, David's eyes darted to her chest. The lech.

"Did you bring my old contract?" she asked.

Looking smug, David said, "Of course. I've got a copy here." He pulled an envelope out of his back pocket.

Something so slim couldn't be that big a problem, could it?

She pulled it from his hand a little too sharply. Inside were three sheets of paper, which seemed short. Clearly, these words packed a punch.

He said, "You might want to take a look at paragraph twelve." She flipped to the second page, realizing that of course this wasn't the original. That would be in a safe place somewhere back at his home or his office.

Paragraph twelve had been helpfully circled, so she read it aloud. "Singer agrees to contribute to the Band's creative endeavors by participating from time to time in music writing sessions. Singer further agrees that all of Singer's creative musical output shall result in intellectual property to be owned exclusively by the Band, whether such creative output (henceforth, 'Music') shall be created jointly in a session with the full Band, while working one-on-one with any individual member of the Band, or written solely by Singer. This clause shall survive the termination of this agreement."

She raised her eyes to him. "So?"

"So," he said. "Those new songs you've got online with the Sutter Boys? That new duet you sang tonight? Everywhere I look, I see the band acknowledging that you're a co-author of this new stuff. And this contract?" He pointed his thumb at his bulky chest. He'd been stocky and muscular before, but now he seemed bear-like. "This contract means that we have rights in that music. I think you and your boy's band owe me and my band a portion of your proceeds from those songs. Don't you think?"

She couldn't decide if seeing the actual contract made her think his case was weaker or stronger.

"I signed this agreement twenty years ago. Do you really think a court would enforce this and give you part of the royalty stream from the Sutter Boys products?" She wanted to project confidence, but she was pretty sure she sounded insecure and worried. Because she kind of was.

"All I see is that I've got a valid claim and the paper to back it up, so don't try to weasel your way out of our agreement. Think of the damage it'll do to Kyle. I've promised him I'll introduce him to my kids and nephews and nieces—and my mom, of course. Why don't you and I just keep this quiet, and let him not be any wiser."

She hated this situation, and she hated that she'd ever let David Marshall into her life, but she agreed with him on one thing. She didn't want to derail Kyle's chances of meeting family neither of them had ever known about. So she said, "I was thinking along the same lines myself."

His shoulders seemed to swell. Clearly, that was exactly what he wanted to hear.

He smiled, that practiced smile she sometimes on salesmen on the shopping channel. "Wonderful. And I guess I'll be seeing you at the last show of tour? It will be—um—easier if you just bring a cashier's check. Not a personal one, mind. I wouldn't want this to slip through the cracks or anything."

This was the man who wanted to be in Kyle's life as his family? Willing to blackmail her? Why? What had she done to deserve this, but fall in love with this guy's little brother, love singing, and have a kid who grew up into the amazing performer Kyle had become? It wasn't like she'd lived a terrible life, if you left out the bit about messing around with a married man.

She started to shift away just as David leaned closer and lowered his voice. Quiet. Intimate. Nauseating. "And maybe then, we can spend a little time together again." He lifted his hand like he wanted to touch her hair, but she jerked backwards.

"I think not," she said. Why did she sound so uncertain?

He paused for just a moment, then fondled the bit of hair that had worked itself out of her ponytail—still not touching her skin, thank God. "Aw, Megan. Don't be like that. We're family. We should be close."

Somehow she took a breath, and somehow she turned to walk away. And then he grabbed her wrist.

Megan froze.

She'd utterly forgotten that sensation, the terror of his hands on her, and now she couldn't get out of her head. She knew she was backstage at a Sutter Boys concert, that she'd already raised Kyle, that she was in her forties; but with his hand on her wrist, she was eighteen again, alone in a room with three men, and pretty darn certain she was about to be gang-raped unless she could somehow break free.

She stood with his burning hot hand on her wrist while he spoke again. "Last show of the tour. Phoenix. Be there, and bring my check."

He dropped her wrist and sauntered away through the crowd, like a man who knew he was going to win.

She needed a shower.

She needed to throw up.

She needed to put on her big girl pants and take this man down.

18

The conversation with David brought her crashing even further down from the high of her last show. She'd wanted to savor her night, and he'd stolen it from her.

She was going to get that bastard.

Moments after David disappeared into the crowd, Brandon found Megan and gave her face a good scan. "You okay? You look a bit rattled. He didn't try anything, did he?"

Of course he was asking about David. Because he cared.

"Not really," said Megan, thinking about David's fingers on her wrist and on her hair, forcing back the bile that rose in her throat. Megan was still holding the slim envelope in her hand. There wasn't exactly anywhere to put it, given what she'd worn for the show: skinny jeans and high heels and another scoop-necked shirt, this one deep red and draping loosely from sleeveless shoulders to reveal more cleavage than she'd show in normal life. She held up the envelope. "But he did give me the contract."

"Good. Let's look at that together back at the hotel. Where it's quieter. If you'd like."

"Sure," she said, grateful to have someone she trusted on

her team. Because she did trust Brandon, whether or not he was really interested in her romantically.

"You heading out? My car's almost here." He held up his phone to indicate he'd ordered a car.

"Not yet," said Megan. "I need to say some goodbyes."

"Of course. I'd stay, but I have a call I have to make, and it'll be easier if I'm someplace quiet. But could you catch me at the hotel? I'd like that." He looked at her again, with something like hope in his expression. Eyes wide, but relaxed and expectant. Mouth hinting at a smile, but uncertain.

She bit her lip. "I'll look for you, see if you're still downstairs."

"Text me when you're close?" he said. "We can grab a quick drink or something, celebrate your success on tour. Unwind."

"Okay." She realized, though, that she needed to resolve the situation with David soon. How could she think of a new relationship with David's threats hanging over her?

"It's a plan," he said. Then he leaned in to kiss her cheek, just like she'd done earlier.

Wow. That was nice. She did not want to mess this up.

When he turned toward the exit, she stared after him for a moment, then headed the opposite way, toward the greenroom.

The band was getting on the bus tonight, pushing on to Raleigh. As far as she knew, only she and Brandon would be at the hotel, since he had a plane to catch back to Memphis.

She almost bumped into Theo and a random woman as they stumbled out of a doorway.

"Sorry, Mrs. M. Didn't see you there." Theo had an arm snaked around his date, and gave her neck a little nuzzle. "You smell so good," he said into the woman's hair.

The woman on his arm giggled. She looked like a younger version of Megan, with similar curves and wavy hair that wasn't sweaty from singing a full set.

"I just wanted to say goodbye, Theo. It's been great touring with you."

He stopped and swung around to face Megan, dragging the woman under his arm with him as he turned. He stepped away from his companion. "Wait here," he told the girl, closing in on Megan. He looked her up and down, but he dropped all the lechery he usually put into these glances. Theo's face grew wistful. "That's right. You're out of here. Now, don't do anything I wouldn't do tonight, you hear?"

He leaned over, elbows spread wide as he gave her the sort of awkward, no-excess-body-contact hug young men gave their mothers. Then he held onto her shoulders for a long moment and spoke into her hair. "I'm gonna miss you something terrible. Megan Gamble, you're the best rock-n-roll mom in the business. I hope you know it."

She patted him on the back. "You're a good man, Theo Likonedis. Don't be afraid to show it, okay?"

They stepped apart.

"Aw," she said. "Get outta here. I'll see you at the end of the tour, okay? Kyle promised me tickets for the last show."

He snaked an arm around the girl again, and the pair turned away.

Megan found and said goodbye to the rest of the band, getting a long hug from Li-Fang and an anxious request to "please be discreet with my mom." She promised. She promised to text Charlotte, and Zane promised to keep Charlotte well-fed. She said her goodbyes to Hannah from makeup and Kryssa from wardrobe, who had gradually grown to understand Megan's personal style: dressing her in things like this shirt: sexy, but not as over-the-top as that first bustier she'd worn in LA.

She found Charlie, who was still her favorite roadie after the hassle he'd given her that night in San Jose, when she'd shown up with Keiko and only one backstage pass. "Take care," she told him, giving him a quick hug. "And lay off those cigarettes!"

He gave her a salute. "Yes, ma'am!" he said. "Been twelve days since my last smoke." He pulled up his sleeve to reveal the nicotine patch on his arm, crowded into the clear space next to his largest tattoo, which of course paid homage to his beloved Red Sox.

"Good man," she said, patting him on the bicep and heading away down the hall.

She made one last stop to say goodbye to their driver, Feroz, who told her he would miss hearing her voice on the bus. Then she called a car.

And that was it. Tour was really over.

But she didn't have time to sit around and mope, so on the way to the hotel, she planned. Obviously her biggest priority should be to make the whole David situation go away. She needed a new job. She also brainstormed about a three-song set for her first open mic night. She could do one original, right? Not just covers. Now that she'd started writing songs, she didn't think she'd ever stop, and she certainly didn't want to. But she did need to make certain her songs belonged to her, not to David Marshall and 2 Samuel 6, which brought her full circle to her biggest priority.

She also wanted to be in a relationship again. Twenty years had been enough time as a single woman, and her nasty, semi-permanent hookup with her old boss had been the opposite of a healthy relationship. It had been toxic. Jaimie had never made her pleasure a priority, let alone her mental or emotional well-being.

But Brandon talked to her. He listened. And he was so damned kind and thoughtful.

The driver pulled up to the hotel. Megan grabbed her bag and Kyle's old guitar and checked in.

She was almost to the elevator banks when Brandon called

out from the archway leading to the hotel bar. Behind him, comfortable couches and tables faced the beach through the enormous windows at the rear of the lobby. "I thought you were going to text."

"I meant to," she lied; really, she hadn't thought she could stand the heartache if he wasn't as interested in her as she was in him. "I guess I forgot. Tired and all, and kinda got a lot on my mind."

He looked so good. He had kept his suit jacket on, but had loosened the tie around his neck. "I'd imagine. Speaking of which, how are you doing, knowing that tonight was your last show? Is that as strange a feeling as I think it must be?"

No one else had asked her that.

"Surreal. I almost can't believe that tonight was my last time on stage with the band. I know I'm flying home tomorrow, but I'm still thinking about my entrance on *Don't Fight It*, wondering if I should pump it up more, or hold back so the spotlight is still on Kyle. Like I haven't really internalized that I'm not going to do that again. I'm just all over the place."

He nodded. "Well, you've been amazing. You are a real pro, but I hope you also had some fun."

The handle of the guitar case cut into her fingers, so she set it down on the marble floor of the lobby and rested her roller bag on its wheels. "Of course. It's been the experience of a lifetime."

He followed the motion to look at the guitar at her feet. He raised his gaze, those tiny smile lines just barely visible. "So, Kyle's old acoustic. Still have it, I see."

She nodded, happiness growing in her. "Kyle told me to keep it. He seems to think I'm not a bad songwriter. Who knows, maybe I'll even write some more for the band."

He crossed to her, picking up the guitar and taking the handle of her bag. "Come sit. We can chat in here. I couldn't quite remember if you drank Sauvignon Blanc or Chardonnay."

They'd only had drinks together that one night after the band had deserted them, and now he looked guilty—like he should have paid better attention and remembered her drink order.

He led the way to a table right against the windows, over-looking the dark of the ocean. The stars shone brightly in the moonless sky.

Brandon gestured. His glass of scotch waited, alongside two untouched and dewy glasses of wine. "I got one of each. Hope-fully they're still chilled."

Romantic.

He pulled out a chair for her. When had someone last done that for her? "You should certainly write for the band, if you want. But I hope you also write for yourself. I suspect that your mind and heart twist lyrics into interesting shapes, and that the songs you write for yourself would be worth hearing."

"But what about this stupid contract? Won't David Marshall just come after me and demand everything?"

His smile lines disappeared as he sat across from her, and his eyes were green ice under his lowered brows. "Over my dead body. Let's see that copy of the agreement."

She nodded, bending to take the folder out of her bag's side pocket. When she put it down on the round table, it took up almost the entire space between their glasses.

She shuddered. She hated knowing David's fingers had been all over the paper.

Brandon caught the motion. "Hey," he said. "I told you we'll take care of this."

"Well," she said. "It's just about my worst nightmare. I have to deal with this man who would have happily raped me and shared me with his brothers, and I've put the band at risk. I just hate being this force for evil!"

"That's not what you are." He looked at her calmly, then grew serious and raised a hand to her face. "You've got those little lines right here, between your brows." Then he pressed a thumb there gently, and smoothed the skin from side to side. The simple touch of his thumb made the skin on her face relax.

She closed her eyes. She wanted to walk around this tiny table and climb into his lap, but she just couldn't let herself. Not until she'd begun to figure out the David situation.

Brandon lowered his hand and pulled the contract out of the envelope. After a quick glance at the highlighted section, he said. "No termination? That strikes me as really odd. But we'll get it looked at by an entertainment lawyer. I've got the band's attorney teed up, and he's expecting your call. I keep saying, there's just no way this should be so broadly enforceable. He'll give us some advice we can act on, and then we can take it from there."

Something about the way Brandon kept assuming they were in this together was simultaneously comforting and really troublesome. She drew her lower lip between her teeth, worrying it as she thought. "You keep saying, 'we.'"

"Well, yeah. I mean, we're in this together. You, me, the band. All of us."

"But it's my fight. My problem."

She said the words and felt stronger, because that was exactly it. It was her problem to solve. And she might not solve it easily or gracefully or at all well, but if she could do it herself, she knew it would go a long way toward changing her whole attitude toward life. It was past time for her to be in the driver's seat of her own life, not letting herself be pushed around by everyone else.

Brandon watched her while she thought, his face barely illuminated by the landscape lighting outside the window.

She took a deep breath. "I'll take the name of that attorney, but I want to contact him myself. And I need to do this on my own, hopefully without screwing up Kyle's chance to meet this family. He's so damned excited by the idea; I can't just take that away from him. David's an incredibly slimy man, but I'd like to give Kyle the chance to finally connect with these people who'd shut us out for so long. I'll tell him what David did; I'll have to. But the rest of the family still deserves a chance. They could be decent people, David excepted. And if they're not, then Kyle's a big boy. He'll figure it out."

Now Brandon's eyes were smiling again. "You are a remarkable woman. That's remarkably unselfish of you."

"Stop. I'm just me. Pretty ordinary, actually."

"Nope. Not buying it, not while I'm sitting across from a woman who can upstage her own son."

"I sure as hell hope not. That wouldn't be fair."

He shook a finger at her, playful. "You know what I mean. Own it. You are an incredible musician in your own right, and a terrific performer."

Megan started to smile. "I'm starting to believe that. Which is why I think I'm finally strong enough to try to fight this other battle as well." She started to say something else, then broke off, a blush warming her cheeks.

"What?" asked Brandon.

She looked at those green eyes, the smile lines etched into the skin around them. "I wondered," she said, speaking softly and dropping her eyes. "Am I imagining things, or is there something starting here?" She looked up again and waved a hand at the air between them.

He caught her hand in his own, and at the simple feeling of his fingers holding her palm, his thumb smoothing the thinner skin on the back of her hand, her lower lip went back between her teeth. "Aren't you the brave one?" he asked. "Yeah, I've been wondering the same."

It wasn't so much sexual attraction that awoke with his words, but a flushed anticipation of a partner in her life, someone to care for and who might care for her. A cheerleader, an inspiration. Someone to walk beside.

And someone to touch. Let's not forget about that.

Which set off the libido she'd been ignoring for too long, or feeding the unhealthiest of diets.

"I worried when you pulled away back in the elevator, when we were in Philly."

He looked surprised. "The way I remember that night, you were the one who stepped back."

They'd been in the elevator, talking about Greta. "Well, you said something about how you always loved a woman with a good voice, or something, and I thought you meant your fiancée's sister. So I thought I needed to give you space."

A lovely smile touched his eyes. "I meant you. And when you pulled away, I thought I'd been misreading things. That maybe you weren't ready, especially after what you'd just told me about David. You astonish me. I mean, you're this badass singer who projects a ton of confidence on stage, and you trusted me enough to tell me about David and how he hurt you. That combination, your strength alongside your willingness to show me your weaknesses? It's remarkable."

"You make me sound like a catch."

He just shook his head. "Because you are."

Brandon was still holding her hand atop the table, resting on top of that awful contract.

She pulled her hand away and sat straighter.

"I just don't believe that. Not with that damn contract just sitting here on the table between us. I feel like I won't be ready for a relationship until I can get this thing settled and gone. Because I'm just a liability until then, to you and to Kyle and to anyone I care about."

And he surprised her, because he didn't look disgusted. She'd reminded them both of the glaring ugliness in her past and the way it had opened up this blatant blackmail attempt, and instead he just looked pained. Like he hurt because she did.

"Oh, Megan. You don't need to be perfect to be worthy of

love and respect. No one is. Don't wait until everything in your life is exactly the way you want it to be before you give yourself the chance to be happy. Maybe I'm not the man for you, but don't make yourself wait until some mythical moment when you're convinced that you're suddenly worthy. I think you're amazing. If you feel like you need to wait until after we've vanquished David—and we will!—then I'll wait as long as you need. But know that I don't love you because I think you're perfect. I love you because you're exactly yourself. And if you think you could develop feelings for me." He broke off and closed his eyes for a moment. "If you think that we have a chance, let's turn this into something real. I want to be there for you. I want to help you when you need it, and cheer you on when you just need to know that someone is in your corner. And I want to hear about all the tiny things in your day: the weird person in the coffee shop, and the song you heard on the radio, and what you think of the newest episode of some random series streaming on TV. I want to listen to you play that guitar and make mistakes and stumble through chord progressions until something clicks for you and suddenly you're making music that no one else could dream up. Take a chance on me, Megan Gamble. Take a chance on us."

She kept focusing on this one word he'd said. It rang in her ears. "Did you say the word, 'love?' You've never even kissed me, and you're ready to say you love me?"

He pushed himself back from their table and looked around, taking in the nearly empty bar, the starlit sky over the ocean outside the window, then—her. His face softened into an expression of hope that raised the corners of his mouth and highlighted the smile lines around his eyes. "I guess I did say that."

Then his grin grew wider. "But I'd like to fix that bit about how we haven't even kissed, if that would be okay with you."

She found herself standing, and he did the same. She said,

"I have a room upstairs," her pulse pounding in her neck, her breath so very shallow.

"Yeah," he said. "Kinda knew about that room of yours. Do you want to head up?" He jerked his head toward the door, and her smile grew.

How could smiles feel so different, mean so many things? This one came from deep inside her. It was like her body had emerged from a chrysalis of shame and now stood new and fresh and beautiful around her soul.

Somehow they made it to the elevators, Megan carrying the guitar and Brandon rolling her bag.

Her mind wanted to buzz away into how tough the logistics were going to be if she really began a relationship with Brandon, and into the horrendous 'what if's surrounding the entire situation with David and the contract she'd signed so many years ago. But maybe right now she could just put that aside. Focus on the good in front of her.

The elevator doors opened, and they stepped in. Megan pushed the button for her floor and said, "I sure am glad you made me miss my entrance that first night."

"I sure am glad you convinced me to let you on that stage."

They rode upward in an easy silence. Was this what it felt like, to stand next to the man who believed in you and always had your back? This was wonderful.

When the elevator doors opened, they stepped out and she asked, "Would you like to come to my room?"

"Very much. But I don't want this to be uncomfortable for you."

And then they were inside her room, where it was private. Where she could tease him a little. "Part of me is hoping that something might be a little uncomfortable. In the best of ways."

He laughed at that, his cheeks showing the tiniest bit of pink. "Oh, do you, now?"

That laughter was just what she needed. The tenderness of

his words downstairs had been marvelous, but right now she was just a woman who was thinking about getting naked with a very attractive man, and she was nervous.

Or she had been, until that laugh.

She laid her hands flat against the lapels of his suit, feeling the warmth of his body through the layers of cloth. "Yeah, I kinda do. But you'll go easy on me."

He raised a hand. "The only things that will happen in this room will be the things you want to have happen. And right now, I very much want to put my hands into your incredible hair and kiss you until I can barely breathe. If that's okay."

"More than okay."

His fingers parted the hair beside her face and tilted her face toward his.

She sensed his breath just out of reach, but his lips didn't touch hers until she opened her eyes again. When she nodded, he finally closed that last bit of distance so she could reach his lower lip and give it a first light nibble. He responded, making her remember how much she loved to feel a man's lips and skin against her own.

She licked Brandon's lower lip, tasting the Scotch he'd been drinking, letting her hands slip under the cloth of his jacket to circle his back. "Is this okay?" she asked.

"Oh yeah. Whatever you want to do with your hands is more than okay with me."

They took their time. Unfastened one button, then a second. Traced a single finger along a waistline. Savored the sensation of newly exposed skin touching fabric, of the brush of his beard against her face. Of Brandon's hands finally on her breasts. Of exactly how hard he was.

This was intimacy. It was private. It was the murmured words, "This okay?" The catch of breath. A gasp. The freedom to move and discover. The certainty that when he touched her, it was because he wanted more from her than just physical release. He wanted her mind and her creativity and her courage on stage. He wanted *her*.

And then it was sheets against bare skin, fingers twisted into the edge of a pillow, a heel braced against the mattress. The faint sound of a condom package being torn open. "Let me do that," she said.

It was the sensation of finally being filled, of fitting together. Of eyelashes fluttering, and that need to move, more and harder and faster; to hang on with fingernails just starting to bite, to get her mouth on a bicep or a shoulder or a pec or that glorious mouth of his. It was sensation and awareness all concentrated in one tiny spot, and it was letting go and falling and shuddering back to an awareness of the newly risen moon lighting the room.

It was breath returning to her body.

It was weight blissfully covering her.

"Wow," Megan said, her hand drifting flat against the skin of Brandon's back.

He raised himself up. "Am I crushing you?"

"No," she said. "I've finally got you just where I want you. Don't move. Not yet."

He sunk his head back into the space next to hers, shifting to free his own hand.

When his broad palm traced the side of her body up from her hip, she shivered. "That's nice. So nice."

He nodded against her neck, and her eyes drifted closed.

"Sorry," he said. "Gotta take care of this." And then he was gone for a moment, padding to the bathroom to throw away the condom, returning with a warm cloth so she could wipe herself clean. She couldn't have found the energy to move that far; it was perfect to be cared for.

"All good?" he asked.

"Much better than that," she said.

He let the cloth drop to the floor and scooted under the

covers, rolling onto his side and drawing her back against the expanse of his chest. "Is this okay?" he asked.

"It's exactly what I've been missing," she said.

She wanted to stay awake all night; but for right now, she was too tired and too satisfied and feeling too damned cherished to do anything other than let her breathing slow, let her eyes close, and drift off to sleep.

19

Morning came too quickly, because it meant it was time to leave. But it was wonderful to wake up next to Brandon, the sunlight streaming through the curtains, throwing highlights into the dark curls atop his head, picking out the strands of silver near his ears, where his cheeks were starting to show early morning stubble. The logistics of this relationship weren't going to be easy, but they would do this again: wake together in the morning light.

Each of them had an early flight, but somehow they made it out the door, bags packed. Nothing was left behind after Brandon's compulsive sweep of their room, which involved opening every drawer and checking under the chairs.

"Do you do this every time you check out of a hotel?" she asked, amused.

He looked a little guilty. "Yes? I don't like to forget things."

"I see," she said.

He kissed her then. "Like, I didn't want to forget to do that."

At the airport, they sat together; their flights were leaving from adjacent gates—his to Tennessee, hers to San Jose.

"You are coming to NorCal soon, aren't you?"

He shook his head. "I wish I were, but I don't get there very often. But you could meet me in LA sometime, stay with me."

"What are you talking about? I thought you lived in Tennessee."

He shrugged. "Most of the time. But I'm in LA so much that I bought a condo there, too. It's not much, but I crash there when I'm in town."

When it was time for Megan's group to board, Brandon pulled her in for a hug, then whispered in her ear, "I'd kiss the hell out of you, but I've never liked PDA. I'd rather save that for when we can have some privacy."

She pulled away and smiled at him, lifting her eyebrows. "So we're going to have some privacy again soon?"

"If I have anything to say about it, we are."

His first text message arrived before she'd even pulled her suitcase to her seat. "Miss you," it said. They kept the conversation going until Megan switched her phone into airplane mode.

It almost felt like they'd skipped right past Megan's resistance to the idea of starting a relationship until after vanquishing David, but not quite. What she felt for Brandon was real, and apparently it was reciprocated. But she wouldn't rest easy or be able to fully enjoy Brandon until she had dealt with that contract.

And then? Then she'd truly be all in.

Hours later, Megan got home to an empty house, opened her suitcase (but failed to unpack or start her laundry), and fiddled with her guitar. Everything in the house smelled unused, the air tight with dust and the remnants of wildfire smoke.

It took her two days to work her way out of her post-tour funk and email the attorney Brandon had recommended; but the time wasn't wholly unproductive, at least musically. Her fingers were stronger now, used to spending hours with the guitar. Playing was like relearning a childhood language that had fallen away. Phrases came back to her. Muscle memory, too. She could think in "guitar" again. If she needed a major chord progression, her fingers did the work her imagination demanded, like her voice responded to her need for certain pitches or dynamics or timbre. There was none of the beginner's need to examine which finger depressed which string onto which fret; it just happened.

And there were songs taking shape, too, with the faint thread of a musical through-line tying them together.

So she didn't feel terribly guilty about the dirty clothes still in her bag, or the emails she couldn't quite send in those first few days. Her brain and her body needed time to process the experience of the tour, and to deal with the fact that even though she was home again, the tour was very much still going on.

Kyle was even responding to her texts, though not always, and not very fast. But touring was hectic, and she understood that now in a way she never had before.

At least tour had been a financial win for her, more than covering her expenses, so even after paying her mortgage she had been saving a bit of money. She'd need a new job, but she had a few months or so. And maybe Kyle would even help out, if she really needed it.

Okay. Not going there. She could still stand on her own two feet. She was a grown woman with a brain and she could take care of herself. Except for that damned issue with David Marshall and the old contract.

Her third night at home, she tossed and turned for hours, her brain demanding that she deal with David.

So, in the morning she sat down at her kitchen counter with her morning coffee, looked out at her tiny backyard, and emailed the attorney—a guy named Glen Auricchio. At first she just mentioned that Brandon had recommended she get in touch about a matter that was personal, but which could impact the Sutter Boys. She didn't attach her ancient agreement with David's band, because she wasn't a client yet, but she mentioned that the issue turned on whether an old contract was still enforceable, and to what degree.

The lawyer pinged her back moments later.

You the client, or is the band?

She responded, *I am. I'm guessing you need an engagement letter.*

Sure do. Attached. You can e-sign, and then send me that agreement. I have a free hour this morning, and I'd rather look at this now than work on my other project. New. Shiny.

She laughed. She was going to like this guy.

When she sent off the old contract with David's band, she gave him her cell number and suggested he call when convenient.

Less than fifteen minutes later, while she was still nursing her second cup of coffee, her phone rang.

"Hello?" she said.

"Hey, this is Glen. This Megan?"

"Yep. Thanks for calling. I can't say I expected this kind of service."

"Well, maybe that's because this isn't complicated legally, and it's also a total scumbag move. So, both easy and juicy. My favorite."

She pictured a guy tilting himself back in an old-school detective's chair for some reason. Was there a song there? "So, am I stuck? Do I have to pay this guy? He wants a lot of money."

"Nope," Glen said. He sounded absolutely confident, like this was material he knew so well that he didn't really need to think much at all to get to the answer. "Don't think it's enforceable. Overly broad. I mean, look at *Whitewater West Indus. v. Richard Alleshouse.* That was pretty decisive, even if it is patent law, not copyright. So in the long run, I don't think this guy is actually gonna be able to get what he wants, at least not by enforcing this contract. That said, it might not be a bad idea to get him to sign a broad waiver of claims. I mean, this contract *should* have been limited to stuff that you created while you worked together. A waiver stating that the reasonable time period during which their band could claim rights in your work has long expired should be enforceable. That said, we'd need to be careful to include a Section 1542 release as well. That section can come back to bite you in the butt, but again, I think you have a solid case. Without a waiver, he could probably drag you to court, make your life pretty miserable. And you wouldn't want that. Normally I'd offer to throw something together for you, but I'm just really swamped."

"No," Megan said, down at her copy of the contract. "I can't impose like that. You've already done me a massive favor just by making the call. Besides, I don't think I can afford your rates. But if you have a form or something, I'm sure I could turn it into something that I could wave in front of David's face."

After a pause, she said, "Hello? You still there?"

"Sorry," he said. "I'm just trying to think of a polite way to point something out. Generally attorneys and paralegals are the only people with the confidence to draft their own agreements. And I don't think you'd be calling me if you were a member of the bar. Brandon would have given me a heads up about that."

"I've actually been a paralegal for years; or, I was until about two months ago. I quit during the tour, so I'm out of a job at the moment. Plenty of time on my hands."

Now he sounded very interested. "Really? I mean, I'm sorry you're out of work, but we might actually be able to solve some problems for each other. At the moment I'm down a paralegal. That's why I'm tearing my hair out. It's usually just three of us in the office: me, an associate, and the paralegal, plus a few support staff. But my paralegal had had enough of LA and just moved back home to Wisconsin, so my associate and I are running on fumes. I'm trying to wrap my head around the fact that I need to do a job search, so anyone with experience sounds like a godsend to me. Any chance you'd be interested in working remotely for a bit? I'd pay you standard hourly rates."

That would at least pay the bills until she figured out what to do with herself. "I could do that, but I don't have any entertainment law experience. Also, full disclosure, you should know I only just finished my last credits for my college degree."

Across the line she heard the sound of a pen tapping rapidly against a hard surface. His desk? The headset? "I appreciate the honesty. Normally I wouldn't hire someone right out of school, but how many years did you say you've been doing this?"

"About twenty."

"Shit. I'd be an idiot not to snap you up. Do you have anyone who could give you a reference?"

Thinking of Keiko, Megan said, "I sure do."

Again, the pen tapping. "Well, why don't we see how this goes? Obviously, I won't have you work on the Sutter Boys account, but I've got lots of other client work to keep you busy. I just wish you were local in LA. Some of our work really needs to happen in the office. And one of the perks of entertainment law is the occasional celebrity sighting, which you can't really enjoy from up north. But having you remote would still really help me out, tide me over until I can do a job search."

"Or," Megan said, letting her voice trail off.

"Or what?"

"I've been toying with the idea of getting a fresh start, even thinking about moving to LA for the music scene. I'm looking to get closer to the industry, find some part time work as a session musician, that sort of thing."

And she'd also been thinking about selling the house. It was the only way she had to raise the amount of cash David was talking about, if things ended up going south. She was just really, really lucky she'd been able to buy out her parents' mortgage when they had retired to Idaho.

Glen was still talking. "I could help you if you're looking for session work, too. I've got a fair number of clients that need singers from time to time. That's your gig, right? Voice?"

"Yeah. Maybe some bar gigs or open mics and that sort of stuff, too." It was only a week until the open mic at her own neighborhood bar. She'd have to go over there in the next few days, make sure she understood how to sign up.

By the time they got off the phone, she'd agreed to start doing remote work for him immediately. If things worked out by the end of a two week trial, he'd make the offer permanent, and give her a month or two to find a place in LA.

After they hung up, Megan checked her phone, which had buzzed with a notification during the call.

It was a text from Brandon. *"Hoping you're making progress. I'm working on a trip to the Bay Area. Nothing set in stone, but I'll keep trying. Let me know how things are going. X"*

God, she loved it when he put that little X of a kiss at the end of his messages.

"Just got off the phone with your attorney. Making progress indeed."

Almost immediately she got a single word response. *"Excellent."*

She smiled, pocketed her phone, and looked around the tiny house where she'd raised Kyle. She'd spent two full days so tired she hadn't even been willing to unpack. But that phone call, followed by Brandon's text, got her right out of her slump.

It was time to move on. She was good at her job, even if she'd fought for years for professional respect. She might have started her years as a paralegal as a woman without a college degree, but she'd learned fast and did excellent work. This LA attorney wouldn't wait out the two weeks before making his offer final. No way.

She grabbed a stack of spare grocery bags from next to the recycling bin. Every move started with dozens of trips to Goodwill. Might as well get started. She had a house to put on the market.

Shit was getting real.

Ten days later, she was working remotely and billing around twenty hours a week for Glen. She'd drafted the waiver to try to get David to give up on his bribery scheme, and Glen had signed off on it. Her house was on the market, both to free up cash in case she actually needed to pay off David, and to get her the hell out of the Bay Area. Just going to her old grocery store, driving toward her old office, thinking about Jaimie, made her realize how much she wanted to rip off the Band-Aid. She wanted to start over.

When her phone buzzed late one afternoon with yet another message from Jaimie, she finally broke. "*I heard you're back in town. Stop by so we can discuss a salary raise for you. We'd hate to lose you, me especially.*"

She hit "dial" and waited for Jaimie to pick up. "Jaimie, I quit. I wrote that email, remember? Did you not read my email?"

"Hello to you, too, Megan. Yes, I got your email, but you couldn't be serious. This is a good job for a college dropout."

She interrupted. "I'm not a dropout any longer. I finished my degree."

"That's right," he said. "I heard about that. But even before that, you've always been valuable to the firm. Especially to me. We can discuss a raise, if that's what you want."

"No, Jaimie, it's not. I've already taken a new job, and I won't be coming back. Keiko can grab the photos off my desk for me, but other than that, there's nothing there I want."

"Nothing?" asked Jaimie, with way too many layers of insinuation in his voice. "Not even the chance to go to law school on our dime? And spend time with me, your favorite attorney?"

What was it with this man not taking "no" for an answer? Well, she was going to regret the law school tuition, but it wasn't worth it. She was done putting up with men who were bad actors, and she had plenty to deal with just to get David Marshall to back off. She sure didn't need to deal with Jaimie at the same time. "Nope, I'm not going to miss a thing," she said, feeling like she could conquer the world.

He'd have to find a new side piece, wouldn't he? "Well," said Jaimie. "If you're ever looking for work again, just let us know. We'd be more than happy to have you back."

Way back in LA, that first day she'd sung with the band, she'd been reeling from Jaimie's betrayal; so upset that he had never, ever considered leaving his wife. She'd resolved then that she was done with him, but she hadn't been convinced that she'd actually follow through. And now, look at her. She had a new job, and had cut ties to Jaimie's office entirely. Just now, it hadn't even been that hard to stick to her position. And Jaimie was even offering her a lifeline, not that she ever planned to use it. She was almost touched that he was being that decent.

With that boost to her confidence, she turned to the thornier issue: David Marshall. She was going to get rid of him, too.

She sang at her neighborhood open mic, then hit two more open mics at different bars, checking out the kind of people who showed up to perform. She drafted a singer's resume and started to get it out into the world both up north in the Bay Area and down in LA.

She was really doing this, wasn't she?

She and Brandon texted constantly. Their exchanges were a necessary part of her day, now. Before Brandon, life had been rather hollow. Not anymore. Maybe it was a pipe dream, but she wanted whatever was happening with Brandon to turn into an actual relationship, with in-person visits and sleep overs and all the intimacy of daily life and the bedroom.

But the David thing nagged at her. She didn't want to live her life with a threat hanging over her. She needed to either pay David off or get him to sign the waiver.

One evening around seven she was working at the kitchen table finishing up the details of a trademark application for one of Glen's clients. It was the sort of detailed work she found satisfying in a nit-picky sort of way. And since she was working from home, she could also keep her Spotify music going for this sort of job. She could still focus, except when the Sutter Boys' numbers came up on her playlist. Like one just had.

She was singing along (of course), until they got to the bridge of this number, where Li-Fang handed off a guitar solo to Charlotte. Megan started dancing around the kitchen, tossing the remains of a very unexciting grocery store Caesar salad into the trash and ignoring the two partially packed moving boxes in the corner, when her phone buzzed with an incoming text.

"Just found this," Brandon wrote, including a link to a YouTube video. *"If this is the sort of stuff David Marshall gets up to, there may be more women out there with stories to tell. It should bolster your case, don't you think? And when you talk to Kyle, this will make it clear what kind of man David is, so it won't sound like you're just being mean and denying him access to his family. It's more like you're protecting him from becoming associated with a pretty evil-sounding guy."*

Megan followed the link and pushed play.

On the screen, a woman at a desk interviewed a couple on a couch, just like every late night show filmed in the last thirty years. The couple was identified with captions as David and Sharon Marshall. In the interview, David seemed maybe five years younger than he was now; probably pushing forty, if not north of that. He looked a bit slimmer than when she'd seen him recently, but was already well on his way to being a very hefty man. His wife was tiny. She was pretty, with perfect fresh-faced makeup that made her look younger than she probably was. She had the aura of a one-time high school prom queen: one everyone actually liked because she was genuinely sweet and kind, even to kids who weren't "cool."

Sharon Marshall slipped a hand into her husband's. "David Marshall is a good man. Like all us, myself included, David has sinned before the Lord. But as far as I'm concerned, as far as anyone should be concerned, now that he has confessed to God Almighty and begged His forgiveness, we should all be able to put this whole matter behind us."

"So," the interviewer said, "You don't think we should give any credence to this woman's accusations that David made lewd suggestions to her while she was working with his band?"

A photo of a woman who was probably in her early twenties flashed on the screen.

David seemed about to answer, but Sharon leaned across him toward the interviewer. "No, I do not think we should do that. That woman is a known tramp. She never should have been part of a band whose mission is to preach the word of the Lord. And while my David may be a friendly man, he is not an evil one. Many, many souls have been saved as a result of the concerts David and the boys play, and countless others have been encouraged in the path of righteousness. And while forgiveness is the Lord's, I'm sure many of us women under-stand that forgiveness is also the spouse's. So if I'm willing to forgive my husband for any small sins of the heart which he may have committed—"

Here Sharon turned back to David, squeezing his hand and looking at him adoringly. "If I'm willing to let bygones be bygones, I think it's high time the rest of the world did the same. Christian charity, Melinda. That's what I'm talking about. That's what we need. And buy 2 Samuel 6's new album!

It's just terrific. I know your viewers will all enjoy it. I know I did."

"And it's time for a break. We'll be right back with you," the interviewer said. And the clip stopped.

The strategic part of Megan's brain wanted to celebrate. Yes, she could certainly show this to Kyle to explain why she didn't want him recording with David Marshall or hanging out with the man.

But another part of her just felt mortified. If she'd spoken up years ago, could she have stopped David from terrorizing other young women?

No. That wasn't on her. She didn't need to blame herself for his bad behavior. But maybe she could keep Kyle from getting caught up in this mess. She was fairly certain that Kyle would believe her when she told him exactly what David had done, but she wasn't looking forward to the conversation. He'd been drifting closer to this uncle of his, and whatever Kyle made of this information, it was going to hurt him.

Everything else was moving along nicely. She was confident she could find a place in LA. She'd even lined up an open-mic night down there in two weeks, and planned to play some of her own music. Which was frightening, but exciting. She already had a new job, and the confidence that she could hold it down. Her relationship with Brandon felt more and more real.

And with those parts of her life falling into place, somehow she believed that this David situation would solve itself. She didn't know exactly how, but it finally felt like the future was finally going to bring something good.

20

The band was in Phoenix, and so was Megan. It was the final concert of their US tour, and the night that David had set for their final confrontation.

If things went well, she'd get David to sign the release, and then she'd be able to breathe again. But she also had a cashier's check in her bag, just in case.

David Marshall.

Megan didn't even want to be in the same city as the man, but she would make herself do it this one last time.

Hopefully, it was only one last time.

When she arrived, the band was onstage for sound check. She missed performing so darn much that she couldn't watch; not until the crowd arrived ,and Greta was firmly in place, and it was clear that there was no room for her out there with the Sutter Boys.

Now, when she felt that itch to sing in front of a crowd, she'd do it for her own people. She'd build a career and find her own audience. It would be tiny, just like it had been at those first open mics, but eventually people would come to hear her. What she cared about was making music, and making that connection with the people who wanted to hear her voice singing her own music. Sure, an audience of thousands meant more in-your-face energy than a smaller one, but she'd still have the rapt attention of fans. And she was determined to cherish it.

At the greenroom she stopped in the doorway. Brandon was on the phone about twenty feet away, standing in the corner; and as always, he was dressed to perfection. The suit. A dark green tie (her absolute favorite on him). The bright white edge of cuffs below his coat sleeves. His clothes reminded her of the night she'd brought Keiko backstage in San Jose and she'd practically had to wipe drool away from Keiko's mouth.

Tonight was the first time she'd seen him in four weeks.

He leaned against an amp case, looking like he barely had the energy to deal with whatever emergency currently had him on a call.

Eventually he pocketed his phone, turned, and spotted her. His eyes crinkled with delight, and she couldn't cross the room fast enough. Four weeks was a long, long time.

He wrapped his arms around her, and she laid a cheek against his chest and finally was able to breathe deeply. Eucalyptus and citrus, freshly pressed wool and linen. And Brandon himself. Her whole body calmed, like his physical presence was a drug designed for her alone.

His lips touched her hair, and then he said, "It has definitely been way too long."

"I'm just so glad I'm here. That you're here."

In her bag, the check and the waiver felt like physical weights dragging at her shoulder. Which would she use? Which would she need?

She eased herself away. Her plan was to do this alone, as a strong woman who could deal with tough issues independently. But Brandon was right here, and maybe there was no reason to expose herself to all of David Marshall's ugliness on her own. Maybe sometimes being strong meant being smart; and right now, that meant having backup. Kind of what she'd done for Kyle onstage all those weeks. "Will you come with me to talk to him?"

"Of course. Whatever you need."

"Great. Just be there, by my side, and let me handle it. I think I just want to know you're there, and that you have my back."

His eyes shone, as though every time he saw her, he found more to admire. "Got it."

She asked, "Is he here yet?"

Brandon shook his head. "Any minute now. I've got a room set up where you can sort this through. So, what's your strategy?"

"I was thinking I would give him the waiver before the show so he can stew on it during the set. Then afterward I'll try to get him to sign. What do you think?"

Brandon already knew she would only pay off David if he refused to sign a waiver. He also knew that she'd sold her house to raise money in case she needed funds. Brandon had been incredulous when he had learned about that, but Megan reminded him that it was also her chance to move to LA, and to be in a city where he, Brandon, spent more of his time. Especially since she now had a job down there.

"Sounds like a plan," Brandon said.

She was too nervous to relax, so Megan paced. She planned out a little speech about the waiver, and made certain the right forms were at the top of her bag where she could get them easily.

Not long afterward there was a knock against the frame of the open greenroom door. A man poked his head in. "Excuse me, Mr. Thatch? David Marshall's here. He's waiting in the room you had set up."

"Perfect," Brandon said to the man in the doorway. In a

quieter voice, he turned to Megan and told her, "You've got this."

His words were like an energy drink for her confidence.

With that warming her from the inside out, she and Brandon followed the stagehand to the room where David waited. Just before she opened the door, she set her phone to record. Who knew what this man was going to say?

Megan couldn't imagine what the space was normally used for. There were no mirrors for makeup, no rods for hanging costumes, not enough space to store much of anything. But there was a cheap table and four folding chairs, two on each side.

David Marshall sat in one of the chairs, facing the door and flipping through his phone.

Megan put on the kind of confidence she had used to walk onto the stage and stepped up to the table. "David," she said.

He started to let his eyes roam down her body, but his eyes snapped up when Brandon stepped in behind her. Brandon folded his arms over his chest and took up a place against the wall near the door, looking for all the world like he was her bodyguard.

The door continued its spring-slowed movement until it closed with a soft click.

"Megan," David said. "And you must be the manager? Brandon Thatch, is that right?"

Brandon nodded, then looked to Megan. There was so much at stake for her, but this needed to happen. For herself, and for Kyle and the band.

She opened the scuffed portfolio she'd carried through all her years at her old firm. Legalese came naturally after working for lawyers most of her adult life; and she hoped the jargon might actually work in her favor, and convince Davide to take her proposal seriously. She pointed to the paper inside and said, "This is a waiver saying you hereby give up all rights under the contract dated March 3, 1990, and that I am free to write, create, perform, distribute, and otherwise profit from music at any time and without creating any debt to you or your band. It further waives any rights you may have to any music created by me on or after March 3, 1996, which we chose because it's five years after my last appearance with your band. This waiver of rights includes without limitation any music that I may have created with the Sutter Boys or any other musician or musicians, and any music that I may have inspired or contributed to in any way whatsoever."

Well, that had been a mouthful, but she'd gotten through it.

David barely glanced at the paper. He manspread himself further and asked, "Why on earth would I sign that?"

Taking a very deep breath, Megan said, "You might want to sign it so I don't go public and tell the world that a so-called Christian tried to rape me when I sang for you. While I was still a teenager, mind you. Your reputation says you've done the same thing again and again, and I'm going to find those women, and we're going to flood social media with stories you don't want the world to hear."

Brandon gave her a significant look, and she remembered her next line. "Besides which, I don't think you'll get Kyle performing on any of your albums once I let the world know that you tried to force me into a gang bang."

"Whoa, whoa, whoa," David said, with the assurance of a white man who clearly still thought he could bluster his way to the conclusion he wanted. "We both know that's not at all what happened. We were friends, all of us—you, me, and my brothers." He leaned forward, looking Megan up and down again. "And you were such a flirt—the clothes you wore, the way you'd smile at people—you must have known that men pick up on those kind of signals."

She felt Brandon come to attention behind her, but he kept

quiet. True to his word, he was trusting her to deal with this on her own.

What had he said that night back in Virginia Beach? That he would cheer her on when she just needed to know that someone was in her corner? It sure as hell was working now. She felt like she could headline a show knowing Brandon had her back.

She said, "What, so I'm responsible for you keeping your hands to yourself and your dick in your pants? I don't think so."

"You wanted it, and you know you did."

"If I'd 'wanted it,' I could have said 'yes.' But I said 'no,' and I had to say it about fifty million times because you weren't listening. You left bruises on my arm, you were holding me so tight."

At that, David actually smiled. "Well, now. I know for a fact that some women like that sort of thing. Being held down. Am I right?" David shot a glance at Brandon.

Brandon's nostrils flared. "Watch it," he said, then visibly calmed himself. She wasn't alone in finding David a creepy, entitled asshole, was she? "We've gone off the rails here. You're a married man, and you make your living playing in churches. I know you've fallen on your metaphorical sword before, because I've seen the interview you and your wife gave. I'm also pretty sure you don't want to do it again, and we believe we can establish a pattern of behavior. I'm sure you'd rather sign this perfectly reasonable release than find your name being smeared in public once we track down other women—and there've doubtless been others—and ask them to swear to statements explaining exactly how you treated them. So, sign. I'm not certain how many times your wife will stick up for a philanderer. And you, sir, are a prime example of one of those."

Megan took over. "What you did to me was a long time ago, and the statute of limitations may have expired. But if we find even one other woman with a valid claim, I would be delighted to help finance her legal team." She might not have a lot of money, but that was a cause worth spending money on.

David still looked almost smug. "I think you're forgetting something," he said. "I have a contract, and I can certainly afford to take you to court, draw this out for a while. That would be bad publicity for the Sutter Boys, wouldn't it, to have me claiming rights in your band's music. So your smear campaign would just look like underhand tactics. I have a signed agreement. You have rumors. Not a lot for you to stand on."

Megan said, "You make me sick. You think the Sutter Boys are going to just roll over and let you walk away with their intellectual property? That I helped create? Your damned contract has got to be unenforceable anyway."

David pushed back further, his arrogant spread-legged posture accentuating his potbelly. "But proving that takes time. So I'll just take you to court to enforce my contract, unless you'd care to give me that down payment we talked about."

The two hundred thousand dollars.

"Do you think I'm an idiot?" asked Megan. "If I pay you once, you'll think you have a cash cow forever."

"Now, don't paint me that color," he said. "Me and my band, we do very good work for the Lord. And with the sort of revenue stream that would come from equitably sharing your songwriting profits, 2 Samuel 6 would be able to put on even more shows. And we could do it as mission work, go into communities that really need the good word."

Megan was having a hard time believing this. "You really still believe that you're a good guy, don't you? You think it is completely okay to come on to me, and to other women, and then to try to blackmail me, and that somehow because you're pretending it's to do 'the Lord's work,' that somehow all this shit is okay? Un-fucking-believable."

"Watch your mouth, woman." His chair barked as he jerked to his feet, sounding like he was ready to slap her for swearing.

"I don't think so," she said, staring up at him.

Their eyes held for a long moment. A slow, odd smile crept over David's features. "Feisty," he said. "I like it."

Behind her, Brandon stepped closer, but Megan put her hand out to stop him. "I've got this."

"I can see that," Brandon said, that calm encouragement again working its magic.

"If she's got this, I'm sure you won't mind giving me and Megan here a minute or two alone." David was still holding her gaze, that creepy smile eating away at the confidence Brandon's words had given her.

Brandon looked to her, silently asking if she was okay with being alone with David. Her stomach clenched, but Megan said, "I'll be fine." He was hardly going to try to rape her again. And she'd survived once, so whatever he had up his sleeve, she'd cope. She didn't want to look weak in front of him.

"I'll be fine," she repeated, more firmly this time.

"Okay, then," Brandon said. He put out his hand as if for David to shake, then thought the better of it and folded his arms back over his chest. "We're going to let you think about this during the show. Afterward you'll be signing the waiver, sparing us all a pointless lawsuit, and leaving Megan the hell alone, because by then you'll have figured out there is no upside for you at all. Until then, enjoy the concert. Megan, I'll be right outside if you need me."

She gave Brandon one last nod as he slipped out the door, then turned to David. "What?" she asked him.

Oh, did she hate David Marshall's smile, all arrogance and slime.

He thumbed his phone again, spinning it so she could see. "So, I know you like to think of me as the bad guy, but remember, I'm not the only man in the world who enjoys women."

"What are you saying?"

"That I do know of someone else who might have a little problem if anyone checked out the ages of the women he hooked up with."

David held his phone closer.

And then Megan was looking at photos of Kyle with various girls as David flipped through images. Most of them were backstage, and while none of the photos were pornographic, all of them showed Kyle with his arms around a girl, or his nose in a woman's hair, with plenty of skin showing on each very young-looking and skimpily dressed woman. She even recognized a few of them.

"Where did you get these?"

David's smile grew wider. "Let's just say I'm supplementing the income of a few people on the band's crew, and they thought I might like these photos."

"But they don't prove anything."

"Maybe not. But I've got these ready to post during the concert with some interesting comments questioning the ages of these girls. Anonymously, of course. And I've got a journalist-friend of mine watching for these to go up today. So I'm sure Kyle wouldn't like to be tried in the press and over Twitter, with everyone and their mother getting upset about how young all these girls are, now would he? That won't help record sales, or his relationship with his recording company, now will it? And unlike me, Kyle doesn't have a loving wife standing by his side and swearing that her man would never, ever behave that way."

Megan's head started to pound. "I thought you were trying to milk a relationship with Kyle for your band, to record with him to up your sales, but instead you're trying to destroy his career?"

"No," David said. "I don't want to destroy his career. Not at all. I'd *like* to play nice, keep these photos nice and safe and private, but I still have this cash flow problem, and you can solve that for me, can't you?"

Now her stomach was churning in time with the pounding in her head. "So I give you the check and you don't post the stuff about Kyle?" This man in front of her was the scum of the earth, but she wouldn't let him poison Kyle's reputation. Kyle liked his women, but he'd told her—he'd told her over and over again that all the women he was with were legal and consenting, and she believed him. But the internet didn't work that way. The court of public opinion could turn on a dime, even if the allegations were completely false. Whatever she knew the truth to be, she would not let David Marshall drag Kyle's name through the mud; because once these things hit the Internet, it was just too damned hard for a man to claw his way back to a good reputation.

She wasn't going to get that waiver signed, was she? And David was going to keep kissing up to Kyle, pretending he was just a caring uncle so darned happy to finally be back in touch with his amazing nephew, all while holding these photos and allegations of statutory rape over Kyle's head. Disgusting.

David Marshall was going to claim rights to every song she ever wrote. Because if she tried to make him sign the waiver, he would smear Kyle's reputation. She could keep Kyle from suffering, and "all" she had to do was to pay off the scum-of-the-earth who had tried to rape her.

Fighting off nausea, she reached for the envelope she'd tucked behind the waiver—the waiver that would have set her free.

She pulled it and pushed it across the table. At least her hand didn't shake.

He opened the envelope, checked the dollar amount on the check inside, and gave her his greasiest smile as he tucked it into his wallet. "Thank you," David said. "Very generous of you, to support the Lord's work like this."

She wanted to throw up.

"Now," David said. "I think it's about time we enjoyed the show."

He pulled open the door and disappeared down the hallway.

Brandon poked his head into the room, turned to watch David walking away, then looked back at her. "Megan?" he asked. "What exactly happened in here?"

Her voice didn't even sound like her own. "I gave him the check."

"What? You actually brought a cashier's check with you?" Brandon's voice rang loud in her ears.

She nodded, then cradled her head in her hands, still seated, elbows propped on the table.

"How could you have done that? Did he at least sign the waiver?"

"No."

Brandon looked back down the hallway, still standing in the door he was holding open. "Why on earth? You had a plan. You didn't need to do that! You would win any lawsuit about that old contract, and we've got to have deeper pockets than he does."

"He was going to blow up the Internet. He has photos of Kyle with all his damn women, and is planning to insinuate that a lot of them were underage. Kyle's reputation would have been lost."

"Oh, for fuck's sake," Brandon said. "No one is going to pay attention to a has-been Christian rocker with his own sexual harassment problems."

"He said he's got a journalist teed up."

"Bullshit!"

"Jesus, Brandon! Calm down."

"Calm down? You just gave a con artist two hundred thousand dollars, and you want me to calm down? What were you thinking?"

That made her look up. "I don't know! That I couldn't ruin Kyle's life?"

He let the door close a bit further. Their voices must be carrying everywhere up and down that hallway. "I thought you had a plan, Megan. I know you want the best for Kyle, but looking out for his professional reputation is my job, and I would *never* let him go down for something as unfounded as this. And now you're setting yourself up for a lawsuit to try to get out of this old contract, and David's got the jump on you on the reputation thing, so anything you try to post about him is going to look like sour grapes. It won't hold water."

"I know that! Are you just trying to make me feel like shit? Because you're doing a great job of it." And she'd wanted to build a relationship with this man? What the hell *had* she been thinking?

He took a heaving breath. The way his chest was rising and falling, it looked like he'd been out for a run, not standing guard in a corridor backstage at a concert.

"I'm sorry," he said. "I shouldn't have raised my voice. But I'm gonna need some time to regroup, here. Show's starting soon. We should get over there."

She nodded.

This wasn't the way she'd wanted to spend these last few minutes before the final show of this tour.

At least she didn't have to perform. That would've been too much.

21

M egan and Brandon stood close together just off the stage, but the air between them was frosty with anger. And pain.

Why the hell couldn't Brandon understand that she hadn't wanted to pay off David, but she'd had no choice? Brandon shouldn't be mad at her for protecting Kyle. They should both be supporting Kyle, not fighting because David had put Megan into an impossible position.

At least that jerk was with the rest of the VIP ticket holders on the opposite side of the stage, corralled behind a rope where the people who'd actually bought their tickets were dancing and singing along.

Dammit, this was the last show. She could stew and be pissed at David and Brandon (and herself), or she could loosen up and do what she'd come to do: enjoy herself.

So she shook off that nasty feeling of being at David's mercy and tried to have fun. And the more she danced and sang along, the better she felt. Music did that for her, just made everything better. It was far more fun to get caught up in the concert vibe than to stress about giving away—shit!—two hundred thousand dollars of her own money.

Shit. That was a fortune.

Shit.

She was an idiot, wasn't she?

Nope. Not going there, not now.

She focused on the music, singing and enjoying the off-mic freedom to create new lines now that Greta was handling the bread and butter of the harmony.

She alternated between a roiling stomach and the high of cutting loose, back and forth, like her mood was having some kind of pre-menopausal hot flash.

It was odd to be here, staring at the band and taking in the set but knowing she hadn't even said hello to any of them. She'd lived with them for weeks on a cramped bus, and tonight she was observing them wearing their on-stage personas; they were focusing all their energy outward, toward the audience.

Which meant that the moment Li-Fang caught her eye was lovely, because he grinned outright to see her singing along.

Li-Fang caught Charlotte's attention, and then Zane and Theo's, and soon each of them were turning her way as well. Even Kyle gave her a quick nod in the middle of one of their songs, and then a full-on smile at the end of the number.

Especially after her encounter with David, it felt incredibly reassuring to be welcomed back, even if it was just smiles from the stage, or a slight twang to a bass line that Theo knew she'd laugh at.

It helped her feel better, even though Brandon was still mad at her, all rigid attention at her side.

It was so strange to not be on mic. She still felt the energy coming off the crowd, but she couldn't tap into it the way she had as a performer.

Greta was nailing the show, which was good. She held her own, even on the rare duet. Yes, she was still a little too unwilling to step in and go with the flow, but maybe that was more of the normal pattern. Kyle could fire a backup singer pretty much at will if they stepped out of line and ruffled his ego, but Megan hadn't worried about that.

Toward the end of the show, Kyle leaned into his mic and said, "Now I know we all love the lovely Greta Marsten belting out those backing vocals. That's right, give it up for Greta." He smiled back at the blond and waited for the applause and hoots to die down. "But some of you know that earlier on the tour, my own mom, the amazing Megan Gamble, was actually out here with us, strutting her stuff and singing like the star she was born to be."

A voice yelled out. "Mrs. M!"

Brandon elbowed Megan. "They remember you. Get ready."

"Wait, what?" asked Megan, staring at Kyle. Was he going to do what she thought he was going to do?

"Anyhow," Kyle said to the audience. "This next song not only featured Mom's voice; it's a number she helped us write. And I was hoping you all could talk her into singing it with me again. As most of you know, tonight is the final show of the tour,"—roars and cheers erupted from the crowd—"and so I'd like to go out with something special. Mom, what do you say?"

She was about to walk out onto the stage when, from the front of the rope line, David made a hat-tipping gesture in her direction. And now he almost certainly had a record of Kyle's words, admitting that Megan was a co-writer on the song. She was never going to get out from under that damn contract, was she? And even though she'd paid him already, blackmail didn't work as a one-and-done. He would be back time and time again. Which would mean that David could extort royalties from her for a song that she hadn't yet made money on, because while the Sutter Boys had given her a writing credit, it was going to be a very long time before the royalty stream trickled all the way down to her.

At least she had her own conversation with David on tape, and hadn't he basically admitted that he'd tried to force her to have sex? So now she had at least a bit of leverage.

"Mom? Come on out!"

Kyle's voice brought her mind back to the concert stage. Everything in her life was a mess except this.

She knew how to perform.

So Megan handed Brandon her portfolio and walked onto the stage like she was the goddamned queen of the world.

A stage tech had moved Greta's mic downstage for Megan, setting it up side-by-side with Kyle's. Greta headed toward the VIP area across from where Brandon stood. For a moment, it seemed like Greta hesitated as she neared the wings, but that might have been Megan's imagination.

Megan concentrated on the crowd, giving them a smile and a wave. "Hello, Phoenix! Kyle here is giving me a chance to be reborn as a singer, so Phoenix is a mighty appropriate city, don't you think?"

The crowd roared back, and Kyle shot her a look of approval, like her words had just done him proud. She'd been a performer since before he'd even been conceived, and maybe he should remember that he was damn good at what he did in part because of her genes and the way she'd raised him.

Zane started the count behind her, and before she knew it, she and Kyle were flying through the lyrics, his hands fast and sure on his guitar, hers wrapped around the head of her mic. She wasn't in stage makeup or wardrobe, but the audience didn't seem to mind. This was the real Megan, singing her heart out next to her son.

And damn, did it feel good—the affection coming off of the audience! Even better, if possible, than when she'd been on tour. Because then she'd been the band's paid backup singer.

On their dime. Conforming to their stylists' notions of what she was supposed to look like. Trying to be the vocalist Kyle told her he needed.

But tonight, she was Megan. Megan Gamble herself, and she held her own singing next to one of the most popular vocalists recording today. Her own boy, the man right beside her on this stage.

Between verses, she shot a wide smile at Kyle. He not only returned her grin, but actually took a hand off of his guitar to give her a salute. Now that? That felt really good.

She'd come a long, long way since her first night onstage; since her first surprise duet; even since her last official show on tour.

During that first duet, the crowd had been with her. But tonight? She owned it. Absolutely everyone in the massive arena was hanging on each note she sang. All those eyes were on her, and all those ears were straining to catch words she had created. Amazing.

When the number was over, they were a mass of waving arms and enthusiastic voices. Through the din, she heard a chant take hold: "Mrs. M! Mrs. M!"

She laughed from the joy of it, and waved at them one more time. "Thank you, Phoenix! And thanks, Kyle, for letting me sing with you one last time. Folks, enjoy the rest of the show. I know from experience that you won't be disappointed!"

She let the stage tech reposition the mic she'd been using, and retreated toward Brandon.

Brandon picked her up off of her feet like he couldn't help it. "Incredible," he said, kissing her before setting her down. "I was out of line before. We'll talk after the show. Okay?"

She nodded, high from the performance and relieved that she and Brandon should be able to clear the air soon.

And then Greta missed her cue. She was almost a full measure late when she finally opened up her voice.

Megan and Brandon both turned toward the stage. Greta wobbled on her heels for a moment, like she'd either managed to get drunk during the single song Megan had covered, or like she'd suffered a massive shock. The band was about four songs from the end of the set, so there wasn't much for her to get through.

Still.

"What's going on?" asked Megan, turning to Brandon. "Does she look okay to you?"

His eyes, too, were now glued to the stage. "No. She's definitely pale. Like something freaked her out."

"Yeah, and look what that 'something' is." Megan gestured between Greta and the VIP section, where the young woman's gaze kept straying to one David Marshall.

Brandon followed the gesture, then turned back to Megan. "Wow. Did not see that coming."

Feeling uneasy, they waited out the rest of the set. What connection could Greta have with David Marshall?

Eventually Megan got caught up again in the energy of the show. The tour was minutes from being over, and then the band would be moving on to new projects.

Well, first they would head to their homes and collapse; but with the new material they'd been writing, they'd want to get into the studio soon. So, not much of a hiatus.

But for right now? This exact moment? This moment was for fireworks from Li-Fang's guitar and violin. Chest-pounding bass flying from Theo's fingers. Grace notes and unexpected texture from Charlotte's keyboards. Solid rhythm and musical punctuation from Zane.

And Kyle's voice. Always Kyle's voice, and his body moving to the music, and his soul shining through his voice and his body, and his joy and passion pouring from him, buzzing into the atmosphere every single moment he was on stage.

It took her breath away, even now, even after performing

with him for weeks, to realize that this powerhouse was the man her little boy had become. That the seeds of all this had been nascent in all those moments of his childhood that she had cherished.

"Why are you standing still?" Megan shrieked at Brandon. "Move, man! This music means you've gotta dance!"

And for the seventeen minutes left in the show, that's what they did.

22

While the audience's final cheers were still in the air, Greta stormed off the stage and slapped David Marshall full in the face.

"What the hell?" asked Megan, looking at Brandon, her eyebrows bounding up to her hairline. They darted across the stage together.

As they approached, David rubbed his jaw and said, "Good Lord, woman, what did I do to deserve that?"

Greta folded her arms across her chest. "You know exactly what you did, you perverted bastard. I never should have taken that gig working for you and your brothers. In case you were wondering, no, I haven't changed my mind about you, your brothers, or the prospects of a 'private party' for the four of us."

"Wait," Megan said. "He propositioned you, too?"

Greta turned to Megan. "If you can even call it that. He just seems to think he's so irresistible that any woman would be into sleeping with him, especially to keep their place on his band's payroll. And he sure as hell doesn't seem to understand that I said 'No!' when he asked if I wanted to 'get it on' with

David here and his brothers. But hold on, what do you mean, 'too?'"

"He pulled the exact same thing on me when I was in my twenties," Megan said. "Except in my case, I left with bruises on my arm."

"Damn, girl. You get a police report or anything?"

Megan shook her head. "I should have, but no. I never did. I just didn't think that way back then."

Brandon was in damage-control mode, guiding David and the two women away from the rest of the VIP crowd, but Greta continued talking to Megan. "Why the hell didn't you? Press charges, I mean."

Despite Brandon's efforts to get them off to the side, their voices carried, which led Kyle their way. "Hey, Uncle David. Press charges about what, Mom?"

"Nothing," Megan said.

"Attempted rape," Greta said, and the two women looked at each other again. Greta should never have had to go through that. No woman should.

Kyle's eyes went wide. "Mom?"

Now what should she do? "Kyle, can I speak to you privately?" Not that there was much privacy with the VIP crowd to one side, the band grabbing drinks to the other, and roadies everywhere in between starting their final load out.

Kyle stepped slightly to the side, pulling Megan in close so he could speak more quietly. "Uncle David tried to *rape* you?"

When she nodded, he shook his head like he was trying to clear it, then put his hands over his face, wiping them down to reveal wide-open and glistening eyes. "He tried to rape *you*? Are you okay? Were you okay? Jeez, how the hell didn't I know this?"

"I didn't want to burden you. It happened before you were even born. And I didn't think it mattered anymore."

"Of course it matters! You're my mom! No one treats you like that!"

Kyle looked away, then back at her. "Now I'm practically committed to recording with him! That ain't happening, that's for damned sure." Kyle raised his hands again, this time pressing the tips of his fingers against his temples.

"Hey," she said. "It's not your fault. It was years and years ago."

"That doesn't exactly help. And then—shit!—then when he got in touch with me and you saw us jamming in my hotel room, no wonder you freaked. Damned abuser! I wish I'd never wasted a minute on him."

This was why she'd never told him. Because she must have known how much it would hurt him to find out.

But it was in the open now. And while she didn't exactly feel great right in this moment, later she'd feel relieved. This secret had been festering forever, and now that Kyle knew, maybe she could fully heal.

She squeezed Kyle's hand, then dropped it. Her voice was quiet, but she didn't think it was shaking. "I should have told you, but it's harder to talk about than you could possibly imagine. I never told anyone at all until about a month ago. I thought it was one of those creepy things women had to put up with, because back in the day, that's pretty much how it worked."

Kyle looked over his shoulder at where Brandon was apparently making it clear that David Marshall shouldn't be going anywhere until they got to the bottom of things.

"Well, that's not the way it works anymore, not around me and my band," Kyle said. "We're going to go over there and I'm going to tell that hypocritical piece of filth that I'm done with him, and that he's out of our lives."

"Well," Megan said. "There's a problem with that. Two problems, actually. There's an old contract hanging around from when I sang for his band, and David says he'll tie us up in court to enforce it, because it gives him rights in any music I write. Including stuff like the duet with you." She didn't want to even look at Kyle, she was so ashamed of that stupid legal landmine.

"Well, that's bullshit. That can't be legal, and, besides!—you and Greta both have stories to tell that should shut him up fast."

"But I'm not going to tell mine, and we need to get Greta to stay quiet, too."

"Why the hell would we do that? It just encourages that pathetic excuse for a man to keep on doing the same thing. The bastard." Kyle looked like he was about to completely lose his shit.

"We can't talk because David's got a bunch of photos of you and some of the groupies you've been seen with. He's going to release them and claim that a bunch of them were underage. And lots of people are going to believe it and you're going to be digging yourself out of a hole for years. I told him I'd keep quiet, because I couldn't stand the thought of it hurting you."

"Oh, Mom, you wonderful, crazy woman." He shook his head again, and this time there actually was a tear glistening in the corner of his eye. "Seriously, you would do that to protect me?"

She nodded.

"Well, I appreciate it and all, but no. Just no. It's not going down like that." Kyle broke away and strode across to where David, Brandon, and Greta stood—Greta with her hands on her hips, clearly explaining things to David in no uncertain terms.

Megan tried to get in front of Kyle, feeling that this was her battle, not his; but Kyle shook his head at her. "Mom, I know this is mostly your business, but part of it is mine; and I want to make a couple of things really clear to this piece-of-shit human being." He turned to face his uncle. "David, you can publish whatever BS you want about me. I truly don't care, because I don't sleep with underage women. Never have, and never will. But you, sir, seem to be exactly the kind of pervert who would."

Greta said, "I was about two weeks past my eighteenth birthday when he propositioned me. And I here I was, thinking I was getting a big break, singing with a nice Christian band for my first touring job."

"Now, now, now, everybody," David said. "No need to get all excited. Kyle and me, we both know that there's no forcing going on with these women after shows." David waved in the direction of the VIP crowd, where most of the women were indeed very, very interested in looking at Kyle.

"Bullshit," Megan said. "You left bruises on my arms. If that's not force, I don't know what is."

"That was twenty years ago. And you can't prove anything." David wasn't giving up.

"Well," said Megan. "I got you on tape before the concert, when you basically admitted to it. So I'm pretty sure I can."

"And," Greta said. "I sure as hell would give a sworn statement about how creepy this guy is. Hell, I'll do an interview, post something. You name it and I'm in."

Especially since watching that interview Brandon had sent to her, Megan had known that David had treated other women the same way he'd treated her. But with Greta standing right in front of her, taking Megan's side, and willing to help face down David; Megan truly began to understand that she wasn't alone. "You'd do that?"

Greta nodded. "Hells to the yes, I would. People need to know what kind of man he really is."

Brandon spoke quietly to Megan. "Don't forget...."

She interrupted. "The waiver, I know. And I'm getting back that check, that's for damned sure. Will you hand me my portfolio?"

He put it in her hands, and she flipped it open. "David, perhaps you'd like to sign here? Or are you going to keep holding that unenforceable contract over my head, so I'll have the pleasure of taking you to court?"

David started to pale, his skin looking loose over the bones of his face. "I can still post what I've got on Kyle."

Megan said, "He's already told you he doesn't care."

She and Kyle exchanged a glance, and Kyle gave David a withering stare. "Really, man. Post away. I don't give a shit because I don't sleep with underage girls."

"Which means you might as well save yourself the effort of posting. Because it isn't going to buy you anything. And I'll take my check back, thank you very much. I don't owe you a dime for song royalties, and I never did. So the only possible reason for you to cash this check is because you're willing to admit that you planned to slander Kyle's name if I didn't pay you off. Or maybe you want the world to know that you have a side-business in extortion?" Megan put out her hand and waited, with Brandon close by her side.

Finally, David reached into his jacket pocket and handed Megan the envelope. She peeked inside to confirm that the check was still there, then tucked it into her portfolio and took the pen from its holder.

She tried not to hold her breath, but David did what she needed him to do. He took the pen and dragged it across the signature line while she held open the leather case.

And Megan could breathe again.

Kyle shook his head and stared at David. "You were seriously trying to use a twenty-year-old, completely over-broad contract, to weasel your way into our revenue stream? That's pretty damn ballsy of you."

"It's where he keeps his brain," Greta said.

Megan laughed at that, and turned to give Greta a fist bump.

Theo and Li-Fang, who had been chatting with fans a few feet away, finally picked up on the tension. Which made seven pairs of rather hostile eyes focused on David.

"'Sup?" asked Theo.

Kyle answered. "Not much. But guys, you remember my Uncle David? Well, say hello and then say goodbye. He was just leaving."

The longer this little conversation went on, the less impressive David seemed. In that tiny room before the concert, David had acted like he ruled the world. Now he looked like a has-been suffering a serious defeat.

Li-Fang said, "Okay, there's a story there that you're going to tell us all; but right now, I think we have a meet-and-greet to get to."

Greta threw an arm around Megan's shoulder. "Good work, Kyle's Mom. About time music got rid of another jerk. Too bad you and I weren't on tour at the same time. We might have had a real good time."

Kyle's face went through an interesting contortion. "Now that is a scary thought: Mom and Greta out on the town together."

Brandon waved over one of the road crew, who left the amp he had been unplugging and came over to the group.

"Can I help you with something?" the roadie asked.

"Yes," Brandon said. "Mr. Marshall here was just leaving. Can you see him out?"

The roadie looked back and forth between David and the rest of the group. "Sure thing, boss." Turning to David, he continued, "If you'll follow me?" The roadie threw back his shoulders like a bar bouncer, and Megan had to smile.

"What are you all waiting for?" Brandon asked the band. "Get!" He shooed them in the direction of the fans.

Kyle squeezed her hand. "Great work, Mom. Li, Theo, Greta

—meet-and-greet time. I want to put this part of the evening in the bag, then go celebrate."

As they left, Li-Fang turned to give Megan two thumbs up. Then he pointed at her with both hands. "Great job, tonight, Mrs. M! Always love having you on our stage."

"Back at you," called Megan.

"So," said Brandon, once the band was out of earshot. "You ready to get out of here?"

"I don't have a hotel reservation," she said.

"Hmm," Brandon said, wrapping an arm around her waist. "Wonder what we can do about that? Do you think we should check my room, see if the bed might be big enough to share?"

She nodded. "Yeah. That sounds like a perfect plan to me."

Laughing, he turned her into his body. She raised her eyes and cupped his face with her hands. "I have one more thing I have to do before we hit the road," she said.

"What's that?" His eyes had those wonderful smile lines playing at their corners.

"This," she said, and stretched up to kiss her man.

EPILOGUE

"Hello, Culver City!"

Maybe she was overdoing it a little bit, calling out with the classic big-arena greeting from the tiny raised platform in the corner of the bar. There might be all of twenty people in the building; but for a place this size, that wasn't too bad for a Wednesday night.

Megan pulled a chord from the strings of her acoustic and spoke again. "I hope you'll all be gentle on me for my first solo show ever." A few people chuckled. And yes, she'd done a good handful of open mics, but tonight she was expected to provide a solid forty-five minutes of music. On her own. "I know, I know. Maybe a little late in life for a career switch, but if you'll indulge me, I'm sure we're going to have a real good time. This first number's an oldie, which means most of you probably weren't born when it was written. But my mom used to crank this one up and sing along, so maybe you'd like to do the same."

She pulled harder on the guitar strings, sounding a few driving chords. In the little table just to her right, Keiko raised her hands over her head, clapping and hooting. She had flown down from the Bay Area just for the show, and sat with Megan's new boss, Glen, bonding over the horrors of billable hours.

Leaning into the mic, Megan dove into "Girls Just Wanna Have Fun." She wanted to get the crowd dancing in their seats, at least. A happy crowd was an enthusiastic crowd.

She'd been in LA for five months now, and Brandon had been in town seven times—but who was counting? He was talking about moving into her condo with her, selling his own place in LA. She thought they should hold out for something a bit larger, but the general plan sure had her stamp of approval.

The manager here had been pretty cool, willing to give her a mid-week slot on the strength of a brief audition, even if she didn't have anything to put out on a merch table.

It was nothing like the crowd for a Sutter Boys concert, but it fed the beast within her—the one that needed to be onstage and get a crowd onto their feet. She'd rediscovered her need to perform, not to mention rekindled her love of writing and making music—and it was all because of the tour. Music fed her in so many ways, evening out the lows of settling into a new life in a new city, letting her express the joys of her triumphs. It just made everything more alive.

Not only had she been spending lots of quality time with her guitar in her condo, but she'd been recording a bit, as well. The Sutter Boys had been in the studio off and on since wrapping the tour, and her voice was on more than one of their new tracks, including that duet with Kyle.

She sang out to the crowd, getting to the end of her final chorus of "Girls Just Wanna Have Fun," and shook her head, incredulous, at the thought of her voice on a Sutter Boys album. That was incredible. Who would have thought that a single mom could have a voice that would be heard by hundreds of thousands of people?

"Thank you," Megan called as she wrapped the first number. She launched right into her second, thinking about how the Sutter Boys would be leaving soon for some of the summer festivals. After that, Brandon was organizing a longer tour which would start after the next album dropped. Meanwhile, Megan had her own career to think about.

A few more people walked in during her second song. The bar manager had warned her that things would be pretty thin at the beginning, but she'd been right that people would continue to drift in. The space was filling up nicely.

She took them through some Fleetwood Mac and some Heart, some early Beyonce and even a Fiona Apple number. In between covers, Megan played five different originals, just to see how they'd go over. Keiko filmed those. Before the show, she'd said, "We're gonna need some stuff for your YouTube Channel."

Brandon wasn't around, but Megan wondered if Kyle would make it. She'd texted him about the show, but he did live in San Francisco. A short flight, but still—he was always so busy, that she told herself it would be better for him if he just used the time to rest and recharge. And when she was truly honest with herself, she acknowledged how much it would mean to her if he actually did make the effort. But she wouldn't beg. She didn't want to put that sort of pressure on him. At least he responded to texts now. Their relationship was so much better these days. Since the tour, she felt like she'd gotten her son back.

She wrapped up another song, transitioning directly into the opening chords of a number by Of Monsters and Men called "Little Talks." Gotta keep the music going, she knew, or the crowd would take it as a signal to stand up, head to the bar, take a bathroom break. Ignore her. So she kept the chords coming and spoke over the music. "This next number is traditionally a duet, but I'm hoping you'll enjoy my version, too."

To her surprise, someone began tuning a second guitar off to her left. An amp blocked her view of that corner of the stage, so she couldn't see the musician. But the voice that spoke from the shadows was one she knew well. "I'd be happy to grab the other part if you'd like."

Enthusiastic applause broke out when Kyle joined her on stage. He pulled a stool forward from the back wall, and someone from the bar set a mic in front of him. "Assuming these good folks don't mind? I was thinking it was about time I backed you up for a change."

He shot the crowd the grin that made all the women at his shows go wild; the women in the little Culver City bar all but climbed onto the stage with them.

"Yup," Megan said, unable to stop the smile spreading across her own face. "About time."

Kyle leaned over and kissed her on the cheek. "Hey, Mom. Gotta say, that guitar looks good on you." Stage banter came out of his mouth like it was his job. Because it was.

"What are you doing here?" she asked.

"Just thought it'd be fun to relax a bit, play some tunes with you. These good folks seem to think it'd be a good idea. Am I right?" He used his arm to sweep across the front of the stage, indicating the whole room, and the crowd clapped and hooted their approval. "And really, after you came on tour for me, I wanted to be here for you, too."

"Okay, then," she said, and began to sing.

She and Kyle played three more numbers together, including an acoustic version of one of the Sutter Boys hits.

Even when she'd done duets with Kyle on tour, it had never felt like this. Because tonight she really was the star of the show. Kyle was deferential and quieter, musically. Instead of upstaging her, he made her feel like she deserved to own this stage, and they each sang and played the better for it. But she also didn't feel like she was relying on him for her confidence; rather, that he was just showing her she could claim this kind of stage presence every time she stood in front of an audience.

Because she was good at this. Her son was a rock star, goddammit, and that apple fell from her tree.

The two of them thanked the crowd one last time, and the lights dimmed. Since she'd started, the bar had gotten crowded. Kyle was going to end up signing autographs for a good twenty minutes, and she wasn't going to get anywhere near him with this crowd. So much for chatting during his spontaneous visit.

The manager of the bar stepped over, a heavily pierced and tattooed young woman named Prahbati who wore her sari like it was a pair of blue jeans. Just comfortable stuff to work in, her body language said. Prahbati jerked her chin in Kyle's direction. "I was already going to offer you a regular slot, but whenever you want to bring that guy with you, I'll bump another act. Your boy here is good for business."

"Yup. About sums it up, doesn't it? But are you serious? You'd like me here more often?"

"Absolutely. The crowd loved you, even before Kyle got here. But let's rescue him, shall we?"

Megan nodded, and the manager began to separate Kyle from the crowd, leading him to the tiny break room behind the bar where Megan had stashed her guitar case. She wondered where Kyle's security was. On tour, he'd always had a couple of burly guys around to handle situations like this one.

Ah, one of the familiar guards was leaning against the wall of the venue, pushing away to follow Kyle and the manager to the break room. And next to the guard was Brandon.

Brandon was here!

She left her guitar on the stand on stage, then headed toward the man in the perfect business suit. It took some time to reach him, because more people than she'd expected stopped her to tell her what a great set that had been. A couple even asked her where she'd be playing next. It was nothing like what Kyle had to deal with, but damn! These people really liked her stuff!

Finally Brandon's arms were around her.

When she stepped back, she brushed her hair back out of her face and tried to be chill. "What's a guy like you doing in a place like this?" He wasn't even supposed to be in town. But she was damned glad that he was.

Brandon propped his foot back against the wall in the classic pose of a cowboy leaning back and relaxing; but his feet were in polished leather shoes, not worn boots. He looked every inch the successful businessman, but she knew how much more he was than a pretty face and a pretty body. He was her guy.

"What am I doing? I suppose mainly apologizing for being late. How'd the first part go?"

"Great, I think. I didn't expect you at all! When did you get in?"

"About two hours ago. I dropped my bag off at your place, then headed here. I hoped you wouldn't mind a bit of a surprise."

"Not at all." She kissed him again, and actually forgot the crowd for a moment, so lost in the feeling of his lips and his arms, the firm strength of his back under his coat.

She pulled back, realizing that probably hadn't been as "safe for work" as it should have been, and finally got a good look at him. His beard was freshly trimmed, and his eyes shone at her, their green dark in the dim light of the bar. His face softened the tiniest amount, the planes of his cheeks less chiseled. More relaxed than the face he showed the world. Like he didn't have to hold it all together for her. Like she was a safe place. Which was exactly what she wanted to be for him.

Around them was the chaos of a bar, the frenzy of fans trying to climb all over themselves to get to Kyle. And then here. This spot. The eye of a hurricane. Home was right here.

She asked, "How long are you in town?"

"Just a couple of nights. Or maybe I can move some things around."

She put her hand on the smooth lapel of his jacket, let the tip of one finger move onto the cotton of his shirt, where she could feel the warmth of his skin. "Hmm. Could you, now?"

His own hand covered hers, and he used it to press both their hands against his chest. She moved another half inch closer, and let the length of her thigh settle against his.

Her whole body shuddered.

With her hand on his chest, she felt the vibration of his voice as he spoke. "If I had a reason to stick around, I could."

Tilting her face up to look into his eyes, she said, "What kind of reason?"

"Well, maybe the chance to do this for a bit longer."

His lips touched hers, and she closed her eyes, all her attention on the sensation of lips touching and sliding, the hint of teeth, the brush of tongue.

She turned her head to rest against his chest—so, so content to just *be*. So cherished.

"Excuse me, Megan?" The bar manager, Prahbati, appeared next to them, checking out Brandon and giving Megan the hint of an approving smile. A lotus flower tattoo on her shoulder caught Megan's eye, and the scrollwork that curved onto her upper arm. "I can see you're a bit distracted at the moment. Understandable; but when you have a chance, let's talk about your cut from the door."

"Okay," Megan said, stepping to Brandon's side and tucking herself under his arm. "But maybe Brandon could sit in with us? Music contracts are sort of his thing."

He nodded. "I'd be happy to tag along if you'd like."

"Fine with me," said Prahbati.

Megan willed herself not to blush and turned to the younger woman. "Lead the way."

She brought them back to the break room, where Kyle was lazing on a tiny couch.

Prahbati said, "I'll send you a full report tomorrow, but I've got your $250 now. If you've got time and want to stick around, I'm pretty sure you'll be earning out a bit on your 80/20, but I won't have that figured out until pretty late. So if you want to get out of here, I'll get you the numbers tomorrow. Text me if you agree with them, and then I'll just Venmo you, yeah?"

"Works for me."

Prahbati crossed to the to corner of the room, kneeling to pull open a cardboard box and poke around inside. "I've got some inventory to get through, but you're welcome to use the room for as long as you'd like."

Kyle patted the space next to him on the couch, inviting Megan to sit. "Nice work, Mom. I think I earned about thirty-seven dollars for my first paying gig. Earning out? That's damned impressive!"

"You'd better not be teasing me," she said, collapsing next to him and poking him in the side.

"Hey," he said, swatting her hand away from his side. "Not kidding at all. Seriously. Well done."

She hadn't seen him in weeks, and he looked good. More rested than he'd been on tour. "You probably earn more than that selling guitar picks with the band's name on them."

"Naw," Brandon said from the barstool next to the couch. "We give those away."

"Stop," she said, shaking her finger at Brandon until he took her hand and held it.

Keeping Brandon's hand in her own, she turned back to face Kyle when he started speaking. "Seriously, Mom. You did great tonight. I love singing with you. Our voices? They really work. And I was thinking, whenever you get around to recording your own stuff, let me know. I'd love to sing some backup for you, lay down one of the guitar tracks. Anything you need."

She tried to keep her jaw off of the floor and checked in with Brandon. "Can he do that?"

"He sure can. No contractual problems at all."

"Kyle, I'd be honored." Beyond honored, actually. And to think they'd gone from barely speaking to this: Kyle asking to lay down tracks for her own music.

"Don't be ridiculous," Kyle said. "Just doing my mom a favor. It's not like I can help around the house and fix shit there. Let me do what I do best, okay?"

"Okay then. Since you insist." Talking more to herself than to either of the men, she continued. "I can't believe I just played a show on my own—until Kyle showed up, that is. It's incredible, isn't it—playing for a crowd, hearing them react? Maybe someday I'll be able to quit my day job!" She was still working for Glen, and finalizing her list of law schools.

"I get it," said Kyle. "Caught the bug bad, haven't you? And hey, did I see Auntie Keiko out there?"

"Yep, she's here. Probably had to take off early to get home, though. I think she has an early flight tomorrow."

She stood and tucked herself under Brandon's arm, right where she belonged.

Kyle put his hands up in front of his face like he was frightened. He peeked between two fingers, then hid his eyes again. "Speaking of history that apparently I know nothing about, let's just say that while I think you're cute together, I literally want to know nothing more about what's going on here." Keeping one hand over his eyes, Kyle waved the other hand back and forth between Megan and Brandon.

Megan flicked a bar coaster at her son. "Wise guy. Don't worry. I'm not planning on kissing and telling."

"Oh, my God. Just stop with the TMI!"

There was one more thing she wanted to follow up on. "So, Kyle, did you ever connect with your grandmother?"

His face went rather blank. "Yeah."

After the showdown with David, Megan had reached out to Paul, Jason's youngest remaining brother—the one who had stayed far in the background, and who had actually seemed like a pretty decent guy. She'd explained that, while she never wanted any contact with David, she did feel badly that Kyle had never met his grandmother.

Kyle said, "Uncle Paul set something up for me. I visited last week. Mom, she's in a memory care unit. She looked at me and called me Jason."

Megan's hand flew to her mouth. "Oh, Kyle." It was suddenly hard to swallow.

Brandon moved his hand smoothly up and down her arm, then gave it a squeeze.

"What did you say?" she asked.

Kyle just looked at her. "I called her Mom and pretended to be my dad—you know, like I loved surfing and everything. When she wanted to talk Bible verses and stuff, I got kinda lost, but I just faked it and hoped for the best."

"I'm sure you made her very happy."

It was as if Prahbati and Brandon weren't even in the room.

Kyle looked down at his hands, then back at Megan. "Well, I told her I'd be back. Figured she deserves that, right? She's just a little old lady who can't remember things well. So if I can make her believe my dad is still around, where's the harm in that?"

"Nowhere," Megan said. "No harm at all." She bit her lip, wondering if it was already time to say her goodbyes to Kyle. She'd been so used to seeing him every day on tour, and she'd missed him in the months since. It was hard to let him go all over again. "How long are you down here for?"

"A few days. Let's grab dinner or something while I'm here."

Kyle gestured toward Brandon. "You can bring this guy along. If you need to."

Of course she would jump at the chance, but she tried to play it cool. "Generous, aren't you? Willing to spend time with your own manager."

"That's me," Kyle said. "Mr. Generosity."

"All right then, Mr. Generosity. Let's get out of here and let Prahbati finish her work in peace."

"Sounds good."

Brandon gave her side a firm squeeze, and Kyle stood to give her a hug goodnight before she and Brandon headed out.

On the other side of the small room, Prahbati had closed up the boxes and leafed through a stack of bar tabs. Kyle hung back, his eyes straying over Prahbati's casual style. The tats. The sari. The lush hair in its long, dark braid.

Megan shook her head. In a low voice she said, "What do you want to bet that Kyle is down here some other night trying out new material?"

Brandon rolled his eyes and laughed quietly. They were only a few steps away from the break room. "Not giving you money on that one. Because I'm pretty sure you're completely right about it."

She picked up her guitar case in one hand and took Brandon's hand in the other, letting him push open the door into the back parking lot. The night air was cool. Gorgeous weather for late May.

"I got you something," he said.

"Yeah?" she asked.

He unlocked the rental car two spaces down, then popped the trunk. Megan set her guitar case down on the pavement, which was still radiating heat from the afternoon sun. "What on earth is this?" she asked, taking the flat rectangular package that Brandon pulled from the trunk.

"Something for your new place."

She peeled back the brown paper wrapping to see the back of a frame. On the other side were the words, "Megan Gamble, Live!" above a photo with her head bent over the guitar, hair tucked behind her ear and draping toward her face. She hadn't noticed it when they'd put the poster together, but the ridge of her cheekbone looked exactly like Kyle's.

Staring at the poster, she said, "You got it framed!" She'd meant to grab one for herself, but had completely forgotten.

"I wanted you to remember your first show."

"Thank you," she said, stretching up to kiss him. "You coming over to help me decide where to put it?"

"You bet."

After one more kiss, she propped the poster against her hip and picked up her guitar, then stood tall to put both into the trunk. She stepped to the door and paused with it open. "Hey," she said. "Did I tell you I'm working on a new song?"

Brandon had the door to his own car open. "Yeah? Are you going to play it for me?"

"I could do that. But it isn't exactly finished, yet."

"That's okay," he said. "I'd love to hear what you've got so far. And I'm sure you'll figure it out."

With a burst of utter certainty, she said. "Yeah. I will."

ACKNOWLEDGMENTS

I'd like to thank Cindy Kehagiaras and Lisa Frieden for their enthusiasm and helpful comments on early drafts of this work, Michelle Hazen for her excellent editorial work and helpful guidance on self-publishing, Mary Helen Gallucci for her eagle eyes and exacting standards in proofreading, and Katie Golding for her amazing cover design.

I've benefited from the wisdom of several writing teachers, and would like to thank each of them for contributing to my growth as a writer and novelist: Amy Payne, for teaching my very first in-person writing classes; Holly Lisle, for her online classes and the processes they lay out—processes which continue to serve me years later; and Michelle Richmond, whose online interactive classes have encouraged and inspired.

Several writers' groups have also influenced my journey, and I am grateful to have benefited from their programs. Specifically, I was delighted to participate in the Community of Writers Workshops at Pallisades, Tahoe, a magical writing week in the high Sierras. The San Francisco Writer's Conference introduced me to several of the tools I'd need to pursue writing, self-editing, and publishing my work, which has proven invaluable. NaNoWriMo, the National Novel Writing Month, gave me the push I needed to draft my very earliest novels. The talented writers of my in-person writing group, whose membership has shifted over the years, have also provided critical support, so thank you to: Lisa Frieden, Staci Turner Homrig, Elizabeth Fergason, Jenness Hobart, Hilary Avis, and Harriet Garfinkle.

I'm also grateful for the kind words and enthusiasm of the many early readers of my short stories and other works, but especially to the late Catherine Rudiger, who found time to appreciate my writing even while dealing with devastating health issues.

My high school friends Ri-Shea and Ri-Pen (Rip) were kind enough to seek out the advice of their amazing uncle and help me find the perfect name for Li-Fang, for which they each have my thanks.

In a novel about having a ball singing your heart out, I'd be remiss if I didn't thank the groups and individuals who let me sing with them: the Valley Presbyterian Church Choir, the Peninsula Women's Chorus, the Merlot Notes, Crescendo, and my voice teacher, Dr. Erin McComber.

And even now, years after my childhood, I'm thankful for the love and unconditional support of my parents and grandparents, the people who let me walk into libraries and bookstores to my heart's content and for Suzanne, who was so often my companion on those literary adventures.

COMING SOON...

DEBBIE ROMANI

What does it take to drive a big talent to forsake her gifts? And what does it take to bring her back again?

Marina Carson's beloved voice teacher goes missing in the September 11th attacks, and the concert which was to be Marina's professional opera debut is recast as a 9/11 memorial. Moments before stepping on stage, Marina receives a recovered voicemail from her voice teacher: "Marina, I'm going to fly." Faced with the precipitous drop into the orchestra pit, and convinced her teacher was one of the 9/11 jumpers, Marina fails on stage and flees, her relationship to music utterly broken.

Ten years late, in the Mendocino church where Marina's talent was originally nurtured, she finally begins to confront her fraught relationship to music. If she can conquer her fears, she may once again feel the siren call of the opera. But she will have to choose between artistic fulfillment and her family, who have been her whole world for the last ten years.

COMING SOON...

Coming Spring 2023
Turn the page for a sneak preview inside...

SNEAK PEEK OF MENDOCINO MUSIC

New York City
Tuesday, September 11, 2001
6:30 am

Marina shifted her two-year-old son from one hip to the other and opened the curtains. "Expect a glorious day," said the announcer from the bedside radio. Sure enough, the mid-September sky over New York was clear and blue.

On the bed by her side, James made a sound more like a whimper than a groan. He raised a hand to block the sun, his wedding ring reflecting the light. Maybe twenty-six was a bit young to be married and have a kid, but it sure hadn't gotten in the way of her career. She was fiercely happy to have work she adored, and a man and boy to love. She pulled little Ryan closer for a snuggle.

"Good morning, songbird," said James, eyes barely open. In the mornings, he pulled her pillow tight to his chest as soon as she climbed out of bed; he was snuggled up against it now. Most of the world saw the buttoned-up, intimidating corporate lawyer, not this sleepy and relaxed man. He burrowed his face deeper into her pillow for one more breath, then he flopped his arms wide, taking one final stretch before he swinging his legs out of bed and standing.

Every morning until they were both old and gray, he would do the same thing, wouldn't he? She was still smiling at the thought when he slipped an arm around her waist and leaned in for a kiss.

She pulled back, mock frowning. "Wow. Pretty serious morning breath you've got going there."

He tugged her closer with a teasing grin, opened his mouth wide, and blew out a smelly breath. She giggled and pounded his chest, trying to break free, but James held tight and ruffled her crazy hair, saying, "You're one to talk, oh, my queen-of-bedhead." The tickle fight she started in retaliation only ended when she needed James's help to keep from dropping Ryan.

With one more kiss for Marina, James ran a flat palm over Ryan's hair. Neither of them really used baby voices anymore —Ryan was two, after all; but James did modify his pitch from baritone to mid-range tenor when he spoke: "Morning, little dude. Shower time for Daddy." He unwound his arm and slipped into the bathroom, leaving the door ajar. She sat on the unmade bed and rested her chin against Ryan's downy head.

"You were up late," said James, his voice raised to carry above the running water.

"I got caught up watching a video Dolores lent me. Remember how I told you the director from the Zurich Opera will be at the gala? They're casting for next season; and my manager thinks they might consider me for one of the leads. Anyway, I wanted to see how Schwarzkopf handled her entrances, and—you'll never believe this!—Dolores actually had a recording of one of her performances, and she let me borrow it."

Ryan wriggled away. Still thinking about the opera, she stood to tuck in the sheets and straighten the pillows.

Yesterday she and Dolores had worked on the Mozart for most of their session, chasing some elusive goal of interpretation which had escaped Marina but had been perfectly clear to her teacher. Towards the end of the lesson, the dumpling of a woman had said, "*Ach*, Marina, *mein Schatz*, you and your James are still live in the sweetness of fresh love; but the Countess only remembers and longs for it. No wonder I cannot yet hear the sorrow of the Countess. But you have a heart. Take that heart, rip it from you, and place it in the Countess. *Feel*, Marina. Feel what she feels—how much she misses that sweetness. *Noch einmal*, sing for me."

Marina had sung it again, imagining what it would be like if she no longer had any confidence in James's love. It had ached to even pretend, and her chest had physically hurt. When she had finished the last note of the aria, it had taken her a moment to even recognize Dolores's face, so lost had she been in the world Mozart had created.

A hint of pleasure had dusted Dolores's papery skin, and then her cheeks had rounded and a full smile had bloomed. "Now you understand. You remind me now of how Schwarzkopf sang the role. Come, I have a recording."

Remembering, Marina spoke aloud. "I mean, Elizabeth Schwarzkopf!"

Through the translucent shower curtain, Marina saw James throw up his hands in an exaggerated expression of surprise. "That's amazing," he said. If he had been dry, Marina would have grabbed a pillow off the bed and thrown it. Instead, she smoothed the case and called back, "Do you even know who Elizabeth Schwarzkopf is?"

He peeled back the shower curtain so he could stick out his face and grin. "Can't say I do, but you seem excited, and that's enough for me."

Ryan toddled by, and Marina snatched him for an airplane ride up and over onto the bed. Who needed a perfectly straight cover? She rolled him onto his back and gave his tummy a raspberry. Staring into the little boy's eyes, she said, "One day you'll know all about Elizabeth Schwarzkopf, won't you, Ryan?"

"More," said Ryan. He stood and bounced on the bed until Marina picked up the squirming boy, crooning from Puccini's *"uno studente in bocca la bacio."* Ryan squirmed, sliding down until his feet touched the floor. She opened up her voice on the next line, *"Folle amore! Folle ebbrezza,"* and Ryan turned in the doorway, then ran back. "More," he said, diving into her arms.

Once James was out of the shower and dressing, Marina raised a topic she'd been avoiding for days. "Can you see if Fiona will give us a few more hours? I need to get my head shots updated, and Schornstein made an appointment for me next week."

He paused with his fingers on his cuff, then fastened the button. There was no such thing as office casual in his firm. "We're already at twenty-five hours a week. That's more than we had last year when you were prepping for the competition. I'm sure she'd love the extra time, but I'm not convinced."

Which is exactly why she'd put off talking about it. "It's just that the gala is more important now than ever. Zurich Opera is going to be there, remember? My manager wants to give them an updated package with new photos, and the only time he could get with his photographer was on Thursday. That's not one of Fiona's normal days, so we need to ask her, and you're *so* much better at dealing with that sort of thing than I am."

He finished buttoning his cuffs and threaded a tie under his collar. "Most women don't ask their husbands to negotiate with the nanny, you know. Most women like to do that themselves."

She grinned. "But I'm not most women. I trust you around Fiona. Besides, it's literally your job to deal with contracts." He was a corporate attorney, after all.

He straightened his tie and smoothed it flat. "Not too much extra time, though, okay? I don't want our little guy growing up and not recognizing his mother." That comment did not sit well, but before she could ask him if he was going to quit his job instead, Ryan ran back into the room.

James caught the sleeper-clad boy, tickling him before he escaped to the other side of the bed.

"More, Daddy. Again."

James lifted Ryan high overhead, then swung him down onto the bed for another tummy raspberry, and she completely forgot to be annoyed. A moment later, James put Ryan back onto his feet and pointed out the door. "Now go find your favorite trains so Daddy can say good morning to the engines."

Ryan ran off. Of course he did what he was told when it was something he already wanted to do! James draped an arm around Marina's shoulders, and said, "Seriously, don't get so wrapped up in your opera that you don't have time for Ryan, okay?"

That was too much coming from a corporate lawyer trying to make partner at a New York firm. What was this, the 1950s?

She shrugged out from under his arm and stared up at him. "What am I supposed to do? Opera is not a career for people who want to futz around with a feeble, half-hearted commitment. I'm a good mom, but singing? That's who I am. Don't ever ask me to shortchange my career."

Ryan was back. "Trains, Daddy. Thomas and Percy and Gordon."

"Careful, buddy, you're going to drop some of these." The collection of wooden engines was cradled against the toddler belly, stubby fingers trying to keep five or six little train cars pressed against the matching picture on his pajama top. "Let me carry a few of them, okay?"

Another conversation interrupted by a toddler. Marina sighed and led the way to their tiny excuse for a kitchen. She pulled out Cheerios for Ryan, reached into the cupboard for two mugs and poured their coffee. "This career isn't going to get easier, you know. Wait till I get jobs out of town. For now, I've got to take every audition that comes up—really put myself out there—because I can't balance my career with my family unless I actually have a career. And if I was at a law firm, trying to make partner, you'd understand." He nodded. "Well, then, don't make my job less important than yours, okay? It's like because I'm a woman, and because I'm in the arts and not keeping that good, old engine-of-commerce humming along, somehow I'm the one who's supposed to make the sacrifices."

She could almost see the wheels turning as James filled two bowls with cereal. Marina put Ryan's bowl on the kiddie table while James stood at the kitchen counter. After his first bite, James turned and gestured with the empty spoon.

"You're right, and I'm sorry. I mean, I didn't—crap, Marina. I'm just worried. God knows it's hard for me to make time for you two, and it just doesn't seem fair to our little monster to have both of us running full-tilt all the time. Trust me, I do know the difference between the law and the opera. I've got a job; you've got a calling. But I'll talk to Fiona, get you the extra hours, since that's what you say you need."

He held her gaze, and slowly her she calmed. "Thank you," she said. "We'll just keep talking about stuff like this, and it'll be okay, right?" She wouldn't let little issues like this build up into bigger ones.

"Of course," he said. "And, hey! What did your mom and dad decide? Are they flying out?"

"No," she said, and her lips tightened. As soon as she noticed, she tried to force herself to relax. She couldn't be cavalier about muscle tension in the neck or jaw or even in the tongue. Tension built up over time, became the body's resting state, and tension spoiled the sound. Worse, tension in the wrong places led to the misuse of muscles, which could cause actual vocal damage.

Shoot, Ryan still needed some fruit with his breakfast. She peeled a banana and placed it on the kiddie table, her nose inches above Ryan's head. He smelled like sleep and baby shampoo, subtle under the stronger scents of breakfast: banana, milk, cereal. "How can my mom and dad even think of missing this performance? What is wrong with them?"

Her voice was too loud, and when Ryan's eyes opened wide, James beckoned Marina back into the tiny kitchen. "Clearly, I shouldn't have brought *that* up," he said.

Marina barely stopped talking. "I won the Hollingsworth Competition, for heaven's sake, and I did it as a lyric soprano! Last year was one of the most competitive anyone can remember, and you know that nearly three sopranos in five sing lyric roles. And I stood out from all of them."

James did that thing he did whenever she worked herself up, which meant he nodded continuously while she talked. They both looked down when Ryan laughed at something on the television, and Marina realized she had no memory of either of them turning on the set. Funny how distracted she got at the thought of her parents.

She hopped up to sit on the counter, her shoulders slumped. "Everyone who cares about opera wants to come to this concert, and I can't even get my own parents to fly out and listen."

James put his hands to either side of her, boxing her in and kissing her lightly, his morning breath completely gone. "I get it. Your mom and dad are the people who are supposed to support you, right? But sometimes it just doesn't work that way." He wrapped his arms around her and rested his chin on the top of her head. "Hey, you've got me. And you've got Dolores. And even that guy back at home, from your old church—was his name Delancy?"

"Mr. Delancy, that's right." God, she was the lamest person ever. Were her eyes actually watering? "You're so sweet. Thank you." Enough dwelling on herself. Switching subjects, she asked, "Are you meeting Hank at the gym tonight? Aren't Tuesdays pickup basketball?"

He stepped back and smiled. "Yep. If I can actually get away." He'd missed two weeks in a row, what with work being way too crazy.

"Well, you should go. I can hold down the fort here; you should take some time for yourself."

In the other room, Ryan laughed and pointed at the television. "Elmo," he said.

James and Marina both turned, and then tried not to laugh when they realized they were wearing identical dopey and fond expressions.

James checked his watch. "Shoot, it's getting late. I'd better run."

He kissed her once again. When he stepped away, she hopped off of the counter. "Yeah," she said. "It's that time, isn't it?"

"Pretty much. Have a good one." James tapped her on the nose before grabbing his briefcase and walking out the door. The commute down to the Deutsche Bank Building next to the Twin Towers took a while, and James liked to get in early.

She wondered what she was doing, getting tied up in knots about her parents when she was so incredibly lucky to be living this life. She had James, and Ryan, and the prospect of an amazing career.

Marina was happy, and when she was happy, she sang. She launched into "*Folle amore!*" Crazy love.

Marina set Ryan up with a few toys and settled onto the couch with two different editions of Mozart's *Marriage of Figaro* in her arms. It was a very good thing that Ryan was able to entertain himself for short stretches, otherwise she'd never get anything done on the days when Fiona wasn't around. Most of her classmates from Juilliard weren't married yet, but so what if she'd found the man of her dreams when she was barely twenty? That was good news, not bad. And if she was a young mom as well? That was great, too. She could do this—fit a career and motherhood together.

Marina ruffled Ryan's hair before she opened her scores. Marina would sing one of the Countess's arias during the gala, but today she planned to examine Mozart's deliciously layered Act II finale. The Count and Countess kicked things off with a duet, and then Mozart added voices one by one until seven vocalists were assembled onstage, each singing their own words and melodies. It was some of the most complex and rewarding music ever written for the voice, and she had loved it for years.

If she landed the part with the Zurich Opera, she wanted her performance to be the best it could possibly be: the music demanded it. And if she'd learned one thing at Juilliard, it was that careful study added nuance, and that nuance was what turned a decent performance into something breathtaking. But today it was different, because she was combing through the music knowing that she might actually be asked to sing the role for a major audience.

Marina knew she could make the Countess seem real to an audience, even though she needed to get inside the head of a the wife of a wandering husband. She certainly didn't want life to give her direct experience of what *that* was like. No, thank you. She'd use her empathy to conjure up the right emotions. Accessing those emotions while singing beautifully was pretty much her job description.

297

Meanwhile, there was the music itself to analyze. Marina dug into the scores, watching the changing key signatures as different characters joined the ensemble, paying attention to Mozart's use of orchestral color. As she studied, the music came alive in her head, the imagined voices and instruments intertwining.

When the phone rang in an entirely different key, she startled.

It was James, clearly calling from somewhere outside, talking on that Blackberry she hated so much. She could hear the traffic in the street, and checked her watch to find that it was already ten minutes before nine. "Hi," she said. He would have reached the office a while ago, so he must be heading to a meeting.

"Songbird, turn on the news, will you? Something just happened—like some sort of loud boom near the World Trade Center? Are they covering it on TV?"

Marina juggled the phone to one shoulder and reached for the remote. She had a bad feeling about this. "Where are you? You're not going in there, are you? There might have been another bomb." That bombing in 1993 had been pretty darned frightening.

"I'm walking over for a nine o'clock. And I highly doubt there's been a second attack on those buildings. I mean, what are the odds?" James worked directly across the street from the World Trade Center, and he frequently walked to meetings high in the towers.

She heard an odd clicking noise from the phone. James said, "Damn. Low battery. Forgot to charge it."

"James. Listen to me. If you think something weird is going on, just cancel. Don't risk it. What if there actually is a problem?" So far, the television stations weren't showing anything except their normal morning programming.

"If there's a problem—which I highly doubt—then it's in one of the buildings, not both of them. And the South Tower looks fine." She could imagine him craning his neck as he crossed the street. "But before I left the office, I felt like maybe I saw some smoke. I don't know. Maybe you're right, and it's another one of those crazy bomb threats like in '93."

"I'm trying to check, but I doubt they'll say anything on the news yet. But, James, why risk it?" asked Marina. She switched the station to a different morning news show.

Whoa. She had not expected *that.* Huge billows of dark smoke poured from a hole high on the side of one of the WTC towers. She turned up the volume in time to catch the anchor's words. "James, they say a plane hit the North Tower of the World Trade Center." Her voice shook.

"That's ridiculous. There's a clear sky. What, the pilot couldn't see the Towers? That's gotta be wrong."

The smoke was oddly fascinating. "I know it doesn't make sense. You need to cancel that meeting. *Please.* This is scaring me."

He made a sound like a scoffing laugh, one that she hated, because it meant that he thought that she couldn't possibly understand how important and urgent his meeting was. "I can't cancel. My meeting is in the South Tower, and now that I'm across the street, it's pretty obvious that the smoke is from the other one."

"You've got to be kidding! People are still going in there?"

She pictured him walking briskly across the plaza, watching the doors to the building. "Yeah," he said. "People are still heading in. A few are leaving, too, but it all looks pretty ordinary. Listen, I've really got to hustle. The elevators take forever." His voice turned warm and affectionate. "I'm sure everything is going to be fine, and I'm trying to close this deal on Friday so we can keep those dinner reservations. Look, my battery's almost dead, but I'll call you when I'm back in the office. Love you!"

The line clicked off. Marina looked down at Ryan. His eyes were riveted to the screen with the endless toddler fascination with heavy equipment.

"Fire trucks, Mommy. Look! Fire trucks." They were streaming down Broadway, heading south to the tip of the island. Marina thought of all the people in the North Tower. In 1993, they'd had to walk down the stairs when the building's power went out. It would be a long, thigh-burning descent.

She was too worried to go back to her music. She was too worried to do anything but watch the news.

At 9:03, she watched the second plane dive into the towers live on television.

Smoke still poured out of the North Tower. As the flight approached, the plane seemed to move in slow motion—a brilliant blue sky the gorgeous backdrop as it crept forward, low against backdrop of the building. Then the aircraft turned slightly, its left wing tilted down in a smooth turn as it penetrated the tower.

It looked as easy as driving a spoon through Jell-O, the plane casually cutting into the second tower of glass and steel and plumbing and carpet. And people. She pressed her fingers to her mouth, feeling bile begin to rise and her eyes starting to burn. Okay, James had to be outside somewhere, right?

She couldn't stop the vision of a poor soul sitting at her desk and watching as the plane came closer. She imagined the woman standing and running, making it to the office door. Jesus, what a horrible thing to see!

Her mind snapped back to James. Maybe the people he was

meeting with had tried to call him and cancel. Maybe his phone had died before they got through. Maybe he was safe; but maybe he was in that building, the one that had just been hit.

Her breath began to shallow out on her, ineffectual gasps failing to move oxygen to her lungs. She froze, wanting desperately to pick up the phone, but unable to move.

On the television, the silvery building briefly showed a black, plane-shaped hole, and then an enormous fireball exploded out of the gash.

What about the people on the plane? Were there kids on the flight? Smoke and flames billowed into the sky, and Marina looked down to find Ryan at her feet. He had been holding a fire truck since moments after the first image had flashed on the screen, and now it had dropped to the floor.

"Mommy," he said. His little eyes were enormous. *The fire*, she thought. The fire was probably scaring him.

"I'm here, little man," she said, bending to hold him and taking comfort in the warm, living, child's body. Her breath deepened ever so slightly, but over Ryan's shoulder, she watched the television.

"Mommy? Want Daddy!" said Ryan. The size of that fireball had probably scared him.

He must be picking up on her fears. Of course he wanted his daddy. Marina swallowed and tried to calm her breathing. "I want Daddy, too, buddy. Daddy's at his office." She thought again of James heading into the World Trade Center just a few minutes ago and her legs began to give out.

Abruptly, she sat on the couch, still holding Ryan, and reached for the phone handset. She told herself she didn't need to worry just yet. James was probably outside. And even if he'd reached the building, surely someone in the lobby had turned him away. And then James would call Beth, his secretary, to explain why he wasn't on his way up to his meeting, right? Maybe Beth would know what floor James was heading for, and together she and Beth could figure out if he could have been on one of the elevators. Could James be trapped?

She dialed his office, and the phone went directly to voice-mail. Marina tried not to panic. She called the Blackberry next, and of course that, too, went to the recorded message. That's right. His battery was dead; he'd said so.

Surely there must be someone else she could call, but now she couldn't get a dial tone. Everyone in the city must be calling someone.

While she held the receiver, Ryan broke down into tears and pointed to the phone in her hand. "Daddy. Talk to Daddy." She was so worried about James that she didn't have a lot of bandwidth for dealing with a frantic child. She wished that the nanny were here today, but admitting that kicked off a serious wave of guilt. It's just that she had no idea how to deal with a toddler at a moment when she was trying to figure out if her husband could be dead. Maybe she really was too young to be a mother.

On the television, the news anchor speculated about terrorist attacks. Just like back in '93. She had been a senior in high school then, in the midst of planning her audition trip to New York, when that bomb had gone off. Years later, she heard a story about that day from one of James's colleagues, who had worked in the buildings when the bombing had taken place. The stairwells had been jammed with people. When anyone had stopped—whether they were winded from being out-of-shape or having trouble because of bad knees—everyone above them had been trapped. James' colleague had been a few stair-steps above a woman when she essentially collapsed, making it clear that she wasn't going to be able to walk any further. So James's friend had helped two other people carry the woman down more than fifty flights—just to clear the way and keep everyone above them from getting trapped.

That was almost certainly what was happening right now. There would be streams of people—maybe thousands of them —walking down flight after flight, their legs fighting the strain as the descent went on and on. At the bottom of the tower, the people would be spilling out into the plaza and backing up to get a view of what she was watching on television.

She told herself that James must be outside, or walking down the stairs, at the very least.

She desperately needed to talk to someone, just to make sure the whole world wasn't falling apart. Outside of James and Ryan, the most important person in her life was her voice teacher. She hesitated a moment, though, because although Dolores might make her feel better, Dolores had a son with a brand-new job working in the towers. She was probably frantic, too. Marina dialed her apartment anyway, and the phone rang and rang.

Disturbed, Marina replaced the handset in its cradle.

Marina spent an endless twenty-five minutes sitting on the floor pretending to play trains with Ryan. Then the phone rang, startling her so badly that she ruined a portion of the wooden train track. Oddly, when she picked up, the line went dead. She pressed down on the buttons where the handset normally rested to get rid of the dial tone, and was still holding the button down, lost in thought, when the phone rang again.

She rolled a train forward along the track and released the button to answer. "Hello?"

"Marina, hi. It's Beth, James's secretary." Her voice was distorted, as if the connection was unstable. "Have you heard from James? Things are crazy down here."

That wasn't good. "No. I haven't heard from him. Isn't he with you?"

"No, he isn't here. We got evacuated, and they're trying to do a headcount, but no one knows where James is. I was hoping he'd called you."

"Wait, you got evacuated? Why? You're across the street from the towers." Marina swallowed hard. In front of her, little Ryan had stopped playing with his trains and was staring at the television screen. She had to get Ryan out from in front of this news program. He probably didn't understand what was going on, but she didn't want these images of burning buildings seared into his brain.

Beth said something that Marina made no attempt to listen to. Instead, Marina said, "James did call, but his battery was dying."

There was audible relief in Beth's voice. "Thank God! That means he got out, right? That's great news."

Marina started to panic. What if Beth hung up the phone? "No, no, no. He called me on the way in, not out. I don't even know what floor he was going to."

There was a pause, as if Beth was figuring out how to break something to her. "James was headed to Cranton Downing. They're pretty high up."

Marina tried to keep her voice under control, so Ryan wouldn't hear the panic. "So maybe he's in there right now? He could be stuck! Oh, my God, Beth, you've got to tell someone— do something! Someone needs to find him."

"I'm sure he's fine," said Beth, but Marina didn't believe her. It didn't even sound like Beth believed herself. "I bet James made it out but can't get through. You said his battery was low, didn't you?"

Marina wiped at her dripping nose. That made some sense. "He forgot to charge it."

"Hang in there. I'll get back to you if I hear anything, okay?" Marina ended the call, and picked up Ryan.

If you enjoyed this excerpt, please visit Debbie's website at debbieromani.com to sign up for her mailing list. She'll let you know when pre-orders for Mendocino Music go live.

ABOUT THE AUTHOR

Debbie Romani is a writer living in Northern California. She reads books the way some people watch television: way too often, and for way too long.

When she doesn't have her nose in a book or her fingers on the computer keyboard, she enjoys singing with a few too many choirs, skiing if her knees and the snowpack cooperate, and swimming slowly and steadily. She loves to travel to places where she can pretend to speak the language, to bake and to eat, and to take long walks. You can find out more at www.debbieromani.com.

If you enjoyed *Megan Gamble, Sing Out*, please consider leaving a review on Amazon, Goodreads, or whatever platform strikes your fancy. Reviews help spread the word about independent books, and each review matters.

 twitter.com/dzubrick